A Long Finish

by the same author

THE LAST SHERLOCK HOLMES STORY
A RICH FULL DEATH
RATKING
THE TRYST
VENDETTA
DIRTY TRICKS
CABAL
THE DYING OF THE LIGHT
DEAD LAGOON
DARK SPECTRE
COSI FAN TUTTI

Michael Dibdin

A Long Finish

faber and faber

First published in Great Britain in 1998
by Faber and Faber Limited
3 Queen Square London WC1N 3AU

Typeset by Faber and Faber Ltd
Printed in England by Clays Ltd, St Ives plc

A CIP record for this book
is available from the British Library

ISBN 0–571–19341–2

2 4 6 8 10 9 7 5 3 1

To Pat Kavanagh

Later – when word of what had happened got about and, in variously garbled versions, was for a time the common property of the entire nation – a television crew set up a satellite dish in a clearing on the hillside at the back of the Faigano property, paying what in local terms amounted to a small fortune for the temporary rights to a few square metres of land so poor, so barren, so utterly useless, that it had virtually ceased to exist on anyone's mental map of the vicinity. People scratched their heads and murmured, 'They paid that? For *il Bric Liserdin*?', seemingly as shocked by this anomaly as they had been by the thing itself.

That was how it was always referred to: 'the thing', as though it had nothing more to do with them than the metal bowl which the outsiders from Milan trucked in and mounted for a fat fee on the steep, scrub-covered hillside where rocks perpetually shouldered their way to the surface like moles, infesting the ground on which Gianni and Maurizio's ancestors had expended such futile labour, its only produce the stones used for terracing the slopes on the other side of the hill, the vineyards with the good exposure.

But the exposure that the television people wanted, contrary to every natural law, was apparently right there in that arid wasteland, with line of sight towards some heavenly body, invisible to the naked eye, which they claimed hung in space like the frescoed angels in the local church, motionless above the moving earth, gathering up all the villagers' chat, blather and evasions and then beaming it down again so that they could watch themselves later, being interviewed live at the scene of the tragedy.

He himself couldn't be interviewed, of course, even later. The man they would have paid far more than they gave the Faigano brothers, in return for being able to ask exactly what he had seen and how it had felt, had to watch the whole charade and bite his tongue and pretend that he was just like everyone else, knowing no more than what he heard in the street and saw on television. The frustration bit keenly, like a bad case of indigestion, subverting every pleasure and adding its intimate edge to every other woe and worry. Had his state of mind been known to anyone else, it might have gone some way to explaining – perhaps even preventing – the subsequent events, which, while not in the same class as *la cosa* itself, nevertheless prolonged the unprecedented notoriety which the community was to enjoy.

But all that came later. At the time, he was aware of nothing but the smear of reluctant light to the east, the fat clods of clay underfoot, the mist oozing up from the river valley, the eager breathing of the dog keeping obediently to heel. He was intensely aware of all this, and of everything else in his immediate vicinity, as he walked up the hillside between the rows of vines, a large bouquet of white flowers clutched in one hand, hunching over to keep below the level of the russet and golden foliage sprouting from ancient stumps kept low by intensive pruning. With all the money they were making, the Vincenzo family had been able to replace the traditional canes supporting the training wires with concrete posts stacked neatly across the hillside like the rows of crosses in the military cemetery just outside the village.

His route had been chosen with care. The vines covered him on two sides only, but they were the vital ones. To his right lay the road which ran along the ridge towards Alba. Only one vehicle had passed since he had slipped into the field through a carefully concealed hatch cut in the protecting fence, and it had gone on its way without slackening speed. A more acute danger lay in the other direction, where on a neighbouring hillside about a mile distant stood the Vincenzo residence and its associated outbuildings. If the owner had been up and about at that hour, watching the mist drifting through his vines like the smoke from a cigar, he might well have spotted something moving out there, and gone inside for his binoculars and his gun. Even at his advanced age, Aldo Vincenzo's eyesight was as legendary as his suspicion and intransigence. But the intruder was fairly sure that on that particular morning there would be no one about, for he had chosen not only his route but also his moment with care.

The price he paid for the cover afforded to either side by the ranks of vines was almost total exposure in the other two directions, but here he felt even more confident of passing unobserved. At his back the ground sloped away to a railway cutting whose further edge was so much lower that nothing was visible in that direction except for the faint outline of the village of Palazzuole rising from the mist on its distant hilltop. Ahead of him, at the crest of the hill, was a small, densely wooded hanger which had been left wild, a scrubby north-facing patch too unpropitious for even Aldo to try to cultivate. The road from Alba to Acqui ran through it on a continuous banked curve so steep and tight that drivers still had to slow down, change gear and address themselves seriously to the steering wheel. Back in 1944, the underpowered, overladen, unwieldy trucks had virtually been brought to a standstill by the incline, even before the lead driver noticed the tree lying across the road . . .

It was while they were waiting that Angelin had found the truffle. The two of them had been stationed on that side of the road, while the others were concealed in the continuation of the wood further up the hill, which had then belonged to the Cravioli family. Now it, too, was part of Aldo's empire, together with the unbroken sweep of vines on the hillside beyond the road to the right.

The plan had been simple. When the crew of the Republican convoy, which had hurriedly left Alba after its seizure by the partisans, got out to clear the fallen birch from the road, the men on the upper slope would rake the scene from end to end with a mounted machine-gun captured from a German unit a few weeks earlier. He and Angelin were to pick off any *fascisti* who tried to take refuge in the woods on that side.

Meanwhile they had nothing to do but wait. People nowadays had no idea how much waiting there had been. They thought that war was all gunfire and explosions, sirens and screams, but he remembered it as long periods of tedium punctuated, like a summer night by lightning, by moments of intense excitement such as he had never imagined possible until then. He had been fifteen at the time, and immortal. Death was something that happened to other people. It no more occurred to him that he might be killed than that he might get pregnant.

As it turned out, he was right. Everything went according to plan, except that Angelin caught a stray bullet which emptied what little brains he'd ever had all over the mulch and moss of the underwood. But although no one came right out and said so, Angelin was expendable, and in every other respect the ambush was a textbook success. Mussolini's die-hards were cut down in seconds – all but one youngster who threw down his gun, pleading incoherently for his life, and had to be dispatched at short range.

But during that interminable period of waiting, all he had been aware of was the pallid light reaching down through the trees and the welling silence, fat and palpable as a spring, broken only by the rasp of his companion's digging. Using a small, short-bladed knife, Angelin was painstakingly excavating the hillside in front of the oak tree behind which they were concealed. Eventually the scraping noise got on his nerves.

'What are you doing?' he whispered irritably.

Angelin smiled in a vacuous, almost mocking way.

'I smell something.'

He'd responded with a muttered blasphemy. It wasn't just the noise that was getting on his nerves, it was the whole situation. Everyone knew Angelin was the next best thing to the village idiot, so being relegated to keep him company on the other side of the road from the real action looked like a judgement. He could imagine what the others had said, back at the planning meeting to which he hadn't been invited. 'Let's stick the kid with Angelin. He can't do any harm over there.' They'd never forgotten the time he'd opened fire out of sheer excitement before the order had been given, and nearly compromised the whole operation. In the end no harm had been done, but one of the older men had made a crude joke about premature ejaculation, and ever since then they'd kept him at arm's length when it came to gun-play. His courage was not in dispute, but they didn't trust his judgement.

Angelin had kept digging away, scratching and sniffing, until he had opened up a gash about a foot wide in the soft earth at the foot of one of the trees. Finally he unearthed a filthy lump of something that might have been bone or chalk, shaved a corner off and presented it impaled on the tip of his knife.

'White diamond!' he whispered, as pathetically eager for praise as a truffle hound for the stale crust of bread with which it would be fobbed off after doing the same work.

It was then that they heard the sound of the convoy in the distance, engines revving as they climbed over the col leading up from the valley of the Tanaro. Later, of course, there'd been no time to explain. There were the trucks to turn around, and cartons of documents and records from the Questura in Alba to unload and reload, together with whatever arms and ammunition they could strip off the escort. They'd left Angelin's body where it was. There was clearly nothing to be done for him. Nor was there any way of identifying the bullet which had passed through the back of his skull and buried itself somewhere in the mulch. They all knew that bullets could ricochet in all kinds of crazy ways. Above all, they knew that the sound of gunfire must have been heard over a wide area, and that an enemy detachment would be coming to investigate very soon.

He did not return to the site of the ambush until the following year. By then the war was over and its victims had started to take on the marmoreal, exemplary status of martyrs and mythic heroes. At the bend in the road where Angelin died – but on the other side, as though he'd been part of the main action – a plinth had been erected, bearing his name, a date and the words: 'Here he fell for Italy beneath the lead of a barbaric enemy'. A faded wreath in the national colours garlanded the stone tablet. Angelin's ex-comrade had read the inscription without the slightest flicker of expression. Then, making sure no one was watching, he climbed down into the woods below and commenced his excavations.

For several years it continued like this. Some seasons he got a heavy yield, others little or nothing. Truffles were like that: capricious, female and unpredictable. It was part of their considerable mystique. Lacking the late Angelin's nose for their pungent scent – no doubt nature's compensation for his deficiencies in other respects – he used a *tabui*, one of the carefully bred and trained mongrels which have the ability to home in on any example of *tuber magnatum Pico* within a ten-metre radius.

The lode which Angelin had discovered on this unregarded strip of wasteland at the edge of the Vincenzo property was not his only hunting ground, but returns during the early years had still been modest. He kept a few of the smaller tubers for his own use, and sold the rest either to middlemen in the informal market held every morning in the back streets of Alba, or directly to a variety of restaurants and local connoisseurs. Considering that the outlay consisted only of his time, which was of no value, the returns were reasonable. Along with some casual labour, part-time haulage and odd jobs in the handyman line, it added up to a modest living.

Then, imperceptibly at first, things started to change. One of the first signs – and the most serious, from his point of view – was the barbed wire fence which Aldo Vincenzo had erected around his property. The local wines were beginning to acquire a reputation, and with it a price, exceeding anything previously heard of, and the grapes which produced them became correspondingly precious. There was even talk of Aldo Vincenzo emulating the example of some other local producers by sending his son, Manlio, to study something called 'viticulture', which struck most of the community as an absurdity akin to enrolling the boy at university to teach him the facts of life.

At about the same time as wines of the Langhe started acquiring their international reputation, coincidentally creating difficulties of access to his secret hoard of white truffles, the market for the latter took off in an even more dramatic and indeed literal sense. Since truffles lose their savour after a few days, most of the harvest had previously been consumed locally, with just a small quantity being exported by rail to hotels and restaurants in other regions of Italy, as well as a handful in Austria, France and Switzerland. Then came the era of air cargo. 'White diamond!' Angelin had said, but that proverbial metaphor was soon out of date. Ounce for ounce, *la trifola* made uncut diamond look cheap. International buyers vied with one another to obtain the precious tubers and ship them off to eager consumers in London, New York and Tokyo.

It was a world market, but the supply was strictly local. Some unexplored Russian hillside or Cambodian valley might perhaps hide similar riches, but white truffles could not be cultivated, and for now the only source of any importance was a small area of southern Piedmont centred on the town of Alba. Prices went through the roof, and the *trifolai* became even more reticent about the exact location of their favoured sites. Angelin's discovery thus became of still greater value. No one ever suspected that this slice of forgotten copse at the margins of the Vincenzo territory might be a mine for the white diamonds so much in demand. Like the hillside which the Faigano brothers later leased to the media for a small fortune, it had fallen off the map.

But if anyone saw him digging there, or noticed that the barbed-wire fence designed to protect the vines had been cut, all this would rapidly change. That was why he had not come during the hours of darkness, the traditional season of the 'phantoms of the night', as truffle hunters were known. At night he would have had to bring a torch, which might easily have been seen. People around here were naturally curious. Everything happened according to a time-honoured order and sense. Any exception was a potentially interesting anomaly to be noted and passed on to others. Hence the indirect route which he had chosen to approach the spot, the care he took not to be seen, and above all his timing.

The evening before had seen the *Festa della Vendemmia*, celebrated annually at Palazzuole on the first Saturday in October.

The date of the vintage itself varied from year to year and from vineyard to vineyard, depending on the weather and the degree of risk which any given grower was prepared to accept in return for the possibility of riper fruit. But the date of the village *festa* was invariable, as were the excesses and rituals associated with it. On the Saturday everyone ate and drank and danced and drank and flirted and drank and reminisced and drank, and then grew maudlin and nostalgic and lyrical. The entire community stayed up until well after midnight, slept in late the next morning and then reluctantly hauled themselves out of bed, clutching their hangovers like cerebral cysts, and staggered to church to attend the service invoking divine blessing on the event on which virtually all of their livelihoods depended in one way or another.

So as he picked his way up the muddy alley between the two rows of vines, he knew that the chances of anyone being up and about, never mind vigilant and suspicious, in the misty half-light before sunrise on that particular Sunday morning were as close to zero as made no difference. And while he had put in an appearance at the celebrations the day before – not to do so would inevitably attract comment – he had made a few glasses of wine go a lot further than it had appeared, and had woken fresh and alert at five o'clock that morning, ready for *his* annual, but very private, ceremony.

He thought of this as 'laying flowers on Angelin's tomb', even though the supposed victim of a barbaric enemy was not, of course, buried at the spot where he had been killed. The flowers were real, though: a touchingly artless bouquet of white chrysanthemums he had bought the day before in full view of several witnesses. He had told them that the flowers were for his mother, but with an awkward shrug which both ended the conversation and would be remembered in the event of his being caught and asked the reason for his presence on the Vincenzo land that morning. 'I just wanted to honour my fallen comrade,' he would say, his voice breaking with long-denied emotion. 'People called him simple, but to me he was a friend . . .'

No one would dare question him further after that, he reckoned. His evident sincerity would speak for itself, for the oddest thing of all was that by now he had come to believe this version of events himself. And so as he made his way up the vineyard that autumn morning, he was simultaneously two quite different people on two very different quests: a wary and unscrupulous truffle poacher, and an elderly veteran of the Resistance honouring a dead brother-in-arms.

It was then that he saw something moving among the vines up ahead, heavy with ripe clusters of the fat blood-red grapes which would produce the Barbaresco wine for which the region was famous. All might have been well, even then. He had always been good at moving silently and at speed, and could easily have slipped through the rows of vines to his left and then worked back the way he had come. But Anna had scented the extraneous presence. Restrained by the leash, she couldn't bound forward and investigate and so, as dogs will, she began to bark. The figure concealed in amongst the vines straightened up and turned towards him.

'What the hell are *you* doing here?'

There was no reply.

'Didn't you see the signs on the fence? "No trespassing," it says. Do you know what that means, or are you illiterate on top of everything else?'

The dog stood between them, looking from one to the other as though uncertain which side to take, which one to defend and which to attack. Then the man who had brought her took the initiative, walking forward at a slow, confident lope, his right hand gripping his *sapet*, the adze-shaped mattock used to unearth truffles.

That was how it began.

'Barolo, Barbaresco, Brunello. I am a purist, Dottor Zen. I also happen to be able to afford that classical austerity which is the ultimate luxury of those who can have anything they want. In wine, as in music, the three Bs suffice me.'

'I see,' said Aurelio Zen, who didn't see anything except the bins of bottles stretching away into the gloomy reaches of the vast, cold, damp cellar, its vaulted roof encrusted with a white mesh of saltpetre.

'Barolo is the Bach of wine,' his host continued. 'Strong, supremely structured, a little forbidding, but absolutely fundamental. Barbaresco is the Beethoven, taking those qualities and lifting them to heights of subjective passion and pain that have never been surpassed. And Brunello is its Brahms, the softer, fuller, romantic afterglow of so much strenuous excess.'

Aurelio Zen was spared the necessity of answering by an attack of coughing which rendered him speechless for almost a minute.

'How long have you had that cough?' the other man asked with a solicitude which was all too evidently feigned. 'Come, let us go back upstairs.'

'No, no. It's only a touch of chestiness. A cough won't kill me.'

Zen's host looked at him sharply. To someone who did not instantly recognize him – no such person was known to exist – he might have appeared an unremarkable figure: trim and fit for his sixty-odd years, but distinguished mostly by the layers of expensive tailoring which clad him like a second skin, and by a face whose wrinkles and folds seemed an expression not of calendar age but of inheritance, as though it had been worn by countless other eminent and powerful members of the family before being bequeathed to the present owner.

'Kill you?' he exclaimed. 'Of course not!'

With an abrupt laugh, he led the way further into the labyrinth of subterranean caverns. The only light was provided by the small torch he carried, which swung from right to left, picking out stacks of dark brown bottles covered in mildew and dust.

'I am also a purist in my selection,' he announced in the same didactic tone. 'Conterno and Giacosa for Barolo, Gaja and Vincenzo for Barbaresco. And, until the recent unfortunate events, Biondi Santi for Brunello. *Poco ma buono* has always been my motto. I possess an excellent stock of every vintage worth having since 1961, probably the best collection in the country of the legendary '58 and '71, to say nothing of a few flights of fancy such as a Brunello from the year of my birth. Under these exceptional circumstances, vertical tastings acquire a classical rigour and significance.'

He turned and shone his torch into Zen's face.

'You are Venetian. You drink fruity, fresh *vino sfuso* from the Friuli intended to be consumed within the year. You think I am crazy.'

Another prolonged outburst of coughing was the only reply, ending in a loud sneeze. The other man took Zen by the arm.

'Come, you're unwell! We'll go back.'

'No, no, it's nothing.'

Aurelio Zen made a visible effort to get a grip on himself.

'You were saying that I don't understand wine. That's true, of course. But what I really don't understand is the reason why I have been summoned here in the first place.'

His host smiled and raised one eyebrow.

'But the two are the same!'

He turned and strode off down the paved alley between the bins. The darkness closing in about him, Zen had no choice but to follow.

The instruction to attend this meeting at the Rome residence of the world-famous film and opera director, whose artistic eminence was equalled only by the notoriety of the rumours surrounding his private life, had come in the form of an internal memorandum which appeared on his desk at the Ministry of the Interior a few days earlier. 'With respect to a potential parallel enquiry which the Minister is considering regarding the Vincenzo case (see attached file), you are requested to present yourself at 10.30 hrs on Friday next at Palazzo Torrozzo, Via del Corso, for an informal background briefing by . . .'

The name which followed was of such resonance that Giorgio De Angelis, the one friend Zen still had in the Criminalpol department, whistled loudly, having read it over Zen's shoulder.

'*Mamma mia!* Can I come too? Do we get autographs? I could dine out on this for a year!'

'Yes, but who'll pay the bill?' Zen had murmured, as though to himself.

And that was the question which posed itself now, but with renewed force. The celebrity in question clearly hadn't invited Zen to his *palazzo*, scene of so many widely reported parties 'demonstrating that the ancient tradition of the orgy is still not dead', merely to show off his wine collection. There was a bottom line, and the chances were that behind it there would be a threat.

'I can appreciate your point of view,' his host's voice boomed from the darkness ahead. 'I myself grew up in the estuary of the Po, and we drank the local rotgut – heavily watered to make it palatable – as a sort of medicine to aid digestion and kill off undesirable germs. But perhaps there is some other way I can make you understand. Surely you must at some time have collected something. Postage stamps, butterflies, first editions, firearms, badges, matchboxes . . .'

'What's that got to do with wine?'

The famous director, known to his equally famous friends as Giulio, stopped and turned, admitting Zen back into the feeble nimbus of light.

'The object of the collection is as unimportant as the quantities inserted in an algebraic formula. To the collector, all that matters is selection and completeness. It is an almost exclusively male obsession, an expression of our need to control the world.

Women rarely collect anything except shoes and jewellery. And lovers, of course.'

Zen did not reply. His host pointed the torch up at the curved ceiling of stone slabs.

'The nitre! It hangs like moss upon the vaults. We are now below Via del Corso. Young men, my sons perhaps included, are racing up and down in their cars as they once did on their horses, yet not a murmur of that senseless frenzy reaches us here. The wine sleeps like the dead.'

'I used to have a collection of railway tickets,' Zen remarked.

Giulio flashed a smile.

'I knew it!'

A dry rustling amongst the bottles to his left made Zen start.

'Rats,' said the famous director. 'You were saying?'

'My father . . .'

Zen hesitated, as though at a loss, then started again.

'He worked for the railways, and he used to bring them back for me, little cardboard tickets with the name of the destination printed on them, the class and the fare paid. By the end I had one to all the stations as far as Verona, Rovigo, Udine and Trieste . . .'

He paused again, then clicked his fingers.

'All except Bassano del Grappa! I remember someone making a joke about having to wait until I was older before trying grappa. I didn't understand at the time. I was just annoyed at having that gap in my collection. It ached like a pulled tooth.'

'Excellent! Perfect! Then no doubt you will understand how I felt when I heard about this dreadful business involving Aldo Vincenzo.'

Zen frowned, returning reluctantly to the present.

'Vincenzo?' he echoed

The famous director shone his torch around the neighbouring bins, lifted a bottle and held it out to Zen. The faded label read: BARBARESCO 1964. VINIFICATO ED IMBOTTIGLIATO DAL PRODUTTORE A. VINCENZO.

'Aldo Vincenzo was one of the producers I selected more than thirty years ago as worthy of a place in the cellar I then decided to create,' he declared solemnly, replacing the bottle on the stack with as much care as a baby in its cot. 'And now he's dead and his son is in prison, all on the eve of what promises to be one of the great vintages of the century! That's the reason why you have been "summoned here", as you put it.'

'You want to complete your collection.'

'Exactly!'

'To continue your horizontal tastings.'

His host regarded Zen sharply, as if suspecting some irony.

'They might be that,' he remarked, 'if one actually swallowed all the wines on offer. Such, of course, is not the way in which a *vertical* tasting is conducted. But in any case, if you imagine that I have any chance of personally enjoying this year's vintage at its best, you credit me with the longevity of a Methuselah. The patriarch, not the bottle.'

Zen struggled mutely with some internal paroxysm, then sneezed loudly, spraying gobs of sputum over the adjacent wine bins. The famous director grasped him once again by the arm and led him back the way they had come.

'Enough! We'll continue this talk upstairs.'

'I'm all right,' Zen protested. 'It's just this cold I've felt coming on for . . .'

'I'm not worried about *you*! But sneezing in a cellar risks half the bottles turning out corked. So they say, at any rate. As for the presence of a menstruating woman, forget it! The whole business of wine is full of that sort of lore. I both believe and disbelieve, but with an investment like this I can't afford to take chances.'

Giulio closed and locked the massive door giving into the vaults and led the way up a long, winding staircase and through an archway leading to the ground floor of the *palazzo*. They passed through several suites of rooms to the book-lined study where he had received Zen on the latter's arrival, and gestured him into the armchair which he had occupied earlier.

'As I was saying, the idea that I'm collecting the Vincenzo wine of this year – assuming there is any – for my own benefit is, of course, absurd. If the vintage is even half as good as has been predicted, it will not be remotely approachable for ten years, and won't reach its peak for another ten. By which time I will be, if not defunct, at least "sans teeth, sans eyes, sans taste, sans everything", as Shakespeare says.'

'Then why should you care?' demanded Zen, lighting a cigarette, which induced another massive fit of coughing. The other man eyed him keenly.

'Do you have children, *dottore*?'

'No. That's to say . . . Yes. One.'

'Boy or girl?'

'A boy. Carlo.'

'How old?'

There was a long pause.

'He's just a baby,' Zen replied at length.

'Congratulations! But they grow up rapidly. Hence my interest in this year's Vincenzo wines. I have two sons, both in the most repulsive period of their teens. At present they regard my interest in wine as just another example of their father's dotage. If they drink at all, it's some obscure brand of imported beer, although Luca at least shows promising signs of becoming a *collezionista* about that, too, hunting down limited-release Trappist brews and the like.'

He set about the meticulous business of cutting and lighting a massive cigar.

'I believe – I *have* to believe – that in time they will come to appreciate what I have bequeathed them, and perhaps even set about extending the cellar far into the next millennium as a heritage for their own children.'

A triumphant puff of blue smoke.

'But that is to look too far into the future. For the moment, all that concerns me is this harvest! Unless we act now, the grapes will either be sold off to some competitor or crudely vinified into a parody of what a Vincenzo wine could and should be.'

Aurelio Zen tried hard to look suitably concerned at this dire prospect.

'But what can I do about it?' he asked. 'If the son is already under arrest . . .'

'I don't believe for a moment that he did it,' the famous director exclaimed impatiently.

Zen produced a crumpled handkerchief from his pocket and blew his nose.

'Nevertheless, I've been given to understand that the Carabinieri have concluded their investigation. They have pressed charges against Manlio Vincenzo and the case is now in the hands of the judiciary. I don't see where I come in.'

His host exhaled a dense barrage of smoke.

'Perhaps you should be more concerned about where you go out,' he said.

Zen frowned.

'Go out? You mean, from this house?'

For the first time, Giulio smiled with what appeared genuine amusement.

'No, no! All appearances to the contrary, I am not planning to immure you in some lost recess of my cellars. Nevertheless, a not dissimilar fate might well await you.'

He eyed Zen keenly.

'I refer to your next professional posting.'

'That is a matter of departmental policy,' Zen replied, drawing on his cigarette.

Another smile, a shade more meaningful.

'Exactly. And in that regard I wish to draw your attention to various facts of which you are aware, and to another which is as yet privileged information. I shall be brief. Firstly, the current Minister is a man of the Left. Many of his friends and associates in the former Communist Party dedicated their lives to the struggle against organized crime. Some of them were killed as a result.'

His eyes met Zen's, and slid away.

'In addition, you have recently been reassigned to work for Criminalpol after your brilliant exploits in Naples where, as the whole country knows, you were instrumental in smashing the terrorist organization known as *Strade Pulite.*'

'But that was . . .'

'A major coup! Indeed. All this you know, *dottore*. What you do not know – what no one outside the Minister's immediate circle knows – is that he is in the process of forming an élite pool of senior officers who are to be drafted to Sicily to spearhead the coming campaign against the organization which took the lives of his comrades.'

Giulio waved his hand negligently.

'We've all heard this before, of course, every time some judge or police officer was gunned down or blown up. But that was in the days when the Mafia had its men here in Rome, in the highest circles of power. Everyone understood how the game worked. Any over-zealous official who looked like doing some worthwhile work was transferred or killed, the government put up a token show of force, the Mafia made a token show of backing off, and in a few months it was back to business as usual.'

He glanced at Zen, who stifled a cough.

'But this time, so I am assured, it will be different. A fight to the finish, with no quarter offered. The Mafia's links to Rome have all been cut, and the new government is eager to show that it can deliver on what its predecessors endlessly promised. As a result, a process of internal head-hunting has been going on for officers of proven experience, ability and – shall we say? – independence.'

He broke off to relight his cigar, holding the tip at a respectful distance from the flame.

'Your dossier, Dottor Zen, revealed you to have been severely compromised in the eyes of the former regime. This fact, needless to say, put you at the top of the list under the new management. Add to this your evident astuteness and ability to get things done, and you became a natural candidate for the new squad.'

'They're sending me to Sicily?' gasped Zen.

His host nodded.

'Oh, yes. I'm afraid there's nothing we can do about that. There's promotion in it, of course, and a substantial pay rise, but you're definitely going to have to go south. The only question is when and where.'

For a moment Zen looked as though he was about to burst into tears, but all that emerged was another massive sneeze.

'*Salute!*' said his host. 'Speaking of which, Sicily is notoriously insalubrious, particularly for newly arrived policemen who might well be drafted straight to the capital. If one were to arrive a little later, on the other hand, once the central command structure had been set up and all posts in Palermo filled, it might prove possible to secure an assignment in some relatively pleasant spot. Do you know Syracuse? An ancient Greek settlement in the least troubled portion of the island, possessing all the charm and beauty of Sicily without being tiresomely . . . well, *Sicilian.*'

Zen raised his eyes to meet those of his interlocutor.

'What guarantees do I have?'

A look of pain, almost of shock, appeared on the famous director's face.

'You have the guarantee of my word, *dottore.*'

'And your interest is?'

'I thought I'd made that clear. I want Manlio Vincenzo released from prison in time to make the wine this year.'

'Even if he murdered his father?'

A shrug.

'If he turns out to be innocent, so much the better. But let's assume that he did kill Aldo. It's absurd to believe that Manlio Vincenzo poses a threat to any other member of the community. And in the meantime there's a potentially great wine – maybe *the* great wine of the century – which demands the skill and attention only he can provide.'

He shrugged again, more expansively.

'After that, I don't really care what happens to him. In a year the estate will have had time to reorganize, to get another wine-maker or sell out to Gaja or Cerretto, either of whom would be only too glad to get their hands on the Vincenzo vineyards. But for now, Manlio's my only resource. Just as I'm yours.'

Zen sat trying to catch his breath through the layers of phlegm which had percolated down into his lungs.

'Why me?' he demanded point-blank.

The famous director waved the hand holding his cigar, which left a convoluted wake of smoke hanging in the still air.

'I made various enquiries, as a result of which someone mentioned your name and sketched in the details of your record. Most promising, I thought. You appear to be intelligent, devious and effective, compromised only by a regrettable tendency to insist on a conventional conception of morality at certain crucial moments – a weakness which, I regret to say, has hampered your career. In short, *dottore*, you need someone to save you from yourself.'

Zen said nothing.

'In return for the services which I have outlined,' his host continued seamlessly, 'I offer myself in that capacity. I understand that at one time you enjoyed the favour of a certain notable associated with the political party based at Palazzo Sisti. His name, alas, no longer commands the respect it once did. Such are the perils of placing oneself under the protection of politicians, particularly in the present climate. They come and go, but business remains business. If you do the business for me, Dottor Zen, I'll do the same for you. For your son, too, for that matter. What was his name again?'

'Carlo.'

The famous director leant forward and fixed Zen with an intense gaze, as though framing one of his trademark camera angles.

'Do we have a deal?'

Zen was briefly disabled by another internal convulsion.

'On one condition,' he said.

The man known to his friends as Giulio frowned. Conditions were not something he was used to negotiating with the class of hireling which Zen represented.

'And what might that be?' he asked with a silky hint of menace.

Aurelio Zen sniffed loudly and blew his nose again.

'That when you next give a party here, I get an invitation.'

There was a moment's silence, then the famous director roared with what sounded like genuine laughter.

'Agreed!'

19

The meal over, the three men pushed back their chairs and returned to work. At first glance they appeared as interchangeable as pieces on a board. Gianni was slightly stockier than the others, Maurizio was significantly balder, while Minot, who was shorter and slighter than either of the two brothers, wore a foxy moustache above his cynical, down-turned lips. But their similarities were far more striking. They were all of an age, which might have been anywhere from fifty to eighty, worn down by constant labour and near-poverty, with proud, guarded expressions that revealed a common characteristic: the fierce determination never to be fooled again. Their clothes, too, were virtually identical: dark, durable knits and weaves, much patched and mended, each garment a manuscript in palimpsest of tales that would never be told.

They had eaten in silence, waited on by the only woman in the house, Maurizio's teenage daughter Lisa. Back in the cellar, the long-maintained silence continued. It was not an empty silence, the void remaining once everything sayable has been said, nor yet the relaxed stillness which implies an intimacy or familiarity such that speech has become an irrelevance. This silence was tense with unspoken thoughts, facts and opinions not alluded to, a mutual reticence about things better left unsaid. It could be defused only by activity – filling mouths, or bottles.

The only light, from a single forty-watt bulb attached to a huge beam in the centre of the ceiling, died a lingering death in the lower reaches of the cellar, as though stifled by the darkness all around. The only sounds were repetitive and mechanical, muffled by the wooden casks mounted on wooden trestles which lined the walls. For lack of any other distractions, odour had it all its own way – an overwhelming profusion of smells fighting for prominence like plants in the jungle: yeast, mildew, alcohol, damp, fruit, corruption, fermentation. Their luxuriant variety created an olfactory arena whose dimensions apparently far exceeded those of the cellar itself, and this sense of concentration, of too much crammed into too little, gave an almost choking intensity to the musty reek which filled the lungs of the trio working silently in the gloom.

The division of labour had been established years before, and remained constant. Gianni Faigano, the elder of the two brothers, took the bottles from the rack of wooden pegs where they had been turned over to dry after being washed and sterilized. He filled each with a stream of red wine from a plastic tube inserted into one of the barrels, then passed the bottle to his brother, who positioned it under a metal lever loaded with a cork, which he rammed down into the opening. Maurizio then handed the bottle on to Minot, a neighbour who came by every year at this time to help out with this chore by applying the labels and capsules.

'I hear Bruno's got a new car,' said Gianni.

The sound of his words died away so rapidly that a few seconds later it already seemed uncertain whether he had actually spoken, or if it had just been some natural noise arising from the work on hand, or of digestion, superficially mimicking speech. More than a dozen bottles passed from hand to hand, and were duly filled, corked and labelled. Crouched in their dusty sails among the shadows above, gigantic spiders surveyed the scene.

'One of those off-road jobs,' Maurizio remarked. 'And bright red, into the bargain.'

Another six or eight bottles moved from the drying rack to the filling pipe and then the labelling bench before his brother replied. 'It's green.'

For a while everything continued as before. Then the spiders suddenly scuttled away to the furthest corner of their webs and crouched down, making themselves small and still. A bottle had broken, scattering jagged chunks of brown glass about the floor and releasing tongues of spilt wine to scout out the terrain.

'I've had just about enough of this damned argument!' said Minot.

There was a long silence. No one spoke or moved. Then Gianni Faigano filled another bottle, which Maurizio corked and handed to Minot, who pasted on a label. The arachnids above crawled back to their vantage points and took up their octagonal surveillance once more, while the bottles resumed their progress from one end of the cellar to the other.

'You know what gets me most about it?' demanded Maurizio. 'Aldo Vincenzo's turned into a national celebrity! There isn't a man, woman or child from here to Calabria who hasn't heard his name. He deserved to die like a dog – unknown, unburied and unmourned.'

'It's our fault for letting those television people talk us into setting up their equipment on our land,' muttered his brother.

Minot stroked his moustache with a sly expression.

'I hear you did quite nicely out of it,' he said. 'Anyway, if you'd refused, they'd have found someone else.'

'I just wish whoever did it had simply killed the old bastard and left it at that,' snapped Maurizio. 'No one would have taken any interest then.'

They were down to the last few dozen bottles now, all destined for a couple of local restaurants and a select number of private individuals in Alba and Asti who ordered the Faigano brothers' wine year in, year out, knowing it to be at least the equal of that made by growers fortunate enough to own land which fell within the officially classified area of Barbaresco, *Denominazione di Origine Controllata*. The property belonging to Maurizio and Gianni Faigano was only a stone's throw away from that of the Vincenzo family, but unfortunately on the wrong side of the stream which marked the boundary of the DOC zone. Because of this, the resulting product could only be sold on the open market as generic Nebbiolo, which commanded a tenth of the price.

'I ran into the *maresciallo* at market this morning,' said Minot, setting another completed bottle in its crate. 'You know what he told me? Apparently the police are opening their own investigation. Not only that, they're sending some big shot up from Rome to lead it.'

The two brothers exchanged a brief glance, then returned to their work. This went without incident, except when the wine started overflowing and Gianni Faigano ripped off a fingernail grabbing for the spigot. Minot retrieved the severed sliver.

'I'll keep this for good luck,' he joked, as though atoning for his earlier outburst.

Once the final bottles had made their way through the production line, the three men stood up stiffly.

'Not like you to drop a bottle, Minot,' said Gianni, sucking his injured finger. 'You're not nervous, are you?'

'Why should I be?'

Gianni smiled.

'I just wondered, since you mentioned this new investigation of la cosa . . .'

'I'm not nervous, I'm angry!' Minot snapped back. 'As if there weren't enough real problems facing the country, without sending some bastard up from Rome to make our lives a misery.'

'Speaking of bastards . . .' said Maurizio.

Minot whirled round on him.

'What the fuck's that supposed to mean?'

Maurizio held up his hands.

'The canine kind,' he explained, alluding to one of the dialect terms for a mongrel.

'Well?' demanded Minot. 'What about them?'

Maurizio hesitated a moment.

'The day Aldo died, I happened to be outside the house here, clearing my head with some fresh air and a raw egg.'

'And?'

'And I heard a dog barking over on the Vincenzo land.'

'Why do you keep going on about Aldo Vincenzo? Let the son of a bitch rot in peace!'

'By all means. Only if there's going to be another investigation, we'd better get our story straight.'

'My story is straight!'

'Of course, Minot,' said Gianni evenly. 'We know that. But some people may be more awkwardly placed, you understand? The owner of that dog, for instance.'

Minot turned to face him.

'You recognized it?'

Gianni looked at his brother.

'Why don't you two go on upstairs? I'll clean up down here and join you in a minute.'

'An excellent idea,' said Maurizio. 'Come on, Minot. After helping us out like this, the least you deserve is a glass of something. I don't know what we'd do without you, I don't really.'

The earlier silence had been replaced by a verbosity almost equally oppressive. But Minot allowed himself to be taken in hand and steered up to the large sitting room at one end of the brothers' house, where he accepted a glass of the wine he had helped bottle several years earlier. Maurizio left the open bottle on the table and sat down, shaking his head sadly.

'All this, coming so soon after Chiara's death,' he sighed.

Minot sniffed.

'You mean there's a connection?'

'For some of us there is,' Maurizio replied, with a sigh. 'I suppose it's stupid, after all this time, but Gianni was hit hard when she died. In his mind, she was immortal.'

Minot stared into his wine and said nothing.

'And just when he'd started to get used to the idea,' Maurizio Faigano continued, 'this happened. Every time someone mentions *la cosa*, it's as if Chiara's tomb has been desecrated.'

Minot reached out and grasped Maurizio's arm sympathetically.

'I'm sorry. I didn't realize.'

Maurizio nodded sadly. After a while, Minot let go of his arm and took another gulp of wine.

'What was that about hearing some dog in Aldo's vines the night it happened?'

Maurizio looked at him.

'Oh, nothing, I suppose. I couldn't see anything, what with the mist, but I thought I recognized the dog's bark. You know how distinctive they are.'

The door opened and in came Gianni, a large smile on his rumpled, slept-in face.

'Well, that's all taken care of,' he said. 'How's the wine, Minot?'

'*Discreto*,' was the guarded reply. 'Maybe I should have kept more for myself.'

He glanced at Gianni, who waved negligently.

'I expect we can let you have a few bottles, in return for all the help you've given us. Eh, Maurizio?'

'Minot was asking about the dog.'

'Ah, yes! Maybe it was just a runaway. Who knows?'

'Not with those fences that Aldo put in,' said Minot.

Gianni poured himself a glass of wine.

'Perhaps someone found a way through them. Or made one. All I know is that Maurizio heard this *bastardin* barking down there. Which is odd in itself. No one's ever found any truffles on Vincenzo land, as far as I know.'

There was a silence.

'So whose dog was it?' asked Minot.

He knew, as they did, that the hound would have been instantly identifiable. All men of their age in the Langhe either kept a truffle dog themselves or knew someone who did. Their noises and utterances were as familiar as those of neighbouring children.

'I thought it was Anna,' said Maurizio.

'Beppe's dog?'

'I might have been wrong.'

They drank in silence for a while.

'There are two ways we can handle this snooper from Rome,' said Gianni. 'Either we come up with a suitable suspect to hand him on a plate, or we just clam up.'

'There already *is* a suspect,' Minot pointed out.

'But if they're starting from scratch again, that means they don't believe that he did it.'

'And neither do I,' said Maurizio. 'What son would do something like that to his father? And still less a milksop like Manlio Vincenzo.'

'They can be the worst if you push them too far,' observed his brother. 'They take it and take it for years, and then one day they crack. And God knows Aldo pushed Manlio. Remember what he said to him that evening at the *festa*, calling him a faggot and a queer in a voice you could hear all over the hall?'

Maurizio shrugged.

'It doesn't matter what we think. The important thing is to work out what to tell this cop from Rome.'

'Or what not to tell him,' Minot put in.

'Or both,' said Gianni. 'Like in the war. Remember our motto? "Tell them anything, so long as you tell them nothing." That's what we've got to do now.'

Minot knocked back his wine.

'I've got nothing to hide.'

'Oh, really?' asked Maurizio with a sarcastic edge. 'Have you got a valid licence to gather truffles? And what about receipts for all your transactions, showing that sales tax was duly paid? All of which income you will, of course, have declared on your . . .'

'What the hell's that got to do with it? There's a lot of stuff I could tell the cops about you two, for that matter.'

Gianni Faigano nodded earnestly.

'That's the whole point. We're all in this together, like during the war.'

'Except during the war you knew which side everyone was on. And we knew what we were fighting for.'

'For our country, right? For our beliefs. Well, now we're fighting for our community.'

Maurizio sighed.

'A community in which someone stabbed an old man to death and cut off his cock and balls.'

Unexpectedly, Minot laughed, a tearing peal of hilarity with a slightly intoxicated edge.

'That son of a bitch! If he'd known how he would end up . . .'

Gianni nodded.

'But the fact remains that whoever did it is living right here amongst us.'

'Right here in the village,' Maurizio chipped in, 'where I've yet to hear a single person speak a sincere word of regret for the victim.'

'It's us against them,' said Gianni. 'What's done is done. It's time to get on with our lives.'

Minot gave a series of earnest nods.

'You're right,' he said. 'It's just like the war.'

Gianni smiled.

'It's like the war all over again. And we know who the enemy is.'

With trembling fingers, Aurelio Zen unwrapped the medicinal potion from its layers of packaging, each as thin and transparent as tissue paper. A tight rain beat against the windows, while the hard wind behind it exploited every crack and weakness in the hotel's ageing structure, seeping through the shutters and curtains to manifest itself as an intangible but ubiquitous presence in the room. The ancient cast-iron concertina of the radiator gurgled and spluttered and hissed, impotent against such virulently intrusive malevolence.

The phone again rang several times, just as it had earlier, breaking off with the same stifled cheep. Ignoring it, Zen worked patiently to free another clove of garlic from its enclosing membranes with the blade of his pocket-knife. The bulb had yielded eleven cloves in all. A few of the insiders were too small to bother with, but the outer monsters more than made up for these runts. Flakes of the frail integument lay all over the table, stirring sluggishly in the pervasive draught like some nightmare dandruff problem.

His task completed, Zen gathered the peelings into a heap, which he tipped into the waste-basket along with the vaguely pubic stalk. Outside, car horns blared and voices were raised in momentary anger. The sudden appearance of cold winds and relentless rain after so many weeks of glorious late-summer weather was trying enough in itself. But there was a more substantial reason why the tempers of the local citizenry should be frayed, for at least half the town was economically dependent, directly or indirectly, on the wine harvest. Until recently all the indications had been that this would be an exceptional vintage in terms of both quality and quantity. But the Nebbiolo grape from which all the best local wines were made sopped up water like blotting-paper, and the resulting product was thin, pale and insubstantial. Another week like this and the whole crop would be downgraded to one of the marginal years such as '92 or '94. A few more and it would be a total write-off, fit only for bulking up and marketing in litre flasks of generic red like the one which stood at Aurelio Zen's elbow.

For Zen, this would not have represented any great tragedy. As the famous director and connoisseur responsible for his posting to Alba had pointed out, wine came in just two forms as far as Zen was concerned: *sincero* or *sofisticato*. The latter category, in its strictest interpretation, comprised anything not made by a family member or close personal friend with his own hands from grapes grown by him, and most certainly included anything in a bottle with a printed label on sale in shops and supermarkets. The former term of approbation was extended to any wines sold by the glass or jug in a few carefully vetted bars and restaurants, the understanding being that the proprietor had obtained them from producers known and trusted by him, and that they had not been messed about with.

But despite his inability to sympathize with the problems which were aggravating the good people of Alba, Zen had his own reasons for feeling wretched. The slight malady he had felt coming on in Rome had transformed itself into a full-blown, all-stops-out misery for which the word 'cold' seemed completely inadequate. As someone who almost never got ill, Zen found this especially hard to deal with. He knew plenty of people who, without being hypochondriacs precisely, nevertheless always seemed to be suffering to some degree or other from one of a range of minor ailments. They were used to it, indeed appeared almost to welcome it. Above all, they were good at it. Practice had made perfect. They were accomplished patients, well-versed in the skills of home remedies and medical treatment alike. They accepted illness as an old if rather tiresome friend whose visits were nevertheless preferable to solitude, to say nothing of giving them a perfect excuse for a multitude of personal shortcomings or lapses.

But to Zen illness was an enemy he had no idea how to placate or control, a barbarian horde which descended without warning and made life impossible until, just as suddenly, it went off to wreak havoc elsewhere. And as such invasions went, this particular one was not only in the Attila the Hun class, but could hardly have been worse timed.

He had arrived in Alba the previous night after a six-and-a-half-hour train journey from the capital. He had never visited the town before, indeed had barely ever set foot in Piedmont except for a few trips to Turin during his years at the Questura in Milan. Asti, the provincial capital where he had changed trains, meant nothing to him except the sparkling, fulsomely sweet wine one got offered at weddings when the host was too stingy or ignorant to come up with anything better.

There had been nothing sparkling about Asti at nine o'clock the previous night, however, with a blustering and buffeting wind and sheets of rain which spattered on the platform like liquid hail. The user-friendly genius of the State Railways had ensured that the two-coach diesel unit which serviced the branch line to his final destination was waiting on a track as far as possible from the platform where the Rome–Turin express had arrived. Trembling and breathless, with aching limbs and a sinking heart, Zen grabbed his bags and ran the length of the dank, ill-lit underpass, terrified that the connection would leave before he could reach it.

He needn't have worried. Another fifteen minutes passed before the *automotrice* finally revved up its engines and nosed off along the single-line track across the Tanaro river and south to Alba. Zen soon fell into a shallow, confused, snuffly sleep, from which he was awakened by a member of the crew, who curtly informed him that they had reached the end of the line. His interrupted dream had been set back in Naples, his last posting, and as he gathered his belongings together and clambered out of the train he braced himself for the crowds, the noise, the vibrant chaos and confusion of that city . . .

It did not take him long to realize his error. The rainswept streets were as deserted as the small station, the taxi rank empty, the shops and houses shuttered and dark. Fortunately it proved to be a relatively short walk to his hotel, where it took several minutes of continuous ringing on the bell to rouse the night porter, who seemed to have no idea who Zen was or what he was doing there, or even that the establishment over which he presided existed for the purpose of offering accommodation to travellers.

But all this had been as nothing to the discovery, next morning, that getting out of bed and going to the bathroom presented a physical challenge roughly equivalent to walking across Antarctica. He was shivering, aching, sneezing, snivelling, coughing and moaning, and felt utterly exhausted and disoriented. Somehow he made it back to bed and lay down for a few minutes, during which, according to the clock, an hour and a half went by. When he finally surfaced, two hours after that, he crawled to the phone, rang for a waiter and arranged for delivery of the ingredients whose preparation he was now embarked upon.

The remedy was an ancient tradition of the Zen family, a secret nostrum at once venerable and slightly shameful, given its reputed connection with an ancestor who had been Governor of the Venetian stronghold of Durazzo, now in Albania, and who had gone native in such a spectacular way that the Council of Ten had not only recalled him but had had him quietly strangled. For Zen its mystique derived from the fact that as a child he had not been allowed to take it. For *his* colds he was dosed with aspirin ground up in a spoonful of honey. Only adults got the full-strength, gloves-off, no-holds-barred treatment: a whole head of peeled garlic eaten raw with copious quantities of strong red wine.

Despite the acknowledged and indeed almost miraculous benefits of this potion, there had been plenty of adverse comments about it from those forced to associate with the patient afterwards. As one uncle had put it succinctly, 'The symptoms of the cure are worse than those of the illness.' But to Zen's mind this merely confirmed its efficacity, on a par with such harsh and primitive remedies as bleach poured over an open wound, or the ministrations of the local self-taught dentist, with his rack of

31

terrifying implements whose application you didn't want to even think about. Pain could only be cured by pain. Bad power required good power to defeat it, and power of any sort was bound to hurt.

The cloves of garlic, once stripped and chewed, certainly hurt at first, their crunchy fibrous substance disclosing an astonishing saturated strength of oily, burning intensity which coated every surface in the mouth and throat and then, under the benign influence of the wine, turned into a mild but persistent tingling warmth promising to drive out every foreign body and intruder in short order. He had drunk most of the litre of red wine and was biting into the last but one of the fat ivory cloves when there came a knock at the door.

'Well?' he mumbled through a mouthful of half-chewed garlic. Probably the cleaner wanting to make up the room. The service was never there when you needed it, but whenever you wanted a bit of peace and quiet . . .

The door opened cautiously to reveal a plump, dapper, well-dressed man of about Zen's age carrying a large manilla envelope. He took in the scene and coughed in an embarrassed way.

'Ah! Excuse the intrusion, *dottore*. I'll come back later, when you're more . . .'

Zen took another leisurely swig of wine.

'Are you the manager?' he demanded. 'About time, too. I've complained twice about the heating, and that lump of scrap metal over there is still about as warm as yesterday's bath.'

His visitor surveyed the dishevelled, unshaven figure huddled in his dressing-gown on the rumpled bed, gulping wine and chewing raw garlic.

'I think there must be some mistake,' he said.

'I certainly hope so!' Zen retorted. 'The principles of central heating have been known in this country ever since Julius Caesar was wetting his knickers, yet your establishment is apparently incapable of . . .'

The newcomer closed the door. He strode to the phone, set his envelope down on the table and dialled.

'Front desk? Room 314, Vice-Questore Tullio Legna of the *Commissariato di Polizia* speaking. I have come to pay my respects to a very important visitor from Rome who is staying here as your guest. I understand that he has complained about the inadequate heating in his room, but without effect. I suggest that you rectify this situation without further delay, lest I find it necessary to close the entire hotel pending a full investigation, a process likely to take some considerable time.'

He hung up and turned back to Zen.

'Please accept my apologies, *dottore*. We don't get many visitors out of season. They must have been trying to cut costs by turning the boilers off.'

Zen unrolled a strip of toilet paper from the spare roll he had removed from the bathroom and blew his nose loudly.

'I feel dreadful,' he said, rising painfully from his bed, one hand extended. Realizing belatedly that he was still holding the soggy tissue, he looked about vaguely for the waste-basket.

'You're ill,' Tullio Legna observed.

'No, no. I mean, yes, I suppose I am. But that's not . . . Dreadful about receiving you like this, I mean. What must you think?'

'I think you have a bad cold.'

Zen waved at the open wine bottle and the remaining clove of garlic.

'An old family cure. I wasn't expecting visitors.'

He gestured Legna towards the lone chair in the room and collapsed soggily on the bed, pulling the dressing-gown about his legs.

'I tried phoning, but there was no reply,' the local police chief replied, sitting down. 'Since I happened to be passing, I thought I'd just drop by in person.'

Zen coughed, sniffed and lit a cigarette.

'And found what looks like a flop for homeless alcoholic derelicts,' he said, pushing the remaining clove of garlic about the bedside table like an extracted wisdom tooth awaiting the proverbial fairy. 'But it does work. At least, so I've been told.'

'The curative powers of garlic are, of course, well-attested,'

Tullio Legna remarked sententiously. 'But here in Alba, at this time of the year, I think we may be able to do better. Will you allow me to order you lunch? Not from the kitchens here, God forbid. There's a good place a couple of streets away. I'll have them send it up to the room. What are you drinking?'

Zen passed him the bottle. His visitor inspected the label, sniffed the contents, and handed it back.

'No,' he said decidedly.

'Not good?' queried Zen.

'Not even bad.'

Tullio Legna wiped his hands together as if to remove a contaminating stain.

'Leave it to me,' he said. 'In an hour, shall we say? The sooner we start, the sooner you'll be back on your feet. Which brings me to my reason for coming, apart, of course, from the pleasure of making your acquaintance.'

He pursed his lips and gazed thoughtfully at Zen, who felt the full force of his disadvantage for the first time.

'When it was announced that a Criminalpol officer was being transferred here to open an investigation into the Vincenzo case, the news naturally excited much comment,' Legna continued in a studiously neutral voice. 'This case had been in the hands of my Carabinieri colleagues – we had had no hand in it – and they had made an arrest. There has therefore been a considerable amount of speculation as to why the Ministry should suddenly have decided to take a hand, and at such a high level.'

'Naturally,' Zen replied in an equally bland tone.

Tullio Legna smiled sympathetically.

'I don't want to burden you with questions when you're unwell, *dottore*. But it would considerably facilitate my position if you would, however briefly, clarify yours.'

Semi-recumbent, half-drunk, stinking of garlic and feeling like death partially defrosted, thought Zen.

'My position?' he repeated.

'Your interest, let's say.'

'In the Vincenzo case?'

'Exactly.'

Zen put out his cigarette in the dregs of wine remaining in his glass.

'I have no interest in it.'

'Ah.'

'It's a question of someone else's interest.'

'And what is that?'

'To ensure that the Vincenzo wine gets made.'

Legna looked probingly at Zen for a moment, then smiled ironically.

'And who on earth is this well-connected *intenditore*?'

Zen lit another Nazionale. When it became evident that he was not going to reply, Tullio Legna nodded gravely.

'Ah, like that, is it? Excuse my indiscretion, *dottore*. We're just simple country people here in the Langhe. I'm not accustomed to the Roman way of doing things.'

Zen gestured feebly.

'It's I who should apologize. You've been very kind, and I'm not trying to play games. I can assure you that the identity of the person who was instrumental in having me sent here is of absolutely no relevance to the case or to my assignment.'

'Which is to get Manlio Vincenzo out of gaol,' Legna remarked expressionlessly.

Zen shrugged.

'I understand that this year's wine promises to be exceptional.'

The Alba police chief got up and crossed over to the window. He opened the curtains, then wound up the external metal shutters. A bleak, pallid light reluctantly made its presence felt in the room. From the bed, Zen could see nothing but a section of rain-drenched plaster on the building opposite.

'Not if this keeps up,' Legna commented. 'Until a few days ago, it looked like being one of the best years of the decade, possibly even the best since 1990. So the growers decided to delay picking and try to squeeze a little more flavour into the grapes. Now they're out there clearing leaves and thinning clusters and praying that the rain lets up in time to save the harvest.'

He turned back to face Zen.

'Well, I won't tire you any more, *dottore*. You'll need to be fully recovered if you're to have any hope of getting Signor Manlio released in time to oversee the vintage. In my humble opinion, it's a very tall order indeed.'

'You think he's guilty, then?'

A silent glance passed between the two men. Tullio Legna walked back to the bed.

'The real problem is that there are no other suspects. Short of someone else coming forward and confessing, I can't see any way of bringing it off.'

He paused, as though about to take his leave, then continued in a quieter tone.

'And even if you did, it might not make any difference.'

Zen stared up at him through a cloud of cigarette smoke.

'Meaning what?'

Legna eyed him acutely.

'This is a small, tightly-knit community, *dottore*. Aldo Vincenzo may not have been the most popular member of it, to put it mildly, but to die like that! It's the sort of atrocity which people remember from the war years, but which they never thought they'd witness again. Feelings are running very high.'

He placed the envelope he had been carrying on the bedside table.

'All the information we have on the case is in there, together with a map of the district. But, as you no doubt know, Manlio and his father had a public row at the village *festa* on the evening in question. They were seen leaving the family house together later that night, and as far as we know Aldo never returned. If Manlio walks free without clear proof of his innocence, I'm afraid it may only be a matter of time before he . . . meets with an accident, shall we say?'

The two men confronted each other in silence for a moment.

'And now I'll go and order your lunch,' Tullio Legna exclaimed in a loud, hearty voice. 'Eat it all up, and try to get as much rest as you can. You're going to need it.'

When the dog first appeared, snuffling and scratching at his door, Bruno Scorrone had a moment of weakness. Between thirty and forty million lire were staring him in the face, not to mention pawing at his knee, whining confusedly and surveying his hallway as though sighting invisible beings.

Somewhere safely far away – north of Asti, for instance, up in the Monferrato – Bruno could easily have disposed of a trained *tabui* like this for cash with no questions asked. But he had quite enough legal worries already, and knew exactly how much the hound meant to its owner. This made it all the more remarkable that she should be running around loose, her leash trailing behind her, at the mercy of less scrupulous and responsible citizens than Bruno, of whom there was no shortage in the locality. In the end he loaded the reluctant, hysterical Anna into his car and drove the two miles along back roads to Beppe Gallizio's house. The rain had finally stopped, at least for now. The air was cool and slightly hazy, yielding a diffident, diffused light.

When he reached the house, on the outskirts of the village, there was no sign of Beppe. His car was there, but the front door was locked and Bruno Scorrone's increasingly irritated thumping produced no response. Anna was behaving oddly, too. She circled the yard continually, sniffing and searching, running back to Bruno, planting her nose on his shoes and pawing the ground, then scuttling off to one side, where a path led down the hill. Bruno's only interest in dogs was to scare off intruders and undercover tax agents, and in terms of their cash value as sniffers-out of truffles. He had no time to play whatever childish game the bitch was proposing. Fetching a length of rope from the barn, he tied one end to the leash dangling from her collar

37

and the other to a spike protruding from the wall of the house, and then drove away.

Several hours passed. There is no way of knowing what this interval might mean to a dog, let alone one desperate to communicate urgent and terrible news. One of our days? One of our years? At all events, by the time Lamberto Latini showed up, Anna had worn her neck to a bloody mess in her frantic efforts to escape. Appalled at her condition, he freed the dog, which immediately displayed the same behaviour as she had with Bruno Scorrone, sprinting to and fro between Latini and the path winding down the hill between Beppe's vegetable garden and a neighbour's ploughed field.

Like the previous visitor, Lamberto rapped impatiently at the door, then tried the handle. He glanced at his watch. Just past ten. That was the time that they had agreed. By eleven at the latest he'd need to be at work back at his restaurant, which had been booked for lunch by a convention party from Asti who were being taken out for a 'Traditional Langhe Country Meal'. But where the hell was Beppe? If he didn't come through, Lamberto was in deep trouble. The cut-price dealings in truffles which took place in the back streets of Alba would be over by now, and if he had to pay the official price, including commission and tax, he'd hardly break even on the day.

Lamberto stood looking around in growing annoyance. Beppe had never let him down before. It was an excellent arrangement for both of them: truffles for cash, with no extra cut for middlemen or the *fisco*. Since Anna was there, he must have returned from his nocturnal hunting and gathering. Also there was the dented, mud-spattered old Fiat 500 which Beppe had cannily refused to trade in for something more comfortable and ostentatious, even though the sum Lamberto had paid him for a particularly fine specimen a couple of months ago would alone have paid for a new car. Whatever Beppe did with his money, it was nothing that might attract attention.

The dog was still mewling and worrying Lamberto's shoes, making little forays towards the path leading down the hillside, then returning with a series of high-pitched whines. This increased the mystery of Beppe's absence. Even if he'd been called away unexpectedly, or suddenly been taken ill, he would never have left his invaluable truffle hound tied up outside the house like one of her poor cousins, the half-starved watchdogs of the region.

Unlike Bruno Scorrone, Lamberto Latini liked dogs, to the extent – regarded locally as eccentric, if not perverse – of keeping a spaniel purely as a pet. So when he followed the increasingly distraught Anna round the side of the house, it was purely as a reflex action born of habit. But once they reached the back of the house and the bitch scampered off down the path, encouraged by this first glimmer of comprehension in the dim yet dominant species she had to deal with, Lamberto did not follow. He had no clear idea how to resolve the problem of Beppe's dereliction, but taking his dog for walkies was certainly not it.

At a loss, and feeling vaguely ashamed of himself, he went over to the back door of the property and made a big show of knocking and calling out Beppe's name. There was no reply, but the door opened a crack, as if under its own volition. Lamberto stared at it an instant. Then, ignoring Anna's frantic entreaties, he stepped over the threshold, shutting the dog outside.

'Beppe! Beppe? It's Lamberto!'

He already knew that there would be no answer. The silence had that coherent quality, like settled soil, which houses only have when they are empty. Lamberto stepped cautiously into the large kitchen, with its board floor and bare walls where islands of brickwork showed through the crumbling plaster. The air was cold, the room empty. Moving into the hall, Lamberto continued his search, occasionally calling Beppe's name aloud, less loudly now. Outside he could hear Anna's persistent keening, as though she were answering him, but within the house the solid, complacent silence was unbroken. There was clearly no one there.

Lamberto returned to the kitchen and looked around, reluctant to admit failure. On the table stood a dirty dish with some sauce dried to a crust, an empty wine glass and a chunk of bread.

The fireplace was cold, the ashes holding no ember. Lamberto picked up the bread and squeezed it. Yesterday's. So Beppe had eaten, presumably before going out, but had not been back since. Except that his dog was there, and his car.

Then he noticed another item on the table. He picked it up and inspected it. At first sight it resembled a general-purpose knife such as might be used for slicing salami or cheese, except that the blade and handle were stained with a dark tawny substance resembling dried blood. Before he could begin to think what this might signify, his attention was diverted by the sound of a key being inserted into the front door.

Lamberto started to put the knife back on the table, then thought better of it. The silence had suddenly turned malign, no longer placid and compact but tense and still, loaded like a gun. Gripping the knife tightly, Lamberto stepped to his right and concealed himself as best he could beside a huge *credenza* where unused heirloom bowls and plates gathered dust. Steel-rimmed heels clacked steadily down the hall. Lamberto couldn't think of anyone who wore boots like that, certainly not Beppe. Lamberto grasped the knife still more tightly, feeling simultaneously ridiculous and terrified.

At the doorway to the kitchen, the heels paused. There was a long moment of silence, broken only by one of Anna's despondent yowls. Then the intruder moved forward into the room, revealing himself as a portly man in black uniform and hard cap trimmed with red braid and a gilt badge showing a flaming torch. Catching sight of Lamberto, he started slightly.

'Signor Latini.'

'*Buon giorno, maresciallo,*' Lamberto replied automatically.

The two men looked at each other for a moment. Then the Carabinieri official nodded towards the window.

'Looks like it's clearing up, finally.'

'I came to see Beppe,' Lamberto blurted out. 'His car's outside, and his dog, Anna. But he's not here.'

Enrico Pascal nodded slowly.

'No, he's not here.'

Lamberto Latini finally became aware of what he was holding. 'I found this on the table,' he said, displaying the knife. 'It's got blood on it.'

Again Pascal nodded, as though this was the most ordinary thing in the world.

'Why don't you put it back where it was?' he suggested.

Latini did so.

'I thought something might have happened to Beppe,' he mumbled haltingly. 'And when I heard someone coming in . . . How did you open the front door?'

'With a key.'

'A key? Where did you get it?'

The Carabiniere did not reply at once.

'Why don't you sit down, Signor Latini?' he said at length. 'No, in that chair, please, away from the table.'

Latini did so.

'You were asking where I got the key. I got it from Beppe. And how did *you* get in?'

Lamberto gestured behind him.

'The back door. It was open.'

'Open, or just unlocked?'

'It wasn't fastened. It must stick slightly. It opened when I knocked.'

The *maresciallo* raised his eyebrows.

'So you took advantage to come inside the house. Why?'

'I just wanted to make sure that Beppe was all right.'

'Why shouldn't he be all right?'

'We had an appointment to meet here at ten o'clock. He's never let me down before.'

'When did you make this appointment?'

The Carabinieri official's tone had become more peremptory. Lamberto Latini appeared to reflect.

'Let's see. Yesterday, it must have been. No, the day before. I phoned and suggested we get together for a chat, you know . . .'

'It's a long way to come for a chat, Signor Latini, particularly on a working day.'

41

Lamberto started to say something, then checked his watch and got up.

'That reminds me, I must be going.'

'I'm afraid that's not possible.'

Lamberto Latini frowned.

'I've got a business convention coming to lunch. They've booked the whole restaurant.'

Enrico Pascal sighed heavily.

'No one appreciates the importance of good food more than I, Signor Latini, and your establishment is without doubt one of the finest in the region – although the last time I ate there, it seemed to me that the lamb was a trifle oversalted. But certain matters must take precedence even over gastronomy. Murder is one of them.'

Lamberto Latini gave an irritated frown.

'Murder? What's the Vincenzo affair got to do with it?'

'Where were you at five o'clock this morning, Signor Latini?'

The question seemed to rebound from Lamberto Latini's face and strike various surfaces in the room before returning for a belated answer.

'In bed, of course!'

'At home?'

'Where do you think I sleep?'

'Alone?'

Now Latini's anger was naked.

'What the hell is that supposed to mean?'

The *maresciallo* appeared unperturbed.

'I'm asking if you can name any witnesses to substantiate your claim to have been at home, asleep, at five o'clock this morning.'

For the first time, Lamberto Latini's expression was one of open hostility.

'My wife is dead. You know that.'

Enrico Pascal inclined his head.

'And when you finally woke up, you got into your car and drove over twelve miles to have "a chat" with Beppe Gallizio. On a day when your entire restaurant has been reserved for an important business lunch.'

'Ask Beppe! He'll confirm what I say.'

Enrico Pascal stared at him in silence for some time. Then he went to the table, bent over and inspected the knife which Lamberto had been holding. He did not touch it, but his pudgy, rather feminine fingers drummed out a brief tattoo on the table-top. With a dismissive sniff, Lamberto Latini got up.

'I've had enough of this!' he proclaimed, heading for the door.

In one smooth gesture, the *maresciallo* undid the flap on the holster of his service pistol.

'Don't do anything rash, Signor Latini,' he said equably. 'You're in quite enough trouble as it is.'

Latini turned, gazing at him in apparent incredulity.

'I can't stand here playing games all day, Pascal! I've got a business to run.'

'It's going to have to manage without you.'

Lamberto Latini squared up to his opponent.

'Are you saying I'm under arrest?'

'I am placing you in detention pending further investigation. If you hand over the keys to your car, I won't bother about the handcuffs.'

'You must be out of your mind! The night Aldo Vincenzo was killed I was . . .'

'Who said anything about Vincenzo? We've already made an arrest in that case, and it's all in the hands of the judges. My concern now is with Beppe Gallizio.'

Latini sighed with theatrical emphasis and spread his hands in gestural surrender.

'All right, I admit it! I came here today to buy some truffles from Beppe for this lunch, which thanks to you is now going to be ruined, along with my reputation. I know that it's technically an illegal transaction, and you know that everyone around here does the same thing. I thought you cared enough about the good things of the Langhe to overlook a minor matter like this. Apparently I was wrong. Very well.'

He drew a bunch of clinking metal from his pocket and tossed it on the table.

43

'Here are my keys, *maresciallo*,' he said in a tone of sarcastic deference. 'If I promise not to make a run for it, will you please try not to shoot me?'

Enrico Pascal watched this performance with a cool, slightly clouded gaze.

'But what about Beppe?' he murmured.

'What do I care about Beppe? Let him look after himself!'

The Carabinieri officer looked at Latini for a moment.

'He can't. He's dead.'

A long silence.

'Dead?'

'Shot. Down in a coppice by the stream. His whole face and half his head blasted away.'

Lamberto Latini staggered as though he had been struck. He said nothing.

'Then I come up to his house and find you here, armed and in hiding,' Pascal went on. 'You have no verifiable reason for being here, nor any alibi for the time of the incident. Under the circumstances, Signor Latini, you'll understand that I have no choice but to take you into custody pending further investigations.'

He awoke naked and covered in blood. A series of mirrors revealed the scene from every angle. In an intriguing *trompe-l'œil* touch, there was also real blood on the glass, blotching out large portions of the reflected gore. This came as no surprise. The stuff was everywhere: on the walls, the gleaming taps, the fluffy white towels. Some had even ended up in the toilet, staining the water pale pink. More to the point, it was all over him, trickling down his face, finding its way in irregular rivulets down his chest, belly and legs, and then dripping off to further complicate the pattern of crimson splotches, spatters and spots on the tiled floor.

A classic murder scene, in short, just like the illustrative pictures of carnage in the training manual, except that this was in sharp, rich colour, not poorly exposed black and white. There was even the obligatory clue, to reinforce the message that the criminal always gives himself away. Looking behind him in the mirror, he saw a smudged handprint on the wall next to the light switch. That's how they'd get him, that and the traces of blood that would linger in the cracks and crevices, no matter how hard he tried to clean it up.

But was he the criminal or the victim? He examined himself more closely in the mirrors surrounding the blood-drenched sink. There seemed to be a deep gash above his left eye, up near the hairline. That must have been where it had landed, the savagely hard blow which had come from nowhere and stunned him out of his dreams into this waking nightmare.

He unclenched his hands, sticky with drying blood, turned on a tap and grabbed a towel, soaked it thoroughly and set about cleaning himself up. The wound on his forehead looked even worse once it was fully exposed, a clammy mouth oozing a frightening quantity of bright red vomit. The half-dried stains covering his body and the floor and walls seemed to take an amazing amount of time and energy to clean up, even superficially. Again and again he wrung out the towel, depositing a stream of rose-coloured water in the basin, then rinsed it out and started in again.

When he couldn't find any more visible blood, he flung the filthy towel in the bath and went into the next room. Apart from a diffuse glimmer behind the closed curtains, it was in darkness. The air was stuffy and musty, with an odd, pervasive odour similar to that of sweat, but subtly different. He found the switch and turned on the light. His forehead was starting to hurt badly, and when he dabbed at the wound with a tentative finger, it came away bright red. He fetched another towel from the bathroom, pressed it to his face and stretched out on the bed.

A manilla envelope was propped against the lamp on the table beside him. It bore the words 'Vice-Questore Aurelio Zen' in black felt marker. The name seemed familiar. He wasn't entirely convinced that it was his, but it was a working hypothesis. Which left the question of where he was. After some considerable reflection, which yielded nothing, he opened the drawer of the bedside table and rummaged around until he found a booklet with instructions for using the telephone. The cover was stamped with a stylized picture of a large building and gold letters reading 'Alba Palace Hotel'.

Alba, he thought. His memory, which seemed to be short on essential facts but chock-full of arcane trivia, promptly supplied the information that this was a form of the Latin word for 'white'. As in 'albino', it added pedantically, before appending a list of other things which were associated with the word: towels, wine, truffles . . .

Tartufi bianchi d'Alba! Now he was getting somewhere. That was the source of that sweet stench – stronger even than that of blood – which perfumed the whole room, the bed sheets, and indeed his skin itself. They'd been grated over a meal he'd eaten the day before: shavings of moist, fragrant tuber with the colour of fine marble, the texture of raw mushroom and a flavour which permeated every internal membrane of your body until it seemed to glow in the dark. And, beneath, an egg with a yolk as orange as the setting sun smothered in a savoury cheese *fonduta* . . .

The faint smile which had appeared on his lips at this fugitive memory abruptly vanished as his earlier panic returned. What about the blood? What about the cut on his forehead? What on earth had happened? He remembered arriving at the station in the rain and lugging his suitcase to the hotel. All that was clearly documented and archived in his long-term memory. The record since then was more contentious, relying on the usual circumstantial evidence, unsupported inference and informers' reports.

He'd been ill, that was the gist of it: feverish, aching all over, tossing and turning in fitful sleep. There was the wrecked and sodden bed to prove it. Somewhere that meal had to be fitted in, and an amiable stranger in a suit who had watched him get drunk and eat garlic. This section was badly focused and confused, with lots of gaps, but nevertheless basically sound.

But what had come afterwards? All he could recover was a mishmash of tortuous, anxiety-ridden dreams, like a film patched together from discards and out-takes trying to pass themselves off as a coherent narrative. The only scene he still remembered – a child standing before him, one hand outstretched like a beggar – made no sense in retrospect, and yet he knew that at the time it had been imbued with an infinite power to hurt and rebuke.

None of which began to explain how his head had been cut badly enough to drench himself and the entire bathroom in blood. One moment he had been lying in bed, perhaps still feverish, racked by vivid and disturbing dreams. Under the circumstances, that was to be expected. The next thing he knew, he was standing in the blood-stained bathroom with a searing gash on his brow. How had he got there? What had happened in between? There was a gap in the story, a hiatus which nothing could explain.

He was aroused from these speculations by the telephone. It sounded cheery, normal and welcome.

'Tullio Legna, *dottore*. Are you feeling any better?'

'I'm, er . . . Yes, thank you.'

For it was only then that he realized that, despite his brutal awakening and its associated mysteries, he *was* feeling better. His cold seemed to have disappeared as if by magic. His limbs no longer ached, his temperature felt normal, and he wasn't shivering or sneezing.

'Good,' said the local police chief, 'because there has been a new development.'

'I know. It's going to need stitches, I think.'

The line went silent.

'Stitches?' Tullio Legna repeated.

'I'm sorry to burden you with my medical problems yet again, but can you recommend a doctor?'

Another brief silence.

'Saturday is always difficult. Let me make a few phone calls and get back to you. But what happened, *dottore*?'

'I slipped in the shower.'

Tullio Legna made sympathetic noises and rang off. Still pressing the towel to his face, Zen walked over to the window, drew back the curtains and gasped. The rain had moved on and the clouds had transformed themselves into a radiant mist through which dramatically slanted sunlight irradiated the piazza where booksellers were setting up their booths under the pine trees.

Thirty minutes later he was out in it all, badly shaved and clumsily dressed, walking up the Via Maestra with Tullio Legna. The latter had not only set up an appointment with a certain Doctor Lucchese, whom he described to Zen as 'one of the best in Italy, if one of the laziest', but had also brought a selection of adhesive bandages, one of which currently adorned Zen's forehead.

'And your cold?' the police chief asked, as they picked their way through the promenading throng of Saturday morning shoppers.

'It's quite extraordinary! The garlic and wine treatment usually works in a few days, but this is like a miracle. It's as if I was never ill in the first place. Even after this stupid accident, I feel better than I have for ages!'

'*Bella, no?*' Legna replied, catching Zen's eyes on a well-endowed woman walking towards them. 'Yes, they have that effect too.'

'What do?' asked Zen, turning round to check out the back view.

'*Tuberi di Afrodite*, as we call them here. I take it you enjoyed the lunch I had sent up yesterday?'

'It was delicious.'

'But it's not just a matter of gastronomic pleasure! I made sure they doubled the usual ration of truffles to increase the therapeutic effect. Some people here will tell you there's nothing but death that they can't cure.'

He turned left into the carriage entrance of an ancient three-storey *palazzo*, its sober façade relieved by ornate wrought-iron balconies and an elaborate plaster cornice. After a brief colloquy with the porter, they were admitted to Doctor Lucchese's apartment on the first floor. The room into which they were ushered gave no hint that medical consultations might take place there. Lined with books, maps and prints, comfortably furnished with leather armchairs, antique tables and writing desks, it looked more like a scholar's sanctum than a doctor's consulting room.

Nor did the physician's appearance inspire confidence. Gaunt, with a shock of long grey hair streaked with silver, wearing a silk dressing-gown and smoking a cigar, he replaced the battered book he had been reading on a table and greeted his guests with a vaguely reluctant, world-weary urbanity which did not seem to augur well for his medical skills.

'Michele Gazzano,' he said to Zen, indicating the book, once introductions had been made. 'From Alba, eighteenth century. I've just been leafing through his chapter on blood feuds in Sardinia. He spent fifteen years there as a judge. We Piedmontese ruled the place then, of course. If we can believe what he says, very little has changed in two hundred years. Should we find that depressing or encouraging?'

Zen shrugged.

'Both, perhaps.'

Lucchese eyed him keenly.

'You know Sardinia?'

'Not as well as your author, no doubt. But we – the Italians, that is – still do rule the place. A few years ago I was sent there to investigate the Burolo murder. You may remember it.'

Doctor Lucchese shook his head.

'I find it hard to take anything that's happened since I was born very seriously,' he said. 'Anyway, what can I do for you?'

With an energy which suggested that he had been fretting on the sidelines, Tullio Legna intervened with an account of the various misfortunes which had befallen Dottor Zen since his arrival.

'He caught the cold in Rome,' he concluded, 'and as soon as I got some *trifola* into his system, it acknowledged defeat and decamped. But now we have this new problem.'

Lucchese removed the plaster and inspected the injury.

'Almost identical to the blow that felled Aldo Vincenzo,' he murmured. 'Were you also attacked?'

'No, I did it myself.'

Once again, the doctor turned his disconcertingly undeceived gaze on Zen.

'I see. Well, we'd better patch you up. Come with me, please.'

The room into which Zen was ushered was a bleak tiled chamber at the rear of the premises. Apparently a converted bathroom, it was small, chilly and none too clean. Lucchese rummaged round in various cupboards, quizzing himself aloud as to whether various necessary supplies existed, or would be usable if they did.

Matters improved once Lucchese got to work. First he injected a local anaesthetic, so painlessly that Zen didn't even realize what had happened until the doctor started to scrub out the wound. Then came the stitches, six in all. Zen felt nothing but an odd sensation that an extra muscle had been inserted into his face and was now twitching experimentally.

'How did this happen?' asked Lucchese casually.

Zen ill-advisedly shook his head, and immediately winced.

'I don't know. I remember tossing and turning in bed, dreaming vividly. The next thing I knew, I felt a sharp blow to my forehead. I didn't know where I was or how I got there. When I turned on the light, I found myself in the bathroom, covered in blood.'

Lucchese tugged at the final stitch.

'What did you mean about the Vincenzo business?' asked Zen. 'I thought he was stabbed to death.'

'That happened subsequently. The first blow was to the temple, with something edged but not sharp. Probably a spade of some kind, since there were also traces of dirt.'

He gave a final wrench and snipped the thread.

'There you are! Bathe it periodically with a pad of gauze soaked in dilute hydrogen peroxide, then come back in a few days and I'll remove the stitches.'

'For someone who doesn't take any interest in recent news, you seem to know a lot about the Vincenzo case,' Zen observed ironically, as he replaced his jacket.

'The doctor who examined the corpse is a fellow member of the Chess Club of Alba. No one's actually played chess there for over a century, of course, but we still show up once a week to smoke and chat, the handful of us who are left. Every so often we make a token effort to elect some new members, but whenever someone is proposed, one of us always seems to feel that he wouldn't quite fit in.'

Lucchese placed the instruments he had used in the sink and peeled off his rubber gloves.

'How much do I owe you?' asked Zen.

'I'm not finished yet. Suturing that cut is something that any competent intern could do. Healing your spirit will be more difficult.'

Zen glanced at him sharply.

'I'll settle for the first, thank you. How much?'

'Nothing.'

'I insist!'

Lucchese turned to him and smiled wanly.

'I'm afraid you can't force me to accept your money, even if doing so might make you feel better about evading the real issue.'

'I'm not evading anything!'

'There's no need to shout, *dottore*. I am simply pointing out that the reason you required medical attention this morning is almost certainly because you experienced an episode of somnambulism, vulgarly termed sleepwalking.'

Zen gestured irritably.

'That's ridiculous! I've never done anything like that.'

'You will yet do many things you've never done before, the last being to die,' Lucchese replied. 'On the basis of what you've told me, I can see no other explanation. But I quite understand your reluctance to accept it. Somnabulism is a profoundly disturbing phenomenon, bridging as it does two worlds which sanity and civilization require us to keep separate. As a policeman, you might like to regard it as a form of dreaming which leaves footprints in the soil – or, in your case, bloodstains in the sink. It is invariably the result of some profound psychic trauma, this being the injury which I loosely termed spiritual. Whenever you wish to discuss it with me, I am at your disposal.'

He opened the door for Zen.

'And then, and only then, will I present my bill.'

Back in the living quarters of the house, Tullio Legna was deep in conversation with a young woman whom Zen assumed must be Lucchese's daughter. The two policemen took their leave and walked down the echoing exterior steps to the courtyard.

'So what's this "new development" you mentioned on the phone?' demanded Zen gruffly. He was still disconcerted by his exchange with Lucchese, as though the doctor had scored a point over him in some way.

Tullio Legna smiled broadly.

'Well, *dottore*, despite this little mishap, it seems that you're in luck!'

'What's that supposed to mean?'

'Come and have a coffee and I'll tell you all about it.'

Legna led the way down the street to the Piazza del Duomo,

where the Saturday morning market was in full swing. The two men skirted the crowded, bustling lanes of stalls and entered a venerable café in a narrow side street on the west side of the cathedral.

Zen stood sipping a coffee and listening with half an ear to some tale about a local truffle hunter named Beppe Gallizio who had been found shot dead in a copse near Palazzuole. The stitches in his forehead were beginning to ache as the anaesthetic faded, but what most bothered him was the doctor's words: 'Healing your spirit will be more difficult.' The man was clearly a charlatan, some sort of amateur psychoanalyst or New Age guru. He would go elsewhere to have the stitches removed.

'. . . holding a knife stained with blood,' Tullio Legna was saying. 'He claimed to have found it on the table, but of course there's no proof of that. On the basis of the preliminary tests the Carabinieri have done, there seems every possibility that it is the weapon which was used to stab and mutilate Aldo Vincenzo. You appreciate what that means, of course.'

'Of course,' murmured Zen vaguely.

'Manlio Vincenzo will be released.'

'He will?'

'Of course! This Gallizio either committed suicide or he was murdered. If it was suicide, the knife must have been in his possession all along, in which case the presumption is that he killed Aldo. If, on the other hand, it turns out that Gallizio was murdered, then his killer – who was also Vincenzo's – must have planted the knife at his house to throw suspicion for the original crime on a dead man.'

Zen frowned.

'Yes, I see,' he said.

Tullio Legna laughed.

'It'll take ages to work out what actually happened, but the beauty of it from your point of view is that it doesn't matter. Your remit was to free Manlio Vincenzo, right? Well, he's been in prison the whole time, and therefore can't have had anything to do with Gallizio's death and the incriminating knife. He's off the hook, and so are you. The whole balance of the case has shifted. You've successfully fulfilled your assignment, and without even getting out of bed!'

The police chief of Alba paid the bill and led the way outside. He turned to Zen and shook his hand vigorously.

'In a perverse way, I'm sorry it's worked out so smoothly, *dottore*. It would have been good to have had you here longer and been able to show you some of the wonderful things which the Langhe has to offer. But I'm sure that you're eager to get back to your family and friends, and at least you had a chance to sample our famous white truffles, eh? It's been a pleasure working with you. If there's anything more I can do for you before you leave, don't hesitate to contact me. *Arriverderci!*'

With that Tullio Legna walked off and was soon lost in the constantly shuffled pack of market shoppers and traders. Zen stood looking after him with the distinct feeling of having been seen off the premises – very elegantly and very painlessly, but also very finally.

He went back inside the café and ordered an *amaro*, a local variety of the sweet, sticky liqueur flavoured, in this case, with truffles. He knocked it back, lit a cigarette and reviewed the situation. According to the local police chief, who did not strike Zen as the type to lie about verifiable matters, the case he had been sent to solve had solved itself without him. There was therefore nothing to stop him from packing his bags and returning to Rome by the first available train. He might as well take a ticket all the way to Palermo, in fact, and save the bother of breaking his journey.

That consideration aside, the prospect of going home just at the moment was far from inviting. His tour of duty in Naples had ended in professional triumph and private turmoil. The most disturbing aspect of the latter had been the discovery that Tania Biacis, with whom he had once had a transient, desultory affair, was pregnant – and that, according to her, he was the father.

He had barely started coming to terms with this development when he was transferred back to the Ministry in Rome, where Tania was also employed, and reinstated in the ranks of the élite *Criminalpol* division as a just recompense for having supposedly smashed a murderous terrorist conspiracy single-handed. But when he cornered Tania in the corridor one day and tried to arrange a meeting to discuss the situation, her response had been brutal.

'There's nothing to discuss, Aurelio. It's all taken care of.'

He literally had no idea what she was talking about.

'I had an abortion,' she explained icily. 'Termination of pregnancy, yes?'

'But you . . . I mean, it's dead?'

'He, actually. Yes, very dead indeed.'

Her tone had an exaggerated brutality about it, a determined refusal to admit feeling directed as much at herself as at him.

'If it makes you feel any better,' she went on, 'I wasn't one hundred per cent sure it was yours in the first place. But after seeing you again, carrying on in that high-handed, arrogant, selfish way, I knew that I couldn't afford to take the risk. So I had it removed. End of story.'

But it wasn't, at least for Zen. His initial sense of shameful relief had quickly proved itself to be illusory – a deceptively fragile crust covering a quagmire in which he was now struggling, as it sometimes seemed, for his sanity, if not his life. Every instinct told him to put the episode behind him, to wipe it out of his consciousness as thoroughly as the foetus had apparently been expunged from its mother's womb. But there seemed to be no surgical procedures prescribed for this particular intervention.

To make matters worse, he had to see Tania every day at work. Not even Zen's current celebrity gave him any leverage over the rigid employment hierarchies of the Ministry of the Interior. He could no more have had his ex-mistress transferred to another department than he could have had the building moved from the Viminale hill to the Aventine on the grounds that the air was more salubrious and the view superior.

As though sensing his discomfiture, Tania appeared to go out of her way to discover or manufacture reasons for crossing his path. Zen had no idea how she herself felt about what had happened. His one attempt to find out had been repulsed with a heavy barrage of rhetoric about a woman's right to choose, all of which he agreed with but which brought him no closer to understanding this particular instance of the general principle.

There was no one he could discuss it with, either. He was no longer on speaking terms with his former friend, Gilberto Nieddu, after what Zen saw as the latter's betrayal in the Naples case when Nieddu had been entrusted with the prototype of a video game, which he had promptly taken off to Russia and sold to the local mafia for a figure which he gloatingly declined to disclose.

His only other resource in a matter as personal as this was his mother, and she seemed to have taken a turn not so much for the worse as towards the far distance, from which zone – like an assiduous but incompetent spy – she relayed incomprehensible or misleading messages, with the names all muddled up and the dates and times confused. Even the unfailing good sense of Maria Grazia, their Calabrian housekeeper, had been tried to the limit at times. To raise the question of dead babies and hypothetical sons with someone who had so recently made startling disclosures about Zen's own paternity – all of which she now denied having ever uttered – would be merely asking for more and deeper trouble.

But if Zen had good reasons for not wishing to return to Rome any sooner than he had to, the prospect of going back to the hotel room where he had been cooped up for the past thirty-six hours, to say nothing of an immediate transfer to a front-line posting in Sicily, held no appeal either. At a loss, he paid for his drink and went outside again.

The sun had now broken through the dispersing mist and was shining wanly, its attenuated light almost as insubstantial as the shadows cast by the buildings at the end of the piazza. Zen made his way slowly through the crowd, only too conscious that he had no set goal or purpose. The shoppers, mostly middle-aged or elderly, all well-dressed and seemingly prosperous, were going about their business without any noise or fuss. Almost everyone he had encountered since his arrival had been like that: pleasant, patient, good-natured, polite. After his experiences in Naples this struck him as slightly sinister, as though it were all some elaborate charade. No one could be *that* nice all the time.

Nor were they, as Zen had known ever since scanning the file on the Vincenzo case. He had obtained this, after the usual delay, from the Defence Ministry in Rome, and read it on the train trip north. Aldo Vincenzo had been killed with a ferocity which almost defied belief; hence the extensive media interest, although this had abated since Manlio's arrest. But the report of a medical witness – perhaps Lucchese's friend – included among the documents which Tullio Legna had brought to the hotel the day before, was even more graphic:

The body was lashed by the wrists and ankles to the wires supporting the laden vines, naked from the waist down. The shirt above was stained black with blood which had trickled down the thighs and legs in coagulating runnels, forming a pool between the legs which had already attracted the attention of a few early flies. The head was thrown back, the eyes wide as a startled horse. He had been stabbed again and again in the stomach and midriff below the breastbone: about forty times in all. The penis and scrotal sac had been hacked off and removed or concealed. No trace of these items has been found.

So the niceness was a pose, a way of keeping strangers at a distance and seeing off inconvenient intruders from Rome. It had happened to him many times before, although usually at the hands of interested parties less suave than Tullio Legna. But the principle remained the same; the door was being closed in his face. Well, too bad, he thought. He wasn't in a mood to be seen off, no matter how politely. He was, in fact, in a mood to make a complete arsehole of himself, to offend as many of these secretive, hypocritical bastards as he could, even though it got him nowhere at all from a professional point of view. This was not business but pleasure.

The grid of the market was defined by the traders' vans and lorries drawn up in rows, their tail-gates opening on to wooden stalls piled high with the goods offered for sale. These were mostly household durables: bedlinen, clothes, kitchen utensils and hardware items, with a few of the usual labour-saving, miracle appliances which salesmen were loudly and enthusiastically demonstrating to a clientele of crumpled, compact women of a certain age, who looked suitably sceptical about these claims but at the same time enthralled by the attention they were receiving.

Near the main door of the cathedral was a separate section, with open-sided vans selling cheese and fresh and cured meats, and stalls offering jars of preserves and honey from the mountains, and, of course, baskets of truffles and wild mushrooms. One of these consisted of a red Fiat truck covered in a tent-like tarpaulin. A hand-painted sign in old-fashioned block lettering above the tail-gate read FRATELLI FAIGANO – VINI E PRODOTTI TIPICI.

Zen stared at it with a deepening frown. Where had he seen that name before? The answer came to him almost immediately. It had been in the report that he had just been thinking of, the one on the Vincenzo case which Tullio Legna had delivered the day before, together with a map of the area and Zen's truffle-laden cure. The Faigano brothers, or one of them, had been among the witnesses who had testified to the loud and public row which Manlio Vincenzo had had with his father at the village *festa* the night before Aldo was killed. This had apparently originated in a series of sarcastic gibes by Aldo on the subject of his son's supposed homosexual inclinations, and had ended with Aldo disclosing in a loud voice that he had read a letter from Manlio's lover, a young man named Andrea. It had been at this point that Manlio had stormed out of the gathering, not to be seen again until after the discovery of his father's body.

The Faiganos' improvised stall was tended by a teenage girl perched on a stool reading a pop music magazine. She looked up with a bored expression as Zen approached.

'Good morning, *signorina*.'

She flashed him a dazzling smile which revealed the embryonic beauty that would soon remake her pasty adolescence.

'Is it possible to speak to either of the brothers?' asked Zen. 'It's a business matter.'

The girl pointed in an over-emphatic manner almost certainly copied unconsciously from one of her teachers.

'They're in the bar over there. The one across from the town hall.'

Zen thanked her and threaded his way through the crowds to the corner of the Via Vittorio Emanuele, which Tullio Legna had referred to as Via Maestra. In a similarly confusing touch, the cathedral square was officially billed as Piazza Risorgimento. The original designations would have been officially changed during the era of reunification – Zen could imagine the ceremony, complete with brass bands playing selections from Verdi – in a fit of patriotic fervour and keeping-up-with-the-rest-of-the-country, but now the ancient names were showing through the scrofulous paint of those discredited ideals.

The bar which the girl had pointed out to Zen was crowded with elderly men whose worn, wary faces and heavy-duty clothing contrasted sharply with those of the townspeople. The air was thick with rumbling dialect and cigarette smoke. Zen told the barman he was looking for someone called Faigano. The latter in turn consulted a group of men standing at the counter, one of whom nodded mutely towards a trio playing cards at a table in the corner. Zen made his way through the throng.

'Signor Faigano?'

Two of the men looked up simultaneously.

'Yes?' one of them replied warily.

Zen took a card out of his wallet and placed it on the table. It was one of those he had had printed during his stay in Naples, identifying him as one Alfonso Zembla.

'Excuse me for interrupting, but I wonder if you could spare a few minutes. I'm a reporter for the *Mattino*, the most important paper in Naples, and I'm working on a story about the Vincenzo case. I've got the basic facts, of course, but I need some colour and comment to round it out . . .'

The man sitting immediately beneath Zen picked up the card.

'Naples, eh?' he said.

'You know it?' asked Zen.

The man laughed shortly.

'The furthest south I've ever been was Genoa, and that was back in the war . . .'

The third man at the table, who had not responded to Zen's

initial greeting, started to whistle a short, melodious refrain. Then he pushed back his chair and stood up.

'Time I was off,' he announced to no one in particular.

'All right, Minot,' said the other man, who had not spoken yet. He, too, stood up, stretching lazily.

'I'd better go back and give Lisa a hand with the stall,' he said through a forced yawn.

'Take care, Maurizio,' said the first man.

'You too.'

'May I?' asked Zen, sitting down in one of the chairs thus vacated.

The remaining man held out his hand.

'Gianni Faigano. It's an honour to meet you, Dottor Zembla, but to be perfectly honest I don't know how much help I can give. I'm just a simple man, and I don't read the papers. To tell you the truth, I can hardly read at all. My brother Maurizio, he's the smart one. He does all the paperwork, but he doesn't like to talk. So there you are! We make a good team.'

'So can we,' suggested Zen, with just the suspicion of a wink. 'You do the talking and I'll take care of the paperwork.'

Gianni Faigano shrugged.

'Why me, *dottore*? Look at all the people in here, and out there at the market. Any of them could have told you what you want to know. Yet you chose me. Why?'

'I'd heard the name.'

'Where?'

Various possibilities presented themselves to Zen's mind, and he decided instinctively to go for the riskiest. What had he to lose, after all?

'Someone told me that it was you and your brother who did it.'

There was a long, intense silence.

'Did what?' demanded Gianni Faigano.

'Killed Aldo Vincenzo.'

Faigano inclined his head and laughed with what seemed like genuine amusement.

'Now who told you that, *dottore*?'

Zen frowned and pretended to consult his notebook.

'Someone called . . . Wait a moment. Ah, here we are! Beppe Gallizio. So when I saw your stall in the market I asked the girl there – Lisa, is it? – where I could find you.'

Gianni Faigano turned his misty brown eyes on Zen.

'I heard that Beppe met with an accident.'

'That's right. Which, of course, would make you even more of a suspect, if I were to tell the police what he said to me.'

Zen paused to light a cigarette.

'But I've no intention of doing that. All I want to know is what happened the night Aldo Vincenzo was killed.'

A brief laugh from Faigano.

'Eh, we'd all like to know that!'

'What people *think* happened, then. What they're saying about it. A bit of background for my story, and the more scandalous and colourful the better.'

Gianni Faigano glanced around, as though to check whether he could be overheard.

'I've heard a couple of stories. I'm not saying there's anything to them, mind you, but . . .'

'Don't worry, this is all off the record.'

The other man looked at him acutely.

'But is it on . . . What do you call it?'

'What?'

'When the people who hired you pay for everything.'

'On expenses? Of course.'

Gianni Faigano smiled slowly.

'In that case, I think we should talk about it over lunch,' he said.

The resulting meal was by no means the first time that Aurelio Zen had had occasion to dine out with men for whom the principal point of the exercise seemed to be to make themselves look good by giving the staff of the restaurant a hard time. Service, food, wine, the menu itself: nothing passed muster by their exacting standards. Other patrons – credulous, ignorant or weak – might be taken in, or too feeble to protest, but not them!

Dishes and bottles of wine would be sent back, or grudgingly accepted after a long critique of their multiple defects. The course of the meal would be interrupted by long negotiations with the waiter, the implication being that while the establishment was capable in principle of producing the genuine product, otherwise they would not have favoured it with their patronage, it equally obviously was not going to do so for just anyone, only for those who had aggressively demonstrated their credentials as true connoisseurs, not to be fobbed off with anything less.

So far from being the type to play games of this kind, Gianni Faigano had struck Zen as someone who would eat whatever was put in front of him and be grateful to have it. This erroneous impression was dispelled the moment they reached the restaurant his guest had suggested, in a side street just off the piazza where the weekly market was now winding down. Even before they were seated, Faigano had pointedly objected to the table they were offered. And once this was rectified, he proceeded to find fault with the selection of daily specials, and, most vociferously, with the truffle with which it was proposed to adorn their meal.

'At least a week old,' he declared, having taken a briefly dismissive sniff. 'And it's not even from the best area.'

A selection of other tubers was brought to the table, and one eventually met with Gianni's grudging – sigh, grimace, shrug, not-much-but-what-can-you-expect-in-a-place-like-this? – gesture of heavily qualified approval.

Next it was the turn of the cellar.

'*Macchè?* Only a couple of bottles I'd drink, even on my deathbed, and they're priced for the Swiss and German tourists. No, no, *dottore*! I may be your guest in one sense, but in another and more important one you're mine. I can't have you come all the way from Rome – I mean Naples – and be held to ransom like this. Wait here.'

He got up and stomped out of the restaurant. Zen sat glumly sipping mineral water and nibbling at a bread-stick, feeling fairly sure that Faigano had used this as an excuse to back out and that he would never see him again. But he was wrong. A few minutes later, his guest returned with an unlabelled bottle which he handed to the waiter and told him to open 'with the greatest care'.

'Our own,' he explained to Zen. 'Not one of the best years, but at least we'll know what we're drinking.'

Nor was that all. When the food began to arrive, Faigano proceeded to denigrate the quality of the *insalata di carne cruda*, finely minced raw veal seasoned with oil, lemon and garlic, then to complain that the *risotto* was overcooked and too dry, and finally to interrogate the waiter in considerable and sceptical detail about the provenance of the hare, which, stewed in wine and its own blood, formed the basis of the main course. Once these formalities had been disposed of, he glanced at Zen in a world-weary, man-to-man way and proceeded to eat his way through the whole five courses on offer while managing to suggest that he was doing so simply as a favour to the management, to avoid them losing face before a distinguished visitor from out of town.

In his spare time, he outlined his views on the Aldo Vincenzo case.

'No one round here ever believed that Manlio did it. Quite apart from anything else, he doesn't have the balls, if you'll excuse the expression.'

'But I was told that he and his father had a big row at the *festa* the night before Aldo died,' Zen replied.

Gianni Faigano gestured dismissively.

'They were always quarrelling about one thing or another. I don't blame the boy. Aldo's mistake was sending him abroad. He learned foreign ways and manners and got strange ideas in his head. When he left, he was a good, obedient son, but when he got back he had changed. Our little world here in the Langhe seemed provincial to him. Aldo tried to bring him back to heel, but the damage had been done.'

He finished the last of his risotto and looked round critically for the waiter.

'That's a nasty-looking cut you've got there, *dottore*,' he remarked, still looking over his shoulder. 'Quite fresh, too, by the look of it.'

'I slipped in the shower.'

Now that the anaesthetic was wearing off, he could feel the stitches as a dull, persistent tugging in his forehead.

'Probably a woman,' said Gianni Faigano, signalling to the negligent minion.

Zen peered at him.

'I beg your pardon?'

'They used to burn them for it, round here.'

'You don't understand,' Zen replied, indignant yet oddly disturbed by the turn the conversation had taken. 'I was completely alone. It was just an accident.'

Faigano smiled.

'There are no such things as accidents, *dottore*. Everything that happens has its cause. And when a healthy man like you injures himself as badly as that, it's almost certainly woman's work. Someone's put a hex on you, maybe even without knowing it herself. But there's a way to break the spell.'

'What's that?' Zen found himself asking, despite his better judgement.

Gianni Faigano leant forward, as though imparting some forbidden mystery.

'Find another woman, one who really loves you. Then the other one won't be able to harm you any more. Despite everything, good is more powerful than evil in the end.'

They were distracted from these abstruse speculations by the arrival of the *lepre al civet*, which Gianni Faigano proceeded to damn with praise so faint as to be practically imperceptible.

'Let's get back to the subject,' Zen interrupted briskly. 'You say that no one here believes that Manlio killed his father. So who *do* they think did it?'

'That depends who you ask. Everyone's got their own theory.'

'And what's yours?'

Gianni Faigano poured them both some more of the dark brick-red wine.

'You like it?' he asked, tapping his glass. The wrinkled skin of his finger contrasted oddly with the smooth, pink tip whose nail had apparently been torn away.

'It's excellent.'

'We don't mess around with our wine,' Gianni Faigano said solemnly. 'We don't make any money off it either. Some people might say that there's a connection.'

'But plenty of people around here do make money from their wine,' Zen pointed out. 'Aldo Vincenzo, for one. Did he mess around with his wine?'

Faigano shook his head decisively.

'No, no! The top producers don't need to. They can make their wine the same way I make mine, using the traditional methods and not cutting any corners, and then charge whatever they want. But that end of the market is very small and very crowded. The rest of us have to try to make a living further down. Most of us manage to get by, but others do rather better. Very much better, in a few cases.'

'And what has this got to do with the Vincenzo case?'

Once again, Gianni Faigano leant forward conspiratorially across the table.

'The Carabinieri are questioning Lamberto Latini about the death of Beppe Gallizio,' he whispered. 'What they don't know is that Latini wasn't the only person at Beppe's house that morning.'

Zen allowed his eyes to open wide.

'Who was the other?'

Faigano returned to eating his meal with the air of someone who has now earned it.

'A little while ago,' he said conversationally, 'Aldo Vincenzo was implicated in a case involving the export of wine which had been falsely labelled.'

'There's money to be made in that?'

Faigano shrugged.

'Wine's not heroin. But buying generic Nebbiolo at a few hundred lire a litre, and then selling it as Barbaresco Riserva *Denominazione di Origine Controllata* at fifty to a hundred thousand a bottle? I'd say there was money to be made.'

Zen paused to swallow a morsel of the succulent hare stew.

'But why would Aldo Vincenzo risk his reputation by getting involved in something like that?'

'Because he was greedy!'

For the first time, Faigano showed some sign of personal feeling. He leant still nearer to Zen, his voice a fervent undertone and his stubby, gnarled fingers stabbing the table to emphasize every point.

'He was one of the richest men in the area, with most of the best land. But he always wanted more. More money, more land, more power, more of everything! And he didn't care what he had to do to get it. He tried to get that son of his to rape my niece so that the Vincenzo family would get its hands on our property when Maurizio and I died! What do you say to that?'

Zen took another sip of wine.

'I'd say that it made you a suspect in his death, Signor Faigano.'

Gianni laughed.

'Ah, but if I'd really done it, I wouldn't have told you that, would I?'

Zen said nothing.

'Anyway, the authorities claim that Aldo and another local producer were involved in a scheme to sell several thousand cases of falsely labelled wine,' Faigano went on. 'Apparently they'd bought off the local authorities, but when the shipment of bogus Barolo was seized in Germany, there was nothing they could do.'

Zen took out his notebook.

'Who was the other man?'

Gianni Faigano paused a moment.

'It's all on record anyway, so there's no harm in telling you. His name is Bruno Scorrone, and he runs a winery near Palazzuole. He buys in grapes from local growers, on a lowest-price-per-kilo basis. Sometimes wine, too, when there's a glut or someone needs some cash fast. I've heard some people say he trucks in wine from down south, too, and uses it for blending, but that may just be malicious gossip.'

He grinned at Zen.

'There's a lot of that around here.'

'I still don't see how Aldo Vincenzo comes into all this.'

Gianni Faigano sighed expressively.

'To sell wine as Barbaresco, you have to be able to show provenance from land in a DOC zone. Scorrone doesn't own any such land, but the Vincenzo family do.'

'But surely they use it to make their own wine.'

'Ah, but here's the trick! With controlled zones, there's a maximum permitted yield – so many grapes to so much ground. Understand?'

Zen nodded.

'But the best grapes are always the fewest. The flavour is denser and more concentrated, and so is the wine. Only the top growers can afford to prune their vines that hard, to keep their yields down and reject any grapes that don't come up to scratch. Men like Aldo Vincenzo, whose wines command the highest prices. That leaves a gap between what they actually produce and the permissible regulated limit, wine which was never actually made but which would have been entitled to call itself Barbaresco if it had. It was that ghost wine that Bruno Scorrone was selling abroad.'

Zen shook his head.

'All right, let's assume that Vincenzo and this Scorrone were involved in a contraband wine racket. Why should Scorrone have killed him?'

Faigano pushed away his plate.

'You asked what people are saying, *dottore*. I'm telling you. They're saying that Aldo Vincenzo was killed just a few weeks before he was due to present himself before a judge in Asti to explain why certificates of origin made out in his name had been attached to a consignment of the cheapest *vino sfuso*. They're saying that it will be much easier now for Bruno Scorrone to argue that he bought the wine in good faith from a renowned grower of the region. How was he to know it was contraband? If Aldo Vincenzo said it was Barbaresco, that was good enough for him!'

He paused significantly and looked around once again.

'They're also saying that Scorrone was seen driving up to Beppe Gallizio's house the morning he was killed.'

Zen finished his wine as the waiter removed their plates.

'So you believe Scorrone did it?'

Gianni Faigano smiled strangely.

'I don't believe anything any more, *dottore*. For me, the world stopped making sense a long time ago. But people around here have long memories. It's all we do have left, some of us. Who knows? Maybe someone had waited years and years before taking revenge for something Aldo thought forgotten, or had even forgotten himself?'

He straightened up as the waiter returned with the cheese tray.

'But that needn't concern you!' Faigano remarked loudly in a jocular tone. 'If you were a policeman, now, I wouldn't envy you the task of trying to solve this case. But as it is, you've got your story and can go home to Naples without bothering your head about it any more. Right, *dottore*?'

'Mombaruzzo, bubbio coazzolo. Sommariva fello fontanile?'

The voice was distant yet loud, reverberant and insistent, with a hectoring tone covering an undercurrent of desperate pleading. It was absolutely essential that he understand! A matter, quite literally, of life and death.

'La morra cravanzana neviglie perletto bene vagienna. Serralunga doglani cossano il bric belbo moglia d'inverno!'

But try as he might, nothing made sense. And the fact that it so nearly did just made matters worse, as if he were at fault. Perhaps if he got closer to the speaker he would be able to hear more clearly and do whatever was expected of him. Stumbling forward in the darkness, he moved in the direction from which the voice seemed to be coming.

'Barbaresco! Santa Maria Maddalena, trezzo tinella?'

In the end, it was his own cry of pain that woke him. This was real in a different way. And – agonizingly, but reassuringly – it was not intermittent or qualified but immediate and continuous, with future consequences built in. A foot was involved, as well as the shin immediately above. He seemed to be naked. The surface beneath his bare soles was as rough and yet yielding as sand, but hard edges lurked in the darkness all around. It was against one of these that he must have struck his left leg.

After an interminable period of exploratory gestures in the surrounding obscurity, he eventually located something that seemed familiar. Further tactile tests seemed to confirm that this was indeed the edge of the bed. Working on this hypothesis, he groped his way along it. Sure enough, he soon came to a table-leg. Not only this, but the lamp was where it should be, according to his folk-memories of the presumed locality. A brief fiddle with the nipple on the base produced light. Stripped of its dream-enhanced pretensions, the room looked absurdly small. No wonder he had come to grief, when his mental chart had been erroneous not in a few details but on a totally different scale, like the map of a city mistaken for that of a continent.

But why had he left the safe haven of his bed in the first place? There had been an urgent reason, he remembered, connected with that resonant voice whose words he could still fugitively hear. It had exhorted him to save someone while there was still time. A life had been in danger, and he was at once deeply implicated and the only person who could prevent the atrocity. Only he hadn't been able to understand the language in which this terrible appeal had been delivered, and so he was guilty. A child had died because he had not been quick or capable enough to save him.

A clamorous noise made itself felt in the room. Another Aurelio Zen – one who lived in the world called real and, unlike his incompetent dream double, understood its signs and portents – picked up the phone and answered.

'*Good morning, Dottor Zen. Did I wake you? My apologies, as they say. But I happened to be awake already, so I thought that we might as well get started.*'

The voice was metallic, neutered, robotic.

'Who is this?'

'*Ah, well, that's the question, isn't it? But don't worry, you don't have to answer it right away. I'll even give you a few clues, to get you started. Here's the first. Via Strozzi, number twenty-four.*'

Zen gripped the receiver with growing anger.

'What the hell is this? Do you know what time it is?'

A tinny laugh.

'*Questions, questions! You're a detective, I hear. Why don't you do a little detecting?*'

'Why don't you go and fuck yourself?'

He slammed the phone down and lay back on the bed. Then, rolling up and over like a wounded animal, he located the bedside clock, rang the front desk and demanded to know why they had put a call through at half-past five in the morning. The clerk,

71

who sounded as though he had been asleep himself, protested that he had not transferred any calls to Dottor Zen's room, and indeed that there had been no calls of any sort to anyone since he had come on duty late the previous evening.

On the floor beside the bed lay the map which Tullio Legna had included with the dossier on the Vincenzo case; Zen had been studying it when he fell asleep the night before in an attempt to get some grip on the layout of the area. It was the standard 1:50,000 sheet covering Alba and the surrounding countryside and villages. He picked it up and located Palazzuole. A railway line ran nearby, and there appeared to be an isolated station which served the town.

His eye drifted away, following the lines of hills and the course of rivers, until he was brought up short by the words Trezzo Tinella. He had heard that before, and recently, too. Then, with an almost superstitious shudder, he remembered the parting shot of the voice in his somnambulistic dream: '*Barbaresco! Santa Maria Maddalena, trezzo tinella?*'

For a moment it seemed as if he had stumbled unawares on some cosmic clue, a previously unsuspected secret passage between worlds believed to be separate. Then he noticed the word Barbaresco on the map. It was, he realized, not just the name of a wine but also of a village, not far from Palazzuole. He searched the sheet until he found Santa Maria Maddalena, Fontanile, Fello, Serralunga and Sommariva. No doubt the others were all there, too. He must have read the names unconsciously the night before and then combined them in his sleep to form those sentences which had hovered so disturbingly on the brink of some painful, urgent sense.

Meanwhile he had been sleepwalking again. On this occasion the experience had left no visible scars, but there was no telling where he might have ended up if he hadn't stubbed his toe and barked his shin on the coffee table. What was happening to him? Was he to believe Doctor Lucchese's theory of psychic disturbance or Gianni Faigano's misogynous ramblings about a malevolent female influence? Or were they both right? And what about that phone call? 'Via Strozzi, number twenty-four.' The address, if that was what it was, meant nothing to him.

He took a shower to rinse away this mood of morbid introspection, then went over to his suitcase and dug out the battered, buff-coloured railway timetable he always carried with him. Alba looked the size of Rome on the 1:50,000 map, but it didn't figure at all on the schematic map of the national railway network printed at the front of the timetable. Zen looked it up in the index, then consulted the schedule for the line wandering off into the hills to the east. The first train of the day left in just under fifteen minutes. On a whim, he decided to try to catch it. He had been spending too much time alone in his room, brooding about his own problems and state of mind. What he needed was to get to work.

Outside the hotel, there was still no hint of the coming dawn. The street was dark and silent, the sky implacably opaque. He walked rapidly back in the direction he had taken when he arrived, glancing at his watch as he passed beneath a street lamp. Somewhere behind him, another set of solitary footsteps resounded comfortingly on the flagstones.

Once he reached the station, it became obvious that there had been no need to hurry. A two-car diesel unit stood dark and silent at the platform, but the booking office was closed and no one was about. Zen lit a cigarette and paced the platform as the clock moved spastically from three minutes to six to three minutes past. As though on cue, a door slammed and two men emerged. One wore the grey-blue uniform of the State Railways, the other was in jeans and a tattered green ski-jacket. Zen walked up to them.

'For Palazzuole?' he enquired, indicating the train.

'Stop at Palazzuole!' the uniformed man called to his unkempt companion, who was heading for the driver's compartment.

'Va bene.'

The engines roared into life amid a cloud of thick black smoke. There was only one other person on the platform, a young woman in a long coat and a hat who didn't seem interested in this train. Zen boarded and took his seat, and after a brief delay the *automotrice* rumbled off into the darkness, crossing numerous sets of points. To all appearances, Zen was the only passenger.

He lay back on the hard plastic seat and turned to the blank screen of the window. It reflected his face back to him: old, tired, defeated, possibly even mad. 'We had no idea! He always seemed perfectly normal.' That's what people said when someone cracked up, as though to reassure themselves that such conditions were invariably obvious and predictable, and so their own lack of symptoms meant that their future sanity was not in question.

Zen sat up and refocused his eyes on the seat opposite. For a moment, the glass had seemed to display two faces: his own, and – some distance behind and to one side – that of a boy about five years old. Only his face, of extraordinary beauty, was visible, the dark eyes fixed on Zen with a look of love and reproach.

'Palazzuole!'

Zen swivelled round. The uniformed man was standing in the doorway at the end of the carriage.

'Palazzuole,' he repeated, as the brakes squealed beneath them.

Zen was about to say that he didn't have a ticket, but the guard had already disappeared. The train jerked to a halt, seemingly in the middle of nowhere. Zen walked hastily to the end of the carriage and stepped down. The train revved up and sidled away, leaving him in total darkness. Almost total, rather, for once his eyes had adjusted, he realized that he could just make out his surroundings by the faint suggestion of light which now tinted the sky, diffused down through a thick layer of mist. The station building was shuttered and obviously long disused. In faded black paint on the cracked and falling plaster he could just make out the letters PAL ZUO E and the information that he was currently 243 metres above mean sea level.

He walked past the station building into the gravel-covered area behind, and along a short driveway leading to a dirt road which crossed the tracks at a slight angle. Here he got out the map and his cigarette lighter, and determined that the village lay east of the railway station which nominally served it. He turned right on to the narrow road, towards the pallid glow which was slowly hollowing out the night.

There was just enough light to distinguish the crushed gravel and glossy puddles of the unpaved *strada bianca* from the ditches to either side. Zen lit a cigarette and walked on through the damp, clinging mist, up the slight incline of the road which crossed the river and the railway. As he climbed out of the valley, the visibility steadily improved. Now he could see that the fields had recently been ploughed and that the turned earth was silvery with dew. The exercise and the fresh air exhilarated him.

Somewhere in the distance, a dog barked. Somewhere else, a church bell began to toll monotonously, summoning the faithful to early mass. By now the light clearly had the upper hand over the mist and the darkness. Every surface glistened and gleamed with moisture, as though it had just been freshly created. As imperceptibly as the dawn itself, the incline of the road increased until he found himself ascending a steep hill which forced the road to twist and turn. Stopping to catch his breath, Zen noticed lights behind him and heard the low growl of a motor.

The vehicle – a red Fiat pick-up truck – neared rapidly, gobbling up the road it had taken Zen so long to traverse on foot. He stepped on to the verge to let it pass, but the truck pulled to a stop and a window was rolled down.

'*Buon giorno*,' said the driver.

Zen returned the greeting.

'Get in.'

The tone was peremptory. After a moment's hesitation, Zen walked around the truck and climbed into the passenger seat, which he found himself sharing with a small black-and-white dog. The cab reeked of a powerful odour to which he would not have been able, a few days before, to put a name, but which he could still smell faintly on his own skin.

'Going to the village?' asked the driver, restarting the truck. Glancing at the dog, which was whining nervously, he snapped, 'Quiet, Anna!'

'I'm going to Palazzuole,' said Zen.

75

'Did your car break down?'

'No, I came on the train.'

The driver laughed humourlessly.

'Probably the first passenger they've had all year.'

Zen studied the man's face as he negotiated the bends in the narrow, steep road. Apart from the thin, weedy moustache which covered his upper lip, it reminded him of pictures he had seen of that iron-age corpse they had dug out of a glacier somewhere up in the Alps. It also reminded him of something else, something more recent, but he couldn't think what.

'The station's a long way from the village,' he replied idly.

'It isn't that!' the man exclaimed. 'But people round here remember the way the railway used to treat us, back when everyone depended on it. I can still remember my mother running to catch a train to town – this was before the war, I can't have been more than a few years old. She was a minute or two late, but people like us didn't have clocks. The guard saw her coming, waving and calling out, but he held out his flag just the same and the train took off, leaving her standing there. Her grandfather died that night, before she'd had a chance to see him for the last time. People round here have long memories, and they don't have much use for the train.'

They were approaching the village now, but all that was visible was the lower row of brick dwellings. Everything above had disappeared behind another thick layer of mist.

'I smell truffles,' said Zen.

His driver glanced at him sharply, and Zen suddenly knew where he had seen him before: in the bar near the market, talking to the Faigano brothers. One of them had called him Minot.

'I got a few. They're easy enough to find if you know where to look. Providing someone else doesn't get there first, of course!'

He barked his short explosive laugh again, and slowed the truck as they entered the bank of mist which enveloped the higher levels of the village. The road had abruptly become paved, and the thuds and rumbling beneath them died away.

'You have friends here?' Zen's driver asked softly.

'I'm on business.'

'What kind of business?'

Zen thought quickly. The man didn't seem to have recognized him, and if he repeated the story about being a Neapolitan newspaper reporter in this context it would be all round the village in no time, and might shut a lot of mouths he would prefer to stay open.

'Wine,' he said.

The truck turned through the mist-enshrouded streets as cautiously as a ship in shallow water.

'Wine, eh?' the man called Minot remarked. 'I thought you people travelled around in Mercedes.'

The engine noise fell away as they emerged on to a broad, level piazza in the upper reaches of the mist.

'I lost my licence a couple of months ago,' Zen replied. 'Drunk driving, they called it, although I was perfectly all right really. Just one of those lunches with clients that go on a little too long.'

The driver drew up in front of an imposing arcaded building.

'Well, I'll leave you here,' he said. 'The Vincenzo house is about a kilometre outside town on the other side. That's where you're headed, I take it?'

Zen got out, and the dog reclaimed its space, curling up on the seat.

'Thanks for the lift,' he said.

The man named Minot gave him an ironically polite smile.

'A pleasure, *dottore*. Welcome to Palazzuole!'

By the time Aurelio Zen finally reached the Vincenzo property, the sun had dispersed the last traces of mist and the air was fresh and warm.

He had spent the intervening period in a café on the main square of Palazzuole, having discovered that there was a bus which stopped there shortly after ten o'clock which would not only drop him off at the gates of the Vincenzo estate but pick him up there on its return and take him all the way back to Alba.

Meanwhile he drank too much coffee, smoked too many cigarettes, read the newspapers and congratulated himself on having done the right thing. He felt a completely different person from the dream-drunk neurotic who had surfaced that morning. In short, he felt himself again. It might be a far from perfect self, but he determined to hang on to it if at all possible.

Two papers were available at the bar in Palazzuole: the Turin national *La Stampa*, and a local news-sheet resoundingly entitled *Il Corriere delle Langhe*. Apart from a filler about a partial eclipse of the sun due the following day, the former paper revealed nothing of any interest except the latest feints and gestures in various political and judicial games which had been going on for months if not years and in which Zen had long ceased to take any interest. The latter, on the other hand, turned out to contain some real news.

'Suspect in Gallizio Killing Released' read the headline. The article below explained that Lamberto Latini, the restaurateur whom the Carabinieri had found at Beppe Gallizio's house when they arrived, had proved to have an unbreakable alibi for the time at which the murder took place. This had been fixed with some precision as shortly after six o'clock in the morning, thanks to a triangulation involving the medical examiner's report, the time shown on the victim's pocket watch, which had been stopped by the shotgun blast that killed him, and the testimony of a neighbour who had heard a shot at about that time.

The witness had taken no particular notice of this event, assuming that it was someone out after game or vermin. People rose early in the country, and they all owned guns. But Lamberto Latini, it transpired, had not risen early that day. When Beppe Gallizio met his death in a grove of linden trees in the valley below Palazzuole, Latini had been asleep in the arms of Nina Mandola, wife of the local tobacconist. What made the situation more delicate, and explained the fact that it had only now been revealed, was that Signor Mandola was sleeping in the next bedroom at the time.

This state of affairs, it turned out, was a long-standing and stable one. Everyone in the village knew about it – Lamberto left his car parked right in front of the house when he came visiting – but it was a private matter and none of them had dreamt of mentioning it to the police. Nor had Lamberto Latini. The truth had only come out when Pinot Mandola himself had called Enrico Pascal, the local *maresciallo dei Carabinieri*, and told him that Latini could not possibly have committed the murder since he was sleeping with the caller's wife at the hour in question.

If truth were told, Pascal was considerably more embarrassed than the complaisant husband himself at having to probe, as delicately as possible, the reasons for this unusual arrangement. Mandola himself was quite straightforward about it. As a result of a glandular illness, he had become impotent. Since he was unfortunately unable to provide for the sexual needs of his wife, his marital duty was clearly to find someone who could.

'I immediately thought of Lamberto. He had long been a close friend to both of us, and I'd always had the idea that he admired Nina. And since his wife's death, he had been running around all over the place having affairs and visiting whores and neglecting the restaurant. I felt it was time for him to settle down.' With two such intimate witnesses, to say nothing of various villagers who came forward, now that the truth was in the public domain, to attest to having seen Latini's Lancia in front of the Mandola house until after eight that morning, the Carabinieri had no choice but to release the restaurateur.

'And so the mystery of Beppe Gallizio's tragic death returns to haunt a community already traumatized by the horror which so recently afflicted the Vincenzo family,' the article concluded. 'Are the two connected in some way? "How can they be?" people are saying. But, in their hearts, they are thinking, "How can they not be?"'

Zen's reading was interrupted by the barman, who alerted him to the arrival of the bus. Ten minutes later, it dropped him before a large pair of wrought-iron gates on an isolated stretch of road outside the village. A deeply rutted driveway of packed gravel curved down a gentle slope between matching sets of poplars as rigidly erect as uniformed guards. To either side, the land flowed away in gentle curves and hillocks, the contours defined as though on a map by serried rows of vines covered in burnt-ochre foliage.

As Zen strode along the drive, the house gradually came into view. It was set a little way down the hillside, so that the first thing visible was the roof. Roofs, rather: a quilt of russet tiles, each section covering a separate portion of the house, the rows all running slightly out of alignment with their neighbours. Stubby brick chimneys covered over with arched spires like miniature bell towers punctuated this mosaic.

It soon became evident that the house itself was as complex and various as its roofs, not so much a single entity as a con-glomerate of buildings of various size, shape and antiquity, hud-dled together along three sides of a large courtyard with a covered well at its centre. Some of the walls were open, consist-ing only of rows of large arches; others had a few ranks of shut-tered windows; still others were blank.

So far all had been silent, apart from the growl of a distant tractor, but when Zen approached the front door, a dog started to howl, alerted by some noise or scent. Judging by its appearance, this entrance had been disused for some time, so he followed the driveway around the outbuildings and into the courtyard. The dog's yelps grew louder and more frantic. A blue farm-cart and a green Volvo estate stood side by side near the inner door, which was opened by a young man holding a shotgun in his right hand.

In his late twenties, he was impeccably dressed in a brown and russet check suit with an English look but an unmistakably Italian cut, a triangle of brown kerchief protruding from his breast pocket echoing the bronze-and-black banded silk tie. A dark mustard V-necked pullover and button-down collared shirt in the subtlest of light blues and a pair of highly polished Oxfords completed the ensemble. His straight black hair, slightly receding from the temples and worn relatively long at the back, was perfectly waved and formed. A pair of wide-rimmed spectacles gave character to a pleasant, open, boyish face.

'Good morning,' he said in a firm, cultivated tone.

Unpleasantly aware of the shotgun – which wasn't exactly pointed at him, but wasn't exactly not either – Aurelio Zen showed his police identification and introduced himself above the frantic barking of the still invisible dog. The young man nodded and set the gun down.

'Shut up!' he yelled loudly.

The dog abruptly fell silent.

'I apologize for the intrusion,' Zen remarked. 'If I'd known there was anyone here, I would have phoned first.'

'Well, someone's been at work on your behalf,' the man replied. 'There have been two calls for you so far this morning.'

Zen looked at him in utter astonishment.

'That's impossible! No one knew I was coming here. I didn't even know myself until a few hours ago.'

'Neither did I, for that matter. I was released at seven o'clock this morning.'

'Released?'

The man stared at him defiantly.

'From prison. I am Manlio Vincenzo. What can I do for you,

81

dottore? My recent experiences have not been such as to endear me to representatives of the law, but I am aware of my duties as a citizen, and still more of the precarious nature of my present position. I repeat, what can I do for you?'

Zen gave an almost embarrassed laugh.

'I'm not sure, to be perfectly honest. I suppose I wanted to take a look at the scene of the crime. To see for myself, I mean, to get the feel of the . . .'

Manlio Vincenzo nodded.

'I quite understand. What we in the wine business call the *goût de terroir*. Well, you're in luck. Whatever else we may lack here in the Langhe, we have any amount of that. Let me get my boots on.'

He went back inside, taking the shotgun with him. Zen turned to face the sunlight streaming into the courtyard. Protected from the slight breeze, to say nothing of the noise of traffic on the road above, it felt incredibly warm and quiet, a haven of sanity in a harsh world. It cost Zen a distinct effort to remind himself that its late owner had walked out of here to an atrocious death, and that as yet no one knew why. When Manlio Vincenzo reappeared, clad in a pair of green rubber boots and a coat, he seemed to have been reading Zen's thoughts.

'My father would have gone this way the morning he died,' he said, leading Zen around the far side of the house.

'The night he died, you mean.'

Manlio shook his head.

'No, *dottore*. He spent his last night in bed. My father snored very loudly. It was not the least of the many things which my poor mother had to put up with from him. I got up in the night to fetch a glass of water, and the whole upstairs of the house was vibrating from that unmistakable stertorous rasping. It was always particularly bad when he'd been drinking heavily.'

Zen frowned.

'There was nothing about this in the reports I read.'

'Of course not,' Manlio snapped bitterly. 'It's only my unsupported evidence, and I was already under arrest. Why spoil a perfectly good case by dragging in the truth?'

'What time was it when you heard him?'

'About half-past three. I've been waking around then ever since I got back from abroad. Or rather I used to. In prison I slept like the dead, as they say.'

They had emerged into the open, with an extensive view of a series of hummock-like hills covered in vines, each surmounted by a clump of low, solid, brick buildings similar to the one behind them. In the washed-out blue sky, patches of cloud massed like foam on water.

'Rosa, your housekeeper, told the Carabinieri that Aldo left the house after returning from the village *festa*, and that you followed him,' Zen remarked.

'Quite right. Rosa preferred to stay here and watch the shopping channel. It's her one pleasure in life, although she never orders anything. Anyway, I left the festivities early, as you no doubt know, following a much-publicized quarrel with my father. When he got back, I tried to talk it through with him. He walked out and I followed. Rosa, who was clearly embarrassed by the whole scene, went off to bed. She was asleep when I returned.'

'Why did your father go out at that time of night in the first place?'

'There was a phone call shortly after he got home. It may have had something to do with that, but when I asked him where he was going, he just said he wanted to clear his head. He'd had quite a lot to drink at the *festa*. I told him that I'd come too, and he shouted that he'd had quite enough of me for one evening. But I tagged along anyway. I didn't like the idea of him going to bed in that frame of mind. Besides, he'd got the whole thing wrong, and I wanted to talk the thing through.'

The lines of heavy-fruited vines stretched away before them across the curve of the hillside. Manlio Vincenzo turned off between two rows and started to walk downhill.

'This is the way we came,' he said. 'My father a pace or two ahead, me following at his heels like a dog.'

'How can you be sure it was this row of vines? It was pitch dark and you admit you were drunk . . .'

Vincenzo turned to him.

'*Dottore*, you could blindfold me and take me to any point on our property and I would know exactly where I was, to the nearest metre. Believe me, this was the way we came.'

They walked on in silence for some time.

'What was the quarrel between you and your father about?' asked Zen eventually.

'There were two causes. The one which has fascinated the press and public, needless to say, is that he had opened and read a private letter addressed to me by a friend, had misunderstood the contents and then used them to abuse me in public. But that was relatively superficial. The real reason for his animus lay much deeper. I'm afraid it will seem quite incomprehensible, if not absurd, to an outsider.'

Zen shrugged.

'Tell me anyway. That's why I'm here.'

Manlio Vincenzo paused to inspect the clusters of grapes nestled amongst the leaves to one side.

'It was about wine,' he said.

Zen looked at him sharply, suspecting a joke. Clearly he was wrong, however.

'Our family has owned this land for about a hundred years,' Manlio went on, striding away again. 'My great-grandfather grew rich in the cotton business, and bought himself a country estate outside the village his father had come from. He made wine for his own consumption, but that was all. When my father inherited the property after the war, those vines and the wine they produced had acquired a significant commercial value, and by the time I was born the market had taken another leap. I managed to persuade him that if we were to continue to compete effectively, we needed to keep track of the latest developments in the field. So when I finished university, he sent me abroad to study viticulture.'

'Where abroad?'

'Initially to Bordeaux, and then to the United States.'

Zen stared at him in amazement.

'America? But all they drink is milk and Coca-Cola!'

Manlio Vincenzo smiled.

'Exactly what my father said when I suggested the idea. But you're both wrong. The University of California at Davis was at that time, and probably still is, one of the best places in the world to study wine production in all its aspects, with no preconceptions and nothing taken for granted. The Americans may have started late, but they've caught up quickly.'

'This doesn't explain why you and your father almost came to blows at the *Festa della Vendemmia* that night,' Zen remarked pointedly.

'I'm coming to that. My father sent me abroad to study because he wanted to emulate the other top growers in the area, people like Gaja, Di Gresy and Bruno Rocca. He resented their growing fame, not to mention the prices they could command, and wanted me to find out how we could match them. As for me, I wanted to travel, to meet new people and to see the world. At that point I didn't even want to be a wine-maker particularly. My degree was in engineering. But I went along with his idea, because it was a way to get out of this place.'

'And away from him?' suggested Zen.

Vincenzo gestured loosely.

'To an extent, yes. In return, I was prepared to do the courses and come back with some useful tips on oak and pruning and fermentation techniques. Instead, I came back as someone quite unrecognizable to him, with ideas he found profoundly disturbing.'

'What sort of ideas?'

'About grape varieties, for one thing. That, of course, had never entered my father's head as a subject for discussion. Like everyone else around here, we grew only one grape, Nebbiolo. That was taken for granted, as though it had been ordained by God. All Aldo wanted me to learn was how to manage and vinify it more profitably. But after my experiences abroad, I had different ideas, which he . . .'

Manlio Vincenzo inspected Zen briefly through his owl-like glasses.

'This is the spot where he told me to go and suck my boyfriend's prick, to quote his expression. Just here in this slight hollow where the water collects. You can feel how spongy the earth is here compared with the well-drained section we've been walking over.'

Zen, who could feel nothing of the kind, nodded. Manlio Vincenzo stood still, looking into the distance.

'Then he turned and walked off without another word. I started after him, but I realized it was useless. I made my way back to the house and went to sleep. I never saw him alive again.'

'What time did you get up the next morning?' asked Zen after a moment's silence.

'About seven.'

'But you didn't see your father?'

'No, he was gone by then. The door to his room was open, but he wasn't there. That didn't surprise me. He was always an early riser, and at this time of year you could hardly drag him away from his vines. I think that's really why he went out the night before, to tell you the truth, even though it was too dark to see anything. As the vintage approached, he would spend hours just tramping the fields, snipping back leaves and checking on the ripeness of the fruit. He was like a mother with a new-born baby.'

Moving quickly, he led the way up the other side of the gulley and over a ridge. The rows of vines were interrupted here by a narrow track to allow mechanical access. Manlio climbed rapidly up the hillside, leaving Zen some distance behind. At last he turned left into the ploughed alley between two rows of vines leading up to a scruffy patch of oak trees at the edge of the field. A lorry lumbered into view, revealing the road by which Zen had arrived.

Suddenly Manlio slowed to a hesitant, stealthy gait, as though stalking some timid creature. He pointed to a bare stretch where three vines had been brutally hacked off just above ground level. The soil showed signs of having been recently turned over.

'That was where they found it,' he said in a stonily neutral tone.

'The corpse?'

A curt nod.

'I had the vines cut right back, of course. There was no question of making wine from *those* grapes. Before that, the spot was well hidden both from the road and from the house. That's why it took so long to find him. My father often used to go off for the day somewhere or other without letting anyone know. If I'd sounded the alarm and then it turned out he'd gone into town on some private business, I'd never have heard the end of it. Things were bad enough between us as it was. I didn't call the police until the evening of the next day, and it wasn't until the following morning that they brought in the dogs.'

'By which time, according to the medical report, it was impossible to determine the time of death with any precision,' Zen remarked in a deliberately casual tone.

Manlio smiled and nodded.

'Yes, I know. The investigating magistrate made great play with that particular point. Nevertheless, the fact remains that I didn't kill my father.'

'Someone did,' Zen said quietly.

'Yes, someone did. And someone else knows who that someone is, and yet another person knows that that someone knows. That's the way it is around here, *dottore*.'

He had spoken with such bitterness that Zen was amazed to hear him add, 'Are you free for lunch, by any chance?'

'Lunch?' he echoed vaguely.

'Well, let's not exaggerate. Rosa has been staying with her daughter since I was arrested, so we'll have to improvise. But the wine will be good.'

He glanced at Zen with an expression of solicitude.

'That's a nasty-looking cut you've got there, *dottore*. Quite fresh, too, by the look of it.'

After Minot had dropped Aurelio Zen in Palazzuole, he drove a few miles out of town to pay calls on some private clients and a restaurant owner with whom he sometimes did business. His pickings that night had not been good enough to warrant going into Alba and selling directly on the street.

His customers initially balked at the discovery that prices had risen by an average of ten per cent.

'Beppe didn't used to charge this much!' they all said, in one form or other.

'God rest him, Beppe's dead,' was the reply. 'If you want to pay market prices, drive into town. If you want home delivery, this is the going rate.'

They paid, all but one, and Minot made his way home a hundred thousand lire nearer to being able to buy Anna from Beppe's sons and heirs. They lived in the city, and not only were they uninterested in owning a truffle hound but they seemed blissfully ignorant of the animal's real value. For the meantime Minot had kindly offered to take care of the bitch, and, needless to say, was putting her to good use, although he kept her in a shed outside the house because of the rats.

The rats had made their appearance some years earlier: a brief incursion here, a nocturnal raid there, some grain missing from the supply Minot fed his chickens, a few chewed sacks of seed, and lots of hard, black droppings. Minot had already tried setting Anna on them once, one night when Beppe had to go to Turin for his younger son's wedding and had let Minot borrow her in accordance with their long-standing arrangement. But Anna had been bred to sniff out truffles, and showed no interest in taking on an army of rodents.

After that, Minot had resorted to the poison and traps, as well as ambushing them one night and shooting a dozen or so. He had even hacked one youngster in half with a shovel in his fury. But they kept coming, until one day – he still wasn't sure why – he had set out some stale bread he had no further use for, unbaited this time. In the morning, it was gone. That evening he put down some more, together with a saucer of diluted milk.

From that moment on, the attacks on his stores of seed and grain gradually diminished, then ceased altogether. It was as if he and the rats had arrived at an arrangement. Minot did not reveal this to anyone else, of course. People already thought that he was a little eccentric. If they learned that he was feeding rats, it would merely confirm their prejudices. But Minot couldn't see why rats had any less right to live than several humans he could think of, always providing that they respected him and his property, of course. After all, they only wanted to survive, like everything else. Was that too much to ask?

It was some months before his dependants risked appearing in person before their benefactor, and, when they did, it was at first the merest glimpse caught out of the corner of the eye, a flurry in the shadows at the edge of the room, the flick of a long thin tail abruptly withdrawn. Perhaps some folk-memory of the shotgun blasts which had decimated the pack still remained, or the squeals of the baby which Minot had cut in two with his spade.

But at length these faded, too, mere myths and old wives' tales that no one took seriously any more. The younger generation knew nothing of this house beyond the food and drink they found there every night. That was real enough; the rest just stories. So out they came, snouts twitching, red eyes alert, tails stirring like autonomous life-forms parasitic upon these parasites. Minot sat on the sofa and watched them take the nightly offering he had put down. From time to time they glanced up at him in ways he might, had he been inclined to sentimentality, have interpreted as gratitude. But Minot was a realist, and knew exactly the extent of the interest which the rats took in him. He liked it that way. Cupboard love was the one kind you could depend on.

By now he fed his pets morning and evening, and they knew him well enough to venture up on to the sofa where he sat, even to the extent of perching on his legs and shoulders. He allowed them to scamper inquisitively about, squinting up at him and scenting the air, their whiskers keenly quivering, until he heard a car draw near and then pull up outside. With a brisk slap of his palms, he dismissed his familiars, stuffed the money which the truffles had brought him under the cushions of the sofa, and went to investigate.

The vehicle parked outside turned out to be a Carabinieri jeep. Out of it, squeezed into his uniform like a sausage in its casing, stepped Enrico Pascal.

'*Marescià*,' said Minot.

Pascal winced.

'My piles are killing me,' he announced with an air of satisfaction, if not pride.

'You spend too much time sitting at a desk!' Minot returned. 'Look at me. I'm out and about all day and half the night, and the old sphincter's still as tight as a drum.'

Pascal shook his head.

'The doctor says it runs in the family. Can I come in?'

Minot waved his hand carelessly. Enrico Pascal walked past him and stopped, surveying the floor in the room within.

'Looks like you've got rats,' he remarked, studying the droppings scattered about.

'Eh, it's hard to keep them out! Care for a glass of something?'

The *maresciallo* grimaced.

'Maybe a splash, just to keep my edge.'

Minot nodded. The customs of the country dictated the consumption of a series of glasses of wine throughout the day, 'just to keep an edge'. One was never drunk, it went without saying, but never entirely sober either.

With his curiously feminine gait, Minot stepped over to the ancient refrigerator in the corner and pulled out an unlabelled bottle of the white wine named Favorita, a grape native to the area since the dawn of time and still cultivated by a few producers for private consumption.

'Even worse than mine,' commented Enrico Pascal, surveying the cluttered interior of the fridge. 'I always assumed the wife was doing it on purpose, to make me lose weight. "You could make a fortune selling this as a miracle diet," I told her. "One look and your appetite disappears for hours." What's this, then?'

He pointed to a glass jar filled with some dark red liquid in which bits of meat were floating.

'Hare,' Minot replied, handing Pascal his wine. 'Shot it just the other day. Do you like hare?'

Pascal did not reply. He tossed off his wine and returned to the centre of the room, where he stood looking around in a lordly way. Minot resumed his seat on the sofa. There was a silence which persisted for some time.

'Saturday morning about six . . .' Pascal began at length, and then broke off.

'Yes?'

Enrico Pascal sighed deeply.

'Where were you?'

Minot reflected a moment.

'Out,' he replied.

'Out where?'

'After truffles.'

With another wince, the *maresciallo* sank into a chair to Minot's right, his back to the bleary light from the one window.

'Yes, but where?'

Minot smiled cunningly.

'Ah, you can't expect me to answer that!'

'I'm investigating the death of Beppe Gallizio. I expect full cooperation from every member of the public.'

The two men exchanged a glance.

'It was over Neviglie way,' Minot replied. 'A likely looking spot I noticed a couple of weeks ago on the way back from making a delivery.'

Pascal considered this for a moment.

'But Beppe had taken Anna out that night,' he said. 'And you don't own a hound of your own, Minot.'

Instead of answering, Minot got up and went out to the kitchen, where he poured himself a glass of wine.

'What's all this about?' he demanded, returning to the other room.

Enrico Pascal shifted painfully from one buttock to the other.

'At first, you see, we assumed that Beppe had killed himself,' he announced discursively. 'We may still come to that conclusion in the end. But in the meantime there are a few things which are bothering us.'

Minot took a swig of wine, leaning against the mantelpiece above the cold grate.

'What sort of things?'

'Well, there's the gun, for instance. It's Beppe's all right, it was lying there beside the body and the only fingerprints on it are his. But Anna had been there, too, and Beppe had his mattock and his torch and all his truffle-hunting equipment with him. Why bother with that, if he'd meant to kill himself? And why bring his shotgun if not?'

He sighed.

'And then the technical people have been on to me with some problems they've been having.'

'Like what?'

'I won't bore you with the details. For that matter, I don't really understand them myself. But when you fire a shotgun, it discharges nitrate on to your sleeve and hand. Now there were traces of nitrate on Beppe's body and clothing, but they were apparently too weak and old to have been done that day. There was also something about the "angle of scatter", or some such thing. They say that for the pellets which hit Beppe to have spread out the way they did, the end of the barrel must have been at least half a metre away, which would have been too far for him to reach the trigger.'

Minot knocked back his wine.

'But what has this to do with me?'

His guest stood up and stuck his thumbs under the black belt of his tunic.

'We have a witness who claims to have seen a truck like yours parked off the road a short distance from the wood where Beppe died.'

Minot turned on him in an instant, his body tensed, ready to spring.

'Who's that? Someone with a grudge against me, I'll bet. They all hate me, God knows why. I've never done them any harm, but they treat me like a leper!'

Pascal did not lose his composure.

'Not in this case, Minot. The witness in question was on his way into Alba early yesterday morning when he saw a vehicle parked in the copse to the left of the road, a red Fiat truck. He recognized it as yours, assumed that you were out after truffles and thought no more about it. Then he heard the news about Beppe's suicide and called me to say that you might have heard or seen something.'

He stared fixedly at his host.

'So now I'd like to hear your side of it.'

Minot sat down again. There was no point in trying to dominate the situation physically. *Minot chit*, they'd used to call him as a child – 'Little Guglielmo' – to distinguish him from another boy of the same name, a swaggering brute and bully known as *Minot gross*. The distinction ceased to have any meaning when the latter Guglielmo broke his neck while exploring the roof of an abandoned farm just outside the village, but somehow the mocking nickname had stuck.

'I said *I* wasn't there,' Minot told Pascal. 'I didn't say anything about my truck.'

The *maresciallo* raised one eyebrow and waited.

'I was out with friends that night,' said Minot, after a pause. 'They brought the dogs, and they drove. When I got back my truck was here, but not where I'd left it. There was mud on the paintwork, too, fresh mud. Someone must have taken it while I was out. The key was in the ignition. I never bother to take it out.

93

No one around here wants to steal an old crock like mine.'

Enrico Pascal considered this.

'And who were these friends?' he asked.

Minot shook his head decisively.

'I'm not going to drag them into the shit.'

Pascal twitched at the seat of his uniform trousers. He sat down again, drumming the fingers of one hand on his knee.

'You're making this very difficult for me, Minot,' he said mildly.

The answer was a laugh.

'You haven't always made things that easy for me, *marescià*! I'm finally getting my own back for . . .'

He broke off abruptly. One of the rats had appeared on the back of the chair in which the Carabinieri official was sitting, and was now perched a few inches from his ear. Minot clapped his hands together loudly. The beast froze, then spun around in the air and vanished. Minot rubbed his palms together as though the slap had been a rhetorical gesture.

'Here's what I'll do,' he suggested in a conciliatory tone. 'Let me have a word with these friends of mine. If there's no problem, I'll call you up and tell you their names.'

'What makes you think there would be a problem?'

Minot shrugged.

'You never know, do you? Look at Lamberto Latini. He didn't want anyone to know where he'd been that night, did he?'

Enrico Pascal shook his head.

'I don't know, Minot. It's very irregular. I mean, you could just go to them and work out a story together, construct an alibi for yourself . . .'

Minot laughed.

'Don't be ridiculous! Who's going to take a risk like that for the likes of me?'

Pascal seemed not to have heard.

'I should really take you in right now,' he murmured, as though to himself.

'You don't want another mistake, though, do you?' Minot returned maliciously. 'First Manlio Vincenzo, then Latini. If you get it wrong a third time, people are going to start making jokes. "Maybe he should save time and just arrest us all!" I don't think you want that, *marescià*. In the city you might be able to get away with it, but out here in the country you need people's respect and cooperation. Lose that, and your job becomes impossible.'

Enrico Pascal stood up heavily.

'You've got the whole thing worked out, Minot. I can't afford another mistake, it's true. On the other hand, I can't afford to have two unsolved murders in my district either.'

'What about this other policeman?' Minot asked him. 'The one who just arrived from Rome. He seemed to have some ideas about the Vincenzo business, at least.'

Enrico Pascal stared at him closely.

'You've met him?'

Minot nodded and smiled.

'Yesterday in Alba, at the market. The Faigano brothers and I were playing cards. He came over and introduced himself as a newspaper reporter from Naples. We pretended to believe him.'

The *maresciallo* seemed staggered by this revelation.

'But how did you know who he was?'

'Because I'd seen him earlier in the street with Dottor Legna, who was treating him with great respect. I knew then he must be this "supercop" they've been talking about in the press. When he turned up in the bar, I recognized him right away.'

He laughed.

'So I started whistling the chorus to this old Fascist song! That's what we used to do back in the war to tip each other off that there was an informer about. They couldn't very well object, could they? We were just being patriotic.'

Pascal sniffed loudly.

'Passing himself off as a reporter, was he? These Criminalpol types, I suppose they're trained to do all that undercover stuff. Well, at least you've seen him and spoken to him. He hasn't bothered to get in touch with me. But then why would he? I'm just a country bumpkin trying to keep order here in the village.'

He nodded to Minot.

'Well, I'd better be going.'

They walked together to the front door.

'Oh, I almost forgot,' said Pascal, turning on the threshold.

He took something from his pocket.

'I think this is yours.'

Minot stood looking down at the knife lying on Pascal's out-stretched palm.

'Where did you get that?' he said.

'It *is* yours, then?'

'I've never seen it before.'

Their eyes locked.

'Then why did you ask where I got it?' asked Pascal.

Minot's eyes narrowed unpleasantly.

'I mean, why are you showing it to me? Why did you bring it here?'

Enrico Pascal examined the knife carefully, as if it might provide the answer to these questions. It was old and well-used, with a worn wooden handle and a long, dull blade. Both were completely clean.

'It turned up at Beppe's house,' he replied at last.

'And what makes you think it's mine?'

The *maresciallo* reflected briefly, as though trying to recall.

'This witness I was telling you about,' he said at last. 'When I showed him the knife, he said he thought you had one like it.'

'Come on, Pascà!' Minot exclaimed angrily. 'Stop teasing me! Just who is this supposed witness of yours?'

Now it was Enrico Pascal's turn to smile.

'If you were under arrest, Minot, I'd have to reveal that information. As it is, I don't see any reason to – how did you put it? – "drag him into the shit".'

Minot's face had become a hard, furious mask.

'Don't play games with me, *marescià*! People who do that . . .'

He broke off.

'Well?' queried Pascal.

Minot looked at him.

'I don't forget, that's all. I don't forget and I don't forgive.

Treat me like a man, and I'll treat you the same way. Treat me like a rat, and I bite back.'

He went inside and slammed the door, leaving Enrico Pascal standing on the doorstep.

'While she was alive, my mother did all the cooking herself, right up to the end, when the pain got too much. So the only time I've ever had any occasion to fend for myself is when I lived abroad. Still, I'll see what I can do. I arranged for a neighbour to come by and feed the hens, so there should be eggs, at least. But first let's crack a bottle.'

Manlio Vincenzo led the way downstairs to a cellar which appeared even larger than the house above. Striding confidently between the bins of stacked bottles, all identical to Zen's untrained eyes, he unerringly selected three from differing locations. Back in the cold, austere kitchen, he unwound a wire cage surrounding the stopper of one bottle and poured a golden froth into two long-stemmed glasses.

'A *moscato* from east of Asti,' he said, offering one to Zen, 'but not like any you'll have had before. This is the authentic thing, made in small quantities for friends by someone who knows what he's doing. It's powerfully aromatic, but very light and barely sweet.'

He sniffed and sipped, staring up fixedly at the exposed beams on the ceiling, then swallowed and nodded once.

'Even better than it was last time I tried it. No one believes this stuff improves, though. The big producers have spent a fortune persuading people that it doesn't, which in the case of their products is true, since they are biologically dead.'

He put his glass down and turned away, waving to Zen to follow.

'Now let's go and see what we can forage. This is rather fun, don't you think?'

He scooped up a trug from a cabinet by the back door and led the way out into the yard. Before long they had gathered a dozen eggs from the hen coop, potatoes and an onion from a vegetable bin, as well as a selection of herbs. Back in the kitchen, Manlio diced the vegetables and set them simmering in oil. Then he went into a room next door, where whole hams and cured sausages hung from hooks in the ceiling, and removed a selection, before disappearing to yet another larder in another part of the house, returning with about a quarter of a wheel of Parmesan.

'There's no need to go to all this trouble,' Zen remarked awkwardly, aware of his ambiguous status.

'It's no trouble,' Manlio returned. 'On the contrary. You have no idea of the pleasure in something as simple as making an omelette without having to think twice or explain what I'm doing or how I'm doing it. But the real reason for all this is that I want to try to get across to you that rather dry subject I broached earlier, but in a more *liquid* way.'

He carved off a chunk of the Parmesan and grated it into a bowl, then added the beaten eggs, tipped in the cooked vegetables in their oil with some salt and pepper, then stirred it all up and returned the mixture to the pan.

'You need to taste the wine,' he declared, as though uttering a philosophical imperative. 'After all, that's what it's all about, in the end.'

With the same darting energy, he set about carving slices of raw ham and salami which he laid out on chipped, hand-painted platters. Then he opened the two bottles of red wine and poured Zen a glass from each.

'Try this one first,' he directed.

Zen did as he was told, and almost spat it out. To his palate, the wine tasted like ink: intense and bitter, *sincero* but distinctly uncharming.

'Now this,' said his host.

Once again Zen raised his glass, more cautiously this time. But this wine was much more welcoming, with a rounder, fuller, fruity flavour. Relieved, Zen immediately took a second gulp.

'Well?' Manlio Vincenzo enquired archly.

Zen pointed to the second glass.

'I prefer this one.'

His host grinned.

'Clearly you don't know much about wine, Dottor Zen.'

'I know that,' Zen admitted sheepishly.

'The first glass I offered you is our 1982 *riserva*. It recently fetched almost two thousand dollars a case at an auction in New York.'

Zen looked suitably impressed.

'And how much does the wrong one cost?'

A pause and a distant smile.

'No one knows. It's never been put on the market, partly because it's "wrong" in a legal sense as well. I made it myself from some stalks I brought back from France and planted on a section of land which got washed out in a landslide a few years back. My father was involved in a legal dispute with the local council about compensation and payment for a new retaining wall. I knew that was likely to drag on for at least a decade – my father was extremely litigious – and so I put in my own plants meanwhile. What you're drinking is the result.'

'Congratulations.'

Manlio Vincenzo got to his feet and went over to check on the eggs.

'This is nothing to what I could make on favoured slopes with fully mature vines. What you're tasting is a blend of Merlot and Cabernet Sauvignon. It would be interesting to try adding some Syrah, and maybe even mixing that in with the Nebbiolo. That's what they've been doing in Tuscany for years now, having finally realized that Sangiovese usually isn't terribly interesting, however "traditional" it may be. But up here tradition is still the word of God, protected by the full force of the law – and God help anyone who suggests otherwise.'

He flipped the *frittata* on to a plate, slipped it back into the pan to cook briefly on the other side, and then brought it to table.

'Take that vineyard I just showed you,' he said, serving Zen, 'the one where my father died. It has good soil and ideal exposure. If we bottled it as a single-vineyard wine and gave it a dialect name, we could charge the same as Gaja does for his *Sorì Tildìn* or *San Lorenzo*. But that would be commercial suicide. We don't have the marketing clout Angelo has, and we need the quality of that field and a few like it to keep our reserve Barbaresco up to par. So we hobble along, producing a good if no longer absolutely first-rate example of what is, in my opinion, a second-class varietal to begin with. Don't tell anyone here I said that, though!'

They had just started to eat when the phone rang.

'Damn!' said Manlio. 'If it's those reporters again . . .'

But it wasn't. After some monosyllabic exchanges, he turned to Zen.

'It's for you.'

Zen stared at him, then went over and took the phone.

'Yes?'

'Hello again.'

It was the same dehumanized voice which had called him at his hotel that morning, a thin crackle like an aluminium can crushed in the hand.

'First of all, a word of warning. Last time you hung up on me. That was a mistake I would advise you not to repeat if you are to have any chance of solving this puzzle before the solution is, so to speak, thrust upon you.'

'How did you know I was here?'

He had spoken without thinking, and was answered with a tinny laugh.

'You still don't seem to understand. I ask the questions. You answer them. A bit of a change for someone in your position, but you'll get used to it. Now, then, have you made any progress with the clue I gave you last night?'

This time, Zen held his tongue.

'No? Via Strozzi, number twenty-four doesn't ring a bell? Odd, really, given how many times you rang the bell there. I wonder if you're really giving this matter your full attention. Let's try clue number two. A name, this time. Amalia. Surely that must mean something? Amalia.

Think about it. I'll be in touch soon, and I hope that next time you'll have something to say for yourself. Frankly, these one-sided conversations are becoming rather boring.'

The line went dead. Zen returned to the table and started in on his lukewarm slab of *frittata*.

'Work?' asked Manlio Vincenzo.

Zen took another sip of the Vincenzo Barbaresco.

'This actually isn't so bad,' he said, to change the subject. 'It stays with you, if you know what I mean. Some wines you drink and they're gone, but this . . .'

'It has a long finish, yes.'

Manlio gouged out another slab of Parmesan from the wheel with the special wedge-shaped tool used for this purpose.

'Try it with this.'

Zen bit into the pungent, siliceous cheese and drank some more wine.

'Even better,' he pronounced. '"A long finish", eh?'

He looked at his host and smiled cunningly.

'Just what we both need in the present case, Signor Vincenzo.'

'Are you suggesting that our interests are identical?'

'Assuming you're not guilty, of course.'

Manlio Vincenzo gave a light, cynical laugh.

'Well, let's assume that, shall we? For the sake of argument. How do our interests coincide, and what do you mean by "a long finish"?'

Aurelio Zen leaned back and lit a cigarette.

'As I understand it, Signor Vincenzo, you've been released on a conditional basis because of a presumed link between the killing of this Beppe Gallizio, which you clearly could not have committed, and that of your father.'

Manlio nodded assent.

'That's good news, but it provides only a presumption of innocence in your regard,' Zen went on. 'Some piece of evidence could come to light at any moment which would tilt the balance the other way, sending you back to prison and me to Sicily.'

'Sicily?'

Zen gave a brief description of the reason why he had been sent to Piedmont, this time – since the reference was unattributable – mentioning the name of the famous director in question. As he had hoped, Manlio Vincenzo was suitably impressed, albeit in a negative way.

'So that's how the system works!' he exclaimed. 'No wonder things are in the state they are.'

Zen smiled thinly.

'"What matter the road, provided it leads to paradise?" I'll find out who killed your father, Signor Vincenzo. But I need a little more time to do that, and to let the front-line posts in Sicily get filled. And you need to make your wine.'

Manlio Vincenzo picked up a lump of Parmesan and started to nibble.

'And just how do we achieve that?'

'I need more information, in particular in an area which may be delicate or painful for you to discuss. You've told me that the real reason for the bad feeling between you and your father was about technical matters relating to wine-making.'

'No, no! You haven't understood. That was just one of the symptoms. What really infuriated him was that by sending me abroad, outside his sphere of control, he had created – as he saw it – a monster of ingratitude who refused to toe the paternal line any longer.'

Zen nodded.

'I've been told that at the village *festa* he specifically accused you of homosexual tendencies, and of a liaison with someone called Andrea. Forgive me prying into your personal life, but is that true or not?'

To Zen's surprise, Manlio Vincenzo laughed.

'It's certainly true that I'm involved romantically with someone called Andrea,' he said in a tone laden with irony. 'But the real reason my father made such a fuss about my supposed homosexuality was that it jeopardized his long-term plans for acquiring the Faigano estate.'

'Gianni and Maurizio Faigano?'

Manlio rose, filled the *caffettiera* with grounds and water, screwed it together and set it on the stove.

'They're neighbours of ours. There's only one daughter – a very late child – and no other heirs, so when the brothers die, she'll inherit the entire property. It's quite extensive, with some very good fields bordering ours, which produce excellent wine.'

'So your father wanted you to marry Lisa Faigano.'

Manlio Vincenzo laughed.

'The idea's absurd! I've only met the child a few times. She's seventeen and I'm almost thirty. My own inclinations aside, there's no possible reason to suppose that she would have any interest in marrying me. In any case, her father would never agree. Maurizio and his brother are no friends of ours. In fact, we're barely on speaking terms.'

'Why's that?' Zen asked.

Manlio shrugged.

'It's just one of those things which are so common around here. You run up against them every so often, and soon learn not to ask questions. No one wants to talk about it, no one will explain. It's just a given, like the lie of the land.'

'Did you point this out to your father?'

'Of course.'

'What did he say?'

Manlio Vincenzo did not answer right away. He came back to the table and took another careful taste of wine.

'He said, "Just get her pregnant, I'll do the rest."'

There was a silence.

'I told him that times had changed, that things don't work like that any more. "Leave that to me," he said. "Just get her in the family way, that's all I'm asking." That was when I made the mistake of mentioning that I was already involved with someone else.'

The coffee came burbling up the spout and spluttered loudly. Manlio removed the pot and poured out two cups.

'What did your father say to that?' asked Zen.

'He said he didn't give a damn where I chose to stick it for pleasure. This was business, and my duty to the family was to marry Lisa Faigano, by force if necessary.'

He broke off, his head cocked to one side like a dog on the scent. Then Zen, too, heard the sound of a car engine, very faintly at first, but rapidly confirming its nearing presence.

'Now what?' demanded Manlio.

The car – a diesel, by the sound of it – pulled up in the court-yard. Manlio had got to his feet and was heading towards the door when it was flung open by a young woman in her mid-twenties wearing a long beige coat over a pullover and jeans. She shrieked something in English, and rushed to embrace Manlio Vincenzo, who reciprocated fervently.

'Have you got any money?' the woman asked, switching to Italian. 'I forgot to change any at the airport and I have to pay the taxi. It's so wonderful to see you, and you're looking so well! I think you've lost a bit of weight, in fact. It suits you.'

Manlio Vincenzo turned to his guest in some embarrassment.

'Do forgive us, *dottore!*' he said. 'I phoned last night when my lawyer told me the good news, but I had no idea . . .'

Zen stood up and bowed politely.

'*Molto lieto, signorina.*'

The formal phrase recalled Manlio Vincenzo to the proprieties.

'But of course you don't know each other! This is Vice-Questore Aurelio Zen, my dear. Dottor Zen, allow me to introduce my fiancée, Andrea Rodriguez.'

'Oh, not so bad,' Minot replied to the brothers' rhetorical enquiry as to how it was going. 'Only too many cops, to tell you the truth. I gave one a lift this morning. You remember that character who showed up at the bar, pretending to be a reporter from Naples? He's trying to pass himself off as a wine dealer now. And no sooner had I got home, than Pascal dropped by.'

Gianni Faigano nodded.

'Thanks for the tip-off. I was able to lead the nosy bastard a merry dance and get a free feed into the bargain.'

'I just wish they'd get the whole thing cleared up, one way or another,' Maurizio said dourly. 'All these cops hanging around makes things like this even more risky.'

He gestured towards the demijohns of wine in the shed beside which Minot had parked his truck. He was to take them to the *cantina* run by Bruno Scorrone, who would subsequently work a miracle of the loaves-and-fishes variety on the contents and split the profits with the Faigano brothers. Minot got paid a flat-rate transportation fee.

'Speaking of which,' Minot remarked lightly, 'I need to ask you both a favour.'

The brothers exchanged a glance.

'What sort of favour?' asked Gianni.

'Let's load the wine, then we'll talk.'

The job took the best part of twenty minutes. Lifting the hundred litre *damigiane* on to the bed of the truck was hard enough, but the really tricky part was ensuring that they were set down carefully enough to avoid breakage. In the old days, the glass was covered with a layer of wicker or rope, but now there was just a sheath of coloured plastic matting with little or no give.

Once the truck was safely loaded, the three men went inside for a glass of the product and a smoke.

'So, two policemen in one day, eh?' Maurizio remarked once they were seated. 'What are things coming to?'

This was just an opening gambit in the match they were about to play, of no importance in itself. Someone had to move first. It was what happened afterwards that would determine the result.

'That's right,' said Minot. 'When I was driving home after a night in the woods, I saw someone walking up from the station towards the village. I naturally stopped and offered him a ride, only to find that it was our friend the spy. I don't think he recognized me, but I knew him all right, with those stitches in his forehead.'

A silence fell.

'Terrible business about Beppe,' remarked Gianni Faigano.

'Terrible,' echoed Minot.

'Why should he want to do something like that?' Maurizio wondered aloud. 'I spoke to him only a few days ago, and he seemed perfectly normal then.'

'Maybe he didn't do it himself,' suggested Minot quietly.

Gianni looked at him.

'How do you mean?'

Minot relit his roll-up, which had gone out.

'Someone told me that you were driving into Alba that morning, and saw a truck parked close to where Beppe was killed.'

'That's ridiculous,' snapped Maurizio. 'We were busy all day filling those demijohns.'

'Well, someone saw a truck there,' said Minot. 'Told the Carabinieri about it, too. That's how I found out, from Pascal.'

He finished his wine and poured another glass.

'Take it easy,' cautioned Maurizio.

Minot laughed harshly.

'Don't worry! If I get arrested, it won't be for drunk driving.'

The silence reformed, a swirling opacity like one of the morning fogs for which the region was notorious.

'What were you two doing the night Beppe was shot?' asked Minot, not looking at them.

Gianni gave a humourless laugh.

'Eh, you've been spending too much time with cops all right, Minot. You're beginning to sound like one yourself!'

Minot smiled.

'Fair enough. But let's say a cop asked you the same question, what would you tell him?'

'The truth, of course,' Maurizio retorted irritably. 'We spent the evening watching TV and then went to bed.'

'Was Lisa here?'

'What the hell is . . .' Gianni began.

'Was she?' Minot insisted, speaking to Maurizio.

'She was at her aunt's house in Alba.'

'So you don't have any witnesses to confirm your story,' Minot concluded. 'In theory, you could have gone out that night, followed Beppe down to the woods and shot him.'

'Are you out of your mind?' yelled Gianni Faigano, pushing back his chair and standing up.

Minot held up his hands in a calming gesture.

'Take it easy, Gianni. I know you didn't kill Beppe. I didn't either, but that didn't stop Pascal from coming round and questioning me about it. Sooner or later it'll be your turn. Just think how much easier everything would be if we all had a nice, solid alibi.'

'Well, that's too bad,' snapped Maurizio, 'because we don't.'

'I do,' replied Minot with his nagging smile.

'Good for you.'

'I was out after truffles that night, miles from where Beppe was shot. And I wasn't alone.'

'Well, that's a stroke of luck. Who did you go out with?'

'With you two.'

The brothers stared at him.

'We met here at midnight,' Minot continued calmly, 'and drove over to a patch I know of near Neviglie. You provided the dogs, I provided the location. We didn't have much luck, as it turned out, but we stuck at it and didn't get home until seven o'clock the next morning. An hour after Beppe was shot.'

Gianni Faigano shook his head.

'Maurizio and I haven't been out truffling for ages, Minot. We're getting too lazy to spend all night tramping through the woods.'

Minot regarded him levelly.

'That's not quite true, Gianni. You make exceptions once in a while. This was one of them.'

Once again, the brothers consulted each other silently.

'Why would we do that?' asked Maurizio at length.

'Why *wouldn't* you? It's in all our interests to have a solid story to tell the cops, right?'

Gianni shook his head slowly.

'I don't want to get involved in this.'

'Ah, but supposing you're already involved?'

'What do you mean by that?'

Minot told them what he meant.

Twenty minutes later, he was back in his truck, the demijohns of wine covered by a tarpaulin. He took a roundabout route to the Scorrone winery, sticking to the back roads. There were risks either way. On the one hand, if any roadblocks had been set up by the police or the *Guardia di Finanza*, they were almost certain to be on the main highway, down in the valley. On the other, the indirect route would take about twice as long to drive, which meant twice as many chances of having a breakdown or an accident which would inevitably bring to the attention of the authorities the fact that he was transporting two thousand litres of unlabelled red wine, for which he had no sales documents, certificates of provenance, tax forms or shipping manifests.

It was a fine calculation, and in the end he decided to compromise by taking a short stretch of the *strada statale* which would cut fifteen minutes off the total transit time. The chances of the uniforms being out at that hour were pretty low. They would have written their quota of tickets that afternoon, lurking in lay-bys to pick off drivers weaving their way home after a long lunch followed by several grappas too many. As for the tax police, both they and their trucker prey would almost certainly have taken Sunday off.

His predictions proved correct, and less than half an hour after leaving the Faigano house Minot pulled off the highway and up a short drive leading to the headquarters of the Azienda Agricola Bruno Scorrone. This looked more like a factory than a winery: all concrete loading bays and stacked plastic crates, pumps and pipes and nozzles and stainless steel tanks. In a region celebrated for its scrupulously traditional approach to wine-making, Bruno Scorrone's main claim to fortune, if not to fame, was a generic Barbera d'Alba, widely available in screw-top, large-format bottles through various national supermarket chains.

Since in most years the Barbera grape is too cheap and plentiful to be worth faking, that particular product was more or less what it claimed to be, although purists might not have approved of the degree of manipulation which the wine had been subjected to, and would certainly have raised an eyebrow at the percentage of even cheaper and more plentiful grape varieties in the final mix. There had even been one occasion when the authorities had taken an interest in Bruno's operation, following the discovery that one batch of wine bottled there had been beefed up with various ingredients of a non-vinous nature, notably antifreeze.

But Bruno had stoutly maintained that this particular lot had been bought in bulk from a third party, who had already been arrested and charged in connection with a similar offence, and that his facilities had served merely as a bottling plant. It had been a trying few months, but in the end he had been released with his legal record, if not his reputation, unspotted. One of the great strengths of Scorrone's operation was that it acted as a depot through which many products of many different provenances passed. Bruno grew no grapes himself, but he vinified others' fruit and blended the results with wine made still elsewhere, until sometimes he himself – or so he claimed – couldn't be sure exactly what was in a given vat. This was true not only at the bottom end of the market, on which he depended for his bread-and-butter, but also on the occasions when he was tempted by an unrefusable offer into the high-margin sector. Which was where the Faigano brothers came into the picture.

Minot had been waiting for almost half an hour when Bruno Scorrone finally showed up in a four-wheel-drive Toyota. Gianni had been right, noted Minot; the brand-new vehicle was indeed green.

'Been over to Lamberto's for lunch,' said Bruno, belching loudly. 'I just wanted to make sure there were no hard feelings. God, you eat well there! I'd forgotten.'

And drink well, too, thought Minot, filing the thought away.

'Why would there be any hard feelings?' he asked.

Bruno Scorrone peered at him. Like everyone else, he was a little taller than Minot, but slacker and paunchier, with the florid, swollen face of a habitual drinker.

'Well, you know, I found Beppe's dog hanging round here after I got back from town. It seemed a bit odd, so I called the *maresciallo* to tell him about it. It's always a good idea to keep in well with the authorities, particularly in my line of business.'

He jerked a thumb towards the laden truck. Minot nodded.

'I understand.'

'I didn't say anything about Lamberto, of course,' Scorrone went on, lighting a small cigar. 'I didn't even know what had happened at that point. But he might have heard that I'd talked to Pascal and thought that I'd said something about him. You can't be too careful in a small community like this.'

Minot looked up at the vacant expanse of sky.

'You certainly can't,' he said.

Bruno Scorrone puffed unsuccessfully at his cigar, then threw it away. He gestured at the truck again.

'Well, shall we?'

Minot backed the truck up to one of the loading bays, Bruno Scorrone lowered the tail-gate, and together they set about shifting the heavy, fragile *damigiane* down to the concrete platform.

'So what's it to be this time?' asked Minot as they took a breather.

111

Bruno huffed and puffed a little.

'Barbaresco!' he exclaimed. 'I just clinched a deal with a buyer from Munich who's in the market for five hundred cases.'

Minot whistled.

'But that's over four thousand litres! There's only half that here.'

'I'll have to cut it, of course. The stuff that Gianni and Maurizio make could *be* Barbaresco. In fact, it's a damn sight better than some I've had. Too good for foreigners, that's for sure. And since they've never had the real thing, they won't be any the wiser.'

Bruno was definitely slightly tipsy, thought Minot, or he wouldn't be prattling away like this.

'How do you know they've never had it?'

Bruno gave him a worldly wise smile.

'Because in Germany, my friend, the real thing costs a minimum of a hundred thousand lire a bottle on release.'

Minot whistled again. Bruno nodded.

'People prepared to pay that kind of money aren't going to buy stuff at half the price with the name of some producer no one's ever heard of. On the other hand, the people who *will* buy it wouldn't dream of paying a day's wages for a bottle of wine that won't even be drinkable for ten years. What they want is something tasty to drink now, at the right price, and with a classy name to impress themselves or their friends. In short, there are two quite different markets, and each one gets what they've paid for. Meanwhile Gianni and Maurizio get a decent price for their excellent wine, I make an honest profit as blender and distributor, and you get your slice as our go-between and cut-out. It beats me why it's even illegal!'

Once the last of the twenty *damigiane* had been heaved into place, Bruno turned to Minot, panting for breath.

'Fancy a glass of something?' he said.

'Looks like you've had a few already.'

Bruno smiled.

'Well, you know how it is. Lamberto prides himself on his collection of grappas, and after I sympathized about Beppe and the whole business about him and Nina Mandola coming out, he brought out a few bottles and then left them on the table.'

He led the way to an office at the end of the loading dock, where he received wine buyers and their agents during working hours. Here he kept a small but select stock of restoratives which he used to tweak moods and swing deals.

'Try some of this!' he told Minot, pouring a grappa illegally made by a neighbour in a disused pig barn.

'So you've been talking to Pascal, eh?' Minot remarked, setting his glass down after an appreciative sip. 'So have I.'

Still savouring the grappa he'd knocked back in one, Bruno Scorrone didn't seem to hear.

'He told me you'd claimed to have seen my truck down by the stream where Beppe was killed.'

Bruno stared at him, all attention now.

'What? I did nothing of the sort. Like I said, I called him to say that I'd found Anna running loose and had taken her home and all the rest of it. I didn't even know Beppe was dead then! Pascal asked where I'd been that morning, and I told him that I'd driven into Alba. I saw people there who could corroborate that – apart from my Munich buyer, I mean – so it seemed the safest thing to do.'

He poured himself another glass of the oily spirit.

'But why bring me into it?' asked Minot, lifting his grappa but not drinking.

'I didn't! He asked if I'd seen anything unusual down where the road crosses the river. I said I thought I might have seen a truck parked in the bushes, but I wasn't sure. He said, "What kind of truck?", and I said I didn't know but it looked a bit like yours. I didn't say it *was* yours.'

Minot looked at him silently.

'So you didn't make a statement under oath or sign any papers?'

'Of course not! It was just a casual chat over the phone.'

Bruno slurped out a third glass of grappa for himself.

'What about you?' he asked Minot. 'You're not drinking.'

'I've got to keep a clear head.'

Scorrone puffed contentedly on his cigar.

'Anyway, I'm glad you told me,' he said. 'That's the sort of thing which can lead to all sorts of misunderstandings if it's not cleared up. No hard feelings, eh?'

Minot shook his head.

'No feelings at all.'

They walked out of the office and along the concrete loading bay to the truck. As they passed a stack of new bottles, Bruno suddenly laid his hand on Minot's arm.

'You weren't really there, were you?' he asked.

Minot looked at him in surprise.

'Where?'

'Down by the stream, the morning Beppe was killed.'

Minot said nothing.

'Only they might ask again, you see, under oath this time. It would help if I knew the truth.'

Minot looked down at the dirty concrete platform for some time.

'If that's what you want, Bruno.'

He removed one of the new green bottles from the stack, examining it as though he had never seen such a thing before.

'The truth,' he said, 'is that I killed him.'

Bruno's face ran through a pantomime of expressions. Then he gave a forced laugh.

'Don't make jokes about something like this!'

Minot looked him in the eyes.

'I'm not joking.'

Neither man said anything for a long time.

'But why?' murmured Scorrone.

Minot stared down at the bottle in his hand and smiled faintly.

'He was on my turf. I discovered that patch of truffles years ago, long before anyone else. But Beppe did an underhand thing. I used to borrow his dog once in a while, when he didn't need her. He took to dipping her paws in aniseed before I took her out, and then tracing my route the next day. I soon found that all my best patches had been cleaned out before I got there. That's why he lent me Anna in the first place, so that she would lead him to all my secret discoveries. So I decided to get even.'

Bruno Scorrone clutched at one of the concrete pillars supporting the roof.

'But that's absurd!' he exclaimed in a wavering voice. 'You don't kill someone over truffles.'

In a single swoop, Minot smashed the bottle he had been holding against the pillar and jabbed the broken end into Scorrone's throat, twisting the jagged glass into the exposed flesh. A whistling spray of blood emerged, accompanied by a gargling shriek which quickly drowned on the pulsing flood. Bruno Scorrone slid down the pillar, emitting vaguely anal sounds and thrashing around feebly on the concrete.

It all went quicker than Minot had imagined. The twin advantages of surprise and sobriety aside, it was a question of will in the end. He wanted Bruno dead more than Bruno wanted to live. There was a lot of mess to clean up, but this was a site designed for spillage, with drains everywhere and a high-pressure hose on the wall. No one had seen or heard what had happened, and the only people who knew that he'd been there in the first place were Gianni and Maurizio Faigano. And he could deal with them.

It was dark when Aurelio Zen arrived back in Alba in a bus packed with football supporters who spent the journey loudly celebrating their victory over a town in the next valley. By the time he disembarked in the inevitable Piazza Garibaldi, Zen had learned several colourful terms of abuse in the local dialect, and even found himself singing along to a rousing chorus which alleged that the players of the Coazzolo team were unable to score in more ways than one.

He started back to his hotel, paying no particular attention to his surroundings until the celebratory yells of the soccer fans brought a uniformed policeman out of a neighbouring building to suggest forcefully that they show a bit of respect, in view of the fact that Juventus had just lost to Inter by a disputed last-minute penalty. This was news to the local *tifosi*, due to poor radio reception on the road and the aforementioned festivities. The upshot was a lively discussion regarding the merits of the latest foreign acquisition by the Turin club, and estimations of how much the Milanese had paid the Roman referee to award the penalty after the Inter centre-forward took a blatant dive inside the area.

While all this was going on, Zen sidled around the group and entered the police station unobserved. He had expected the place to be deserted, it being Sunday, but to his surprise there was a group of five men in the squad room, a plain-clothes officer in the middle of a telephone conversation, and various uniformed patrolmen looking on.

'Sì, sì, sì,' the man on the phone declared in a tone of utter boredom. 'Va benissimo. D'accordo. Senz'altro. Non si preoccupi, dottore. Certo, certo. Non c'è problema, ci penso io. D'accordo. Sì, sì. Ci sentiamo fra poco. Arriverderla, dottore. Buona sera, buona sera.'

He replaced the phone and glanced sourly at Zen, who was hovering in the doorway.

'Well?'

'Excuse me,' Zen began hesitantly. 'I didn't mean to disturb you, but the thing is . . .'

'Yes?'

Zen hesitated.

'Well . . .'

'Get on with it! We're busy here.'

'Well, the fact is, I need a phone tapped.'

There was a long silence. The plain-clothes officer got to his feet. He smiled, not pleasantly.

'Are you sure that's all? You don't want anyone arrested, by any chance?'

'Not at the moment.'

The officer's smile became still more menacing.

'Just the phone tap, eh? And which phone did you have in mind?'

'The one at the hotel where I'm staying,' Zen replied. 'It's called the Alba Palace.'

'The whole hotel? All the calls, eh?'

'Just the incoming ones.'

At this point, the officer evidently decided that he had milked the joke for all it was worth.

'What the hell's Dario doing down there at the door?' he asked, turning to his colleagues. 'Letting some madman push his way in here like this! It's a disgrace.'

'I apologize,' Zen replied. 'I should have . . .'

The officer whirled around.

'As for you, bursting in here and demanding a telephone tap on the leading hotel in town! Are you out of . . .'

He grabbed the identity card which Zen was holding out.

'. . . your mind? Are you out . . .? Are you . . .? Aaaaaaaagh! Ha! Yes. Yes, yes, of course. Dottor Zen! We meet at last.'

He held out his hand with a fixed smile.

'Nanni Morino. Forgive me for not recognizing you, *dottore*.'

'On the contrary, forgive me for interrupting. Nothing important, I hope.'

'No, no, just an accident at a local winery. But the victim was quite a big name round here, so we've had to cancel our plans for Sunday evening and show willing. Still, it's double time, eh, lads?'

With an insincere laugh, he motioned his subordinates to make themselves scarce, which they duly did.

'Now then, this phone tap,' Morino said, once he and Zen were alone. 'No problem, of course, but it may take a while to set up.'

He stared intently at Zen.

'That's a nasty-looking cut you've got there, *dottore*.'

'Yes, and quite fresh, too, by the look of it. Can we get back to the point, please? I've been getting some anonymous calls recently. The first was at the hotel, the second at the Vincenzo house.'

Nanni Morino raised an eyebrow.

'I went out to Palazzuole today, to take a look at the scene of the crime,' Zen explained. 'The son, Manlio, was there, and he invited me back to the house for lunch. While we were eating, the phone rang and it was for me. My anonymous caller.'

Morino brightened up.

'In that case, I should be able to give you a lead right away.'

'How do you mean?'

He lifted the receiver of his own phone and dialled.

'The Vincenzo line has been tapped ever since the crime. Any calls received there today should have been logged. This was at lunchtime, you said?'

Nanni Morino spent over five minutes talking to various police personnel in Asti, running through a repertoire of stock phrases such as those he had used in his previous phone conversation. Then he hung up and turned to Zen.

'That's odd,' he said. 'There was only one call recorded to the Vincenzo house at that time today. It was made at twelve fifty-two.'

'That sounds right. Where was it from?'

'That's what's odd. It was made from the hotel you mentioned, the one where you're staying. The Alba Palace.'

There was a long pause. Then Zen slapped his forehead.

'I'm an idiot. My apologies again for the interruption.'

'Don't mention it, *dottore.*'

At the door, Zen turned, suddenly recalling Tullio Legna's warning about the consequences of Manlio Vincenzo's release.

'That accident you mentioned . . .'

'Yes?'

'Who was involved?'

'A man called Scorrone. He ran a big commercial operation out near Palazzuole and was found dead there earlier this evening.'

'You're sure it was an accident?'

'No question about it! It's something we're all too familiar with around here. He was found floating in a vat of fermenting grapes. Apparently he'd been to a local restaurant and had a long and well-lubricated lunch, then drove straight to his winery to check on some wine he'd started up the day before. He must have leaned over too far and fallen in. The atmosphere above those vats is heavy with carbon dioxide and alcohol fumes. One slip and you drown or suffocate, or both.'

Zen nodded absently.

'Scorrone, you said?'

'Bruno Scorrone. Do you know him?'

'I've heard the name.'

He turned towards the door.

'About that phone tap . . .' Morino said.

'That won't be necessary, thank you. Good night.'

At the main entrance downstairs, Dario was explaining in an authoritative tone to the assembled fans that if only Del Piero had taken down that long ball from Conte late in the second period with the *inside* of his foot and then got in the cross to Inzaghi, who was wide open . . . Zen slipped unnoticed through the opinionated throng and made his way back to the hotel.

The night clerk on duty was the same one who had been there when Zen arrived on the train from Rome, a short balding man with an expression which mingled anxiety, humiliation and aggression, as if he were perpetually haunted by the suspicion that everyone secretly despised him for his frailty and incompetence and was defying them to come right out and admit it.

Zen flashed his identification card.

'Show me a list of everyone staying here,' he said.

'*Staying* here?' asked the clerk, wide-eyed, as though the idea of anyone staying at a hotel was a bizarre and slightly disturbing notion which had never occurred to him before.

'Everyone currently registered at the hotel,' Zen explained.

'Staying here *now*?'

'What do you think I mean, April the first next year? Just show me the book.'

The clerk shook his head violently.

'There isn't one! No one has a book any more! Books are finished.'

He turned away, pressing a series of buttons on a computer keyboard. Paper unrolled to a staccato rhythm from a printer on the shelf beside him. The clerk tore it off and handed it to Zen.

'There! Everyone who's here now! All of them, every one!'

He stared at Zen with a manic intensity which suggested that there were in fact a number of guests not named on the list whose bodies were concealed in the cellar. Zen walked through an archway into the bar and sat down at a corner table, scanning the list. It was more or less what he had expected. Apart from the ten foreigners – three Swiss, four Germans, two Americans and a Frenchman – there was a woman, three couples and four single men, excluding himself. None of the names meant anything to him, but tomorrow he would return to the *Commissariato di Polizia* and ask them to run a search of the records.

'Have you got a light?'

He looked up, his right hand already reaching automatically for his lighter. The speaker was a young woman in black leggings and a leather blouson. Zen vaguely remembered having seen her leaving the room next to his when he got back the previous evening. She lit her cigarette, then slumped down in the armchair opposite him.

'Do you mind if I sit here?'

Zen glanced at her curiously. The bar was empty, and there was no shortage of available seats.

'Suit yourself.'

The woman took a few puffs at her cigarette, then ground it out in the ashtray. Her hair was cropped short in layers, she wore no make-up and the expression of her green eyes was uncompromisingly direct.

'I don't usually do things like this,' she said.

Zen smiled politely.

'No.'

'The truth is, I'm going out of my mind with boredom.'

'I see.'

'Alba is *fantastically* boring, don't you think?'

'I suppose so.'

It couldn't be a pick-up, he decided. She was too straightforward to be anything other than a professional, in which case she would have got to the point by now. Besides, it was hard to imagine that sort of action in the bar of the Alba Palace.

The young woman's eyes met his.

'You're here on business?'

Zen nodded.

'And you?'

'The worst kind. Family business.'

Silence fell. Zen had decided to make no attempt to keep the conversation going. The woman was quite pretty, he supposed, in a rangy, sharp-featured way, but he wasn't attracted to her. For him, the voice was always the key to such things, and hers lacked that special resonance.

'You're a policeman,' she said.

He hesitated just a second.

'Is it that obvious?'

'I heard you talking to the desk clerk. Something about wanting a list of guests at the hotel. He seemed quite amazed, but then he always does.'

She pointed to the scroll of paper on the table.

'Is that it?'

Zen regarded her in pointed silence.

'I suppose I'm being indiscreet,' she said. 'It's just that the idea that anyone in this dump might be of interest to the police seemed irresistibly ... well, interesting.'

Zen thought briefly of telling her to mind her own business. Then it occurred to him that she might be of use.

'It's not an official matter. At least, not yet. Someone's been making anonymous phone calls. I have reason to believe that it's one of the people staying here.'

He handed over the list.

'Have you met any of the men whose names I've marked?'

'This one tried to chat me up in the restaurant last night and then gave me his card. He's a commercial traveller in wines and seems to sample a lot of the product. And one of the others patted my bottom in the lift yesterday. I don't know his name.'

She handed the list back.

'What does your anonymous caller want, anyway?'

'I don't know. But he knows who I am, and ...'

'Speaking of which, we should introduce ourselves.'

She turned the list around and pointed to the name 'Carla Arduini'.

'And you must be Aurelio Zen.'

He looked at her, frowning.

'How did you know that?'

'It was in all the local papers, along with a photograph,' she replied airily. '"Ministry sends top man from Rome to investigate Vincenzo case," that sort of thing. Perhaps that's how your caller found out, too.'

'Perhaps.'

Zen felt slightly put out that this idea hadn't occurred to him.

'But why does he bother phoning you, if he's staying here? If he's too timid to go to your room, he could always accost you in the bar. After all, I have!'

'I haven't the slightest idea, *signorina*. That's what makes it so unsettling. But enough about that. What are you doing here? Or is it too private to discuss?'

Carla Arduini appeared to consider this question for a moment.

'I'm trying to trace a relative.'

Zen looked away.

'A few years ago, a relative traced me. And without even trying,' he said.

'What sort of relative?'

'My father.'

He corrected himself with a gesture of the hand.

'My mother's husband.'

'Is there a distinction?'

Zen did not reply. Carla Arduini got to her feet.

'I'm sorry,' she said. 'I'm being tactless and tiresome. I think it's this place. It seems to be driving me mad.'

Zen stood up, smiling.

'I know what you mean. Look, perhaps we could have dinner together some time. When are you leaving?'

Carla Arduini looked at him intently, as though considering this proposition.

'Don't worry,' Zen went on. 'I'm not going to pat your bottom. That's not my style, and, besides, you're young enough to be my daughter.'

The woman unexpectedly burst into laughter.

'Yes, I am!'

'I'll give you a call. Which room are you in?'

He glanced at the list.

'312? Right next to mine. And how long are you staying?'

She looked at him with her disconcertingly candid green eyes.

'As long as it takes.'

When he emerged from his hotel the next morning, the sky had settled back into a grey, overcast mode which brought it down to a point where it seemed to graze the rooftops. Having stopped in a bar for an eye-opening shot of caffeine, Zen made his way along Via Maestra to the house to which Tullio Legna had led him earlier, ascended to the first floor and rang the bell.

There was no answer. He rang twice more before the door was opened by a young woman in the silk dressing-gown which the doctor had been wearing on Zen's previous visit. He introduced himself and asked apologetically if it were possible to see Lucchese.

'Is it about moths, medicine or music?' the woman demanded.

'Medicine. Your father treated me for . . .'

'My father is dead and has nothing to do with it.'

She pulled back the door with a yawn which was echoed by the silk gown, the two sides gaping open to reveal the upper slope of her breasts.

'Wait in there,' she said, pointing to a doorway on the other side of the hall. 'I'll tell the prince that you're here.'

She strode off down the corridor, her bare feet as soundless as an angel's on the terracotta tiles.

The room in which Zen had been directed to wait appeared to be a library. Taking the only seat visible, a wooden stool positioned in front of a writing desk, he waited.

And waited. And waited. Outside, the sun broke through for a brief and jagged moment, darting in and out of the room like a fugitive memory. Not daring to smoke, Zen got up and started to look over the volumes on the shelves. Old and heavily worn by use, they all seemed to be about musical instruments. There were pictures of pianos and organs, weirdly contorted wind instruments, and stringed ones the shape of a pregnant woman.

'My apologies for keeping you waiting, *dottore*.'

He turned to find Lucchese in the doorway, immaculate in a black suit and tie.

'I have to attend a funeral this morning. One of my relatives has apparently managed to kill himself by falling into a vat of wine. Quite exceptionally inept, even by the standards of the family, but there it is. Hence the delay.'

Zen stood up.

'Please excuse me for disturbing you so early in the morning, *principe*.'

Lucchese sighed loudly.

'Oh dear, has Irena been trying to impress you? That's one of the problems of fucking down, I'm afraid. There are, of course, compensations. Anyway, what can I do for you? Is it about your head, or is it about your head? I mean, sutures or psychoanalysis? Am I babbling? Irena, who studies music at the Academy in Turin, by the way, brought some exceptionally fine hashish with her and I'm afraid that we rather over-indulged last night – in more ways than one, in fact. Sorry, wrong thing to say to a policeman. Look, why don't I just shut up and let you talk instead?'

Zen smiled nervously.

'Actually, I just wondered if there was any chance of getting these stitches out. They make me look like Frankenstein's monster, besides attracting some attention I could do without. But if you're incapacitated, *principe* . . .'

'Incapacitated? I fancy that Irena could vouch for me in that respect.'

He went over to the window, grasping the frame at either side with his pale, articulate hands. As if in response, the sunlight returned in full strength, revealing shoals of dust like minnows in the air.

'It was harpsichords that brought us together,' the prince continued. 'I happen to own two particularly fine models, both seventeenth century. We have since moved on from one form of plucked instrument to . . . No, I don't think I'll finish that thought.

As for your stitches, there's no question of removing them yet. The wound would merely reopen and look even worse than it does now.'

Zen nodded meekly.

'Well, thank you for receiving me, and, once again, please excuse the disturbance.'

'Not at all.'

Zen started to leave, then turned back.

'Would the name of the relative whose funeral you're attending be Bruno Scorrone, by any chance?' he enquired.

'That's him. My cousin twice removed, *da parte di madre*. I never liked the man in the first place and haven't seen him for over a decade, but one's expected to turn out for these things.'

'I'd like you to see him now.'

Lucchese peered at him.

'He's dead, *dottore*. Or so I've been reliably informed.'

'That's precisely why I'd like you to see him. What time is the funeral?'

'Eleven.'

'Here in town?'

'In Palazzuole, the village where he lived. But why should you be interested? God knows I'm not, and I'm family.'

Zen lowered his voice.

'I was sent here to investigate the death of Aldo Vincenzo. Since my arrival, two other men have died violently. In a quiet, rural community like this, it is statistically improbable that three such incidents should occur without there being a connection between them. There is therefore a possibility, to put it no higher, that your cousin's death may not have been an accident. My only chance of proving this is to examine the cadaver before it is buried or cremated. To do so officially, I would need the family's permission, which almost certainly would not be granted. A judicial order would take too long, so I have to improvise. Do you have any insuperable objection to performing a post-mortem examination on a relative?'

Lucchese's lips spread in a wicked smile.

'Nothing would give me greater pleasure! In fact, I can think of three or four kinsmen whom I would be glad to eviscerate without the formalities of a death certificate.'

He frowned.

'But in this case it's impossible. The corpse is laid out at Scorrone's house, closely watched over by the allegedly grieving widow and an indeterminate number of offspring summoned from their niches in Molino.'

'Where?'

'I beg your pardon. My term for the megalopolis which bestraddles us to the north. Torino plus Milano equals Molino.'

Zen nodded sadly.

'I understand. Oh, well, it was worth a try.'

'However, thanks to an ancient family tradition which I have just remembered, there should be no problem.'

Lucchese moved a tall ladder attached to a rail along the shelving, climbed up and produced a large spike made of some dull-coloured metal.

'Careful!' he cried, dropping it down to Zen, who made the catch. 'Apart from anything else, it's solid silver.'

Leaning further out from the ladder, Lucchese retrieved from a still higher shelf a large rubber mallet.

'You're not squeamish, I hope?' he said as he climbed back down the ladder.

'Why?'

Lucchese smiled enigmatically.

'Breaking hearts is a gory business. I'll just get my bag of tricks, and we'll be off.'

Aurelio Zen's second journey to Palazzuole was a marked improvement over his first. They travelled in a pre-war Bugatti exhumed from a former stable in the courtyard of the Palazzo Lucchese and driven by Irena, now clad in a minimalistic black skirt and jacket. Zen reclined on the spacious rear seat with the prince, who proceeded to pursue a discussion which he and Irena had apparently been having earlier, involving quilling techniques in early eighteenth-century harpsichords, with particular reference to the relative merits of raven and crow feathers.

As they crossed the smoky ridge of hills surrounding Alba, Lucchese leant forward and pushed a button on the fascia of the rear compartment. An inlaid rosewood panel opened to reveal a drinks cabinet containing several thick glass decanters. Most appeared to be empty, or reduced to an unappetizing syrupy residue. Lucchese sniffed the two that looked most promising.

'Cognac, query. And something that might once have been whisky.'

Irena passed back what looked like a fat twist of paper.

'Try some of this.'

'Is this wise?' asked Lucchese. 'You may not be aware, my dear, that Dottor Zen is an officer of the law.'

The massive car slowed majestically to a halt.

'You want to walk?' asked Irena pointedly.

Zen glanced confusedly at Lucchese.

'Because the prince and I are planning to smoke some hash,' Irena continued, 'so if you don't want to be a party to a crime you'd better get out now.'

Zen gave her his most intimidating glare, with no discernible effect whatsoever.

'Kindly drive on,' he replied.

Lucchese lit the roll-up, took a few pungent puffs and then offered it politely to his fellow-passenger, who shook his head.

'So who killed Aldo Vincenzo?' asked the prince, passing the joint back to Irena.

Zen looked at him in astonishment.

'*I* don't know!'

'Really? Everyone else seems to.'

'They do?'

The hash-laden cigarette passed back again.

'So who was it?' Zen demanded.

The prince was otherwise engaged for some time.

'Ah, but we're not telling!' he said when he finally exhaled. 'Around here, we like to hoard our little secrets. Keep them dark like truffles. They're the only thing we have, you see.'

'*Cherchez la femme,*' commented Irena.

The car was now filled with fragrant dark smoke. Zen tried to open the window, but the handle spun round without effect.

'So everyone knows, eh?'

The prince laughed merrily.

'Of course! If they didn't, it wouldn't be knowledge.'

'How do you mean?'

'Do you agree that things are either knowable or unknowable?'

'I suppose so.'

'In that case, the identity of the killer is either unknowable, in which case your question makes no sense, or it is knowable and therefore by definition known. I really don't see your problem, *dottore*. To me it's all as clear as day.'

He broke into another helpless fit of giggles and passed the joint back to Irena, who swerved to avoid a truck which had suddenly materialized in front of them.

'Take the conversation which my protégée and I were having before you raised this interesting philosophical issue. Thanks to his treatise *L'art de toucher le clavecin*, we know a considerable amount about Couperin's preferences in quilling and other matters, but we have no idea at all what Scarlatti expected of his instruments – or even if he gave a damn one way or the other. The man was clearly a total degenerate, probably an obsessive gambler, quite possibly a drug addict.'

More gales of giggles.

'But nevertheless he was harpsichord tutor to the Infanta of Spain, and the molecular structure of the stone used to build several rooms in the Escorial must be impregnated with the sounds produced from whatever instruments he used. It's like this eclipse this morning. *We* know how, why and when it will happen, but people used to think it was caused by a dragon eating the sun.'

'The what?'

'*The sun!*' Lucchese replied loudly, as though to a deaf person.

'What son?'

Outside the window, the landscape had started to ripple and break into waves, curling lazily over like the slow, spent wash of Adriatic storms fetching up on a mudbank in Zen's native lagoons. But the sky looked threatening, the light had waned and the wind might get up at any minute.

'Speaking of *L'art de toucher*,' said Irena, hurling the Bugatti round a tight bend, 'how long will it take to plant this relative of yours? Or maybe we could have a quickie at the cemetery? I've always wanted to do it on a grave.'

'*What son?*' Zen shouted at Lucchese. 'I never told you I had a son! And I don't. He's dead. She killed him, and I wasn't even there!'

Eons passed in the blink of a celestial eye.

'Right at the next turning, Irena,' said a voice.

Everything came to a stop. There was a house and lots of cars. People, too, all wearing black.

'I suggest you let me do the talking, *dottore*,' said Lucchese, getting out of the car. Zen followed, hastily wiping the tears from his face. Irena kissed him on the cheek.

'It'll be all right,' she said in a kindly voice. 'It's not your fault.'

Zen watched her fade in and out of focus for a while.

'What was it you said? "*Cherchez la femme*." Do you mean a woman did it?'

But Irena had turned away to join her partner, who was surrounded by a dense knot of family members bent on lengthy and loud commiseration. The prince's voice came floating back towards Zen like the commentary to an unwatched television programme.

'. . . but before we go any further, I regret to say that I have an unpleasant but equally unavoidable duty to perform. Ah, there you are, my dear. This is my niece, Irena Francavilla, whom I have taken under my wing after she fell into some bad company in Turin. I'm glad to say that she's now almost completely recovered, although as a safety measure I am continuing the treatment thrice daily on a regular basis for the moment lest any relapse occur.'

'When's my next shot due, *principe*?' moaned Irena.

'Soon, my child, soon. Where were we? Yes, of course, the unpleasant duty I referred to earlier. As you may be aware, it has been customary since time immemorial for members of my family to undergo cardiac puncture post-mortem. I have no reason to suppose that my dear cousin would have wished to break this tradition, although, given the tragic circumstances leading to his unexpected demise, it was naturally impossible for him to confirm this.'

'What are you talking about?' one of the women in mourning asked. 'What tradition?'

'In principle it dates back at least three hundred years, but in practice it was reinstituted by my great-great-grandfather, Guido Andrea.'

Andrea, thought Zen. *Cherchez la femme!* Suddenly it all made sense.

'Guido's morbid horror of being entombed alive was notorious in our family. Indeed, the memory of it survives to this day. I recall mentioning it on one occasion to my brother, and his replying that all we need do was to bury his portable phone with him! But, joking aside, I feel sure that poor dear Bruno would have wished to receive the usual formalities, and I have therefore come prepared. It won't take long.'

'What won't?'

'A simple medical procedure, my dear,' the prince replied, 'but you might prefer to be spared the details.'

'*Medical?* But Bruno's not . . . I mean, he's . . .'

'Dead. Yes, I'm sure he is, to all appearances. But these things are not always as certain as they might seem. There have been several cases of "corpses" showing signs of life during their own funeral service, which, needless to say, is extremely embarrassing for all concerned. Still more distressing is the case of those for whom reanimation has occurred a little later – too late, in fact. Scarcely a graveyard is excavated without at least one skeleton being discovered in a kneeling position, straining in vain to lift the lid of the coffin lying under several tons of solid earth.'

The women gasped and clutched their throats. Prince Lucchese nodded gravely.

'It was to avoid the possibility of just such a fate that my great-great-grandfather instructed the family physician to drive a spike into his heart prior to the funeral. I believe they originally used a simple nail, but some time later an instrument was specifically fashioned for this purpose out of solid silver by a local craftsman. It is presently in my possession, and I now propose to put it to use, thus allowing my beloved cousin to rest in assured peace. My colleague, Dottor Aurelio Zen, will assist me.'

He waved to Zen, who followed him inside the house.

Afterwards, of course, it was clear to Aurelio Zen that he had been a victim of passive smoking. Although he had declined Lucchese's offer of the hashish-spiked cigarette, the fumes circulating in the closed car had been quite strong enough for him to become drugged by proxy. All this was clear in retrospect, but at the time he had only the evidence of his senses to go on, and they told him a completely different story.

There were, for a start, three versions of Prince Lucchese. One was preparing to do something, the next was doing it, while the third told Zen the results of whatever had been done by the other two. This activity was disturbingly ambiguous, at once a hideous scenario involving a dead body, surgical knives and some very primitive butchery, and an entirely innocent, even praiseworthy activity of vital importance for reasons which, however, were not immediately apparent.

Under the circumstances, Zen decided to take a back seat – literally, in this case. There was a wicker chair near the door where he sat down, watching the trinity of princes at work and responding as best he could to their baffling comments. The centre of the room was occupied by a dining table on which stood an ornate, oblong wooden chest. The threefold Lucchese opened the black bag he had brought with him and set to work on whatever was inside, talking in a low, purposeful voice the whole time.

'No visible injuries apart from some superficial lesions to the thorax . . . Probably gouged himself on some metal edge on the way in . . . Massive loss of blood pre-mortem, though, and visible traumas don't account for same . . . Now let's have a look inside . . . God, look at this subcutaneous fat . . . Just hack through the costal cartilage and whip out the . . . Forgotten how easy all this is . . . That's odd . . . No trace of wine in the lungs, but he must have sucked some in unless . . . Heart attack before he hit the surface, perhaps . . . Let's take another look at that neck . . . Ah . . . Well, now, that's interesting . . .'

The doctor and his two assistants left the room, returning in due course as one person. Confronted by this miracle, Zen emerged from his wake with a sense of panic.

'What? Who? When?' he spluttered, leaping to his feet.

'Probable homicide, person or persons unknown, at or about the stated time of death,' Lucchese replied succinctly, wiping his bloodstained instruments on a filthy rag.

'Are you sure?'

'I'm sure that he was dead when he went into the wine vat. And I'm almost sure that it was not a natural death. That lesion in his neck is a lot deeper than it looks. The artery is severed, and there are small fragments of broken glass embedded in the surrounding flesh.'

'And you'll testify to that?'

Lucchese looked at him haughtily.

'Of course not. I haven't been invited to examine the cadaver, and therefore no such examination has taken place. I'm merely performing the last secular rites for my cousin, according to a long-standing tradition in our family. Speaking of which, I suppose I'd better do the damned thing, just in case anyone checks.'

He took the silver spike and set it down on the dead man's chest, then lifted the mallet. There were a number of dull-sounding blows, the last accompanied by a guttural grunt from Lucchese. Feeling nauseous, Zen went back outside. The cloud had burned off and the sun shone softly in a flawless azure sky.

'The priest is here!' a woman said excitedly. 'Can we proceed?'

'Out of the question,' a voice proceeding from Zen's throat pronounced. 'It is my sad duty to inform you that your late relative's body is evidence in a criminal case.'

Cries of astonishment burst out all around. The door of the house banged shut and Lucchese emerged, clutching his black bag.

'This man,' Zen continued, pointing to him, 'has been apprehended mutilating a corpse in direct contravention of section 1092 paragraph 3A of the Criminal Code. He is now under arrest, and the said corpse is material evidence in the case. This house and its contents are therefore sealed and under my direct and personal jurisdiction. No one can enter and nothing can be removed until further notice.'

'But the funeral!' an elderly woman exclaimed. 'It's all arranged!'

'I regret that it will have to be rearranged. The law is the law, and I'm here to uphold it.'

'Me, too,' said a voice behind him.

Turning, Zen found himself face to face with a plump, stolid man in a dark grey suit.

'Enrico Pascal, *maresciallo dei Carabinieri*,' he said. 'Forgive me, *dottore*, but I'm not familiar with the article of the code you just cited.'

'Of course not. I just made it up.'

The Carabinieri officer stared at him.

'Are you out of your mind?'

'Yes.'

It was only now that he was sure of this. He must definitely have gone out of his mind, because night seemed to be falling. It was not yet dark, but the light had been gutted and thinned down to a tenuous essence with no more substance than moonshine. Luckily no one was paying any attention to him. They were all looking up at the sky, many of them holding up wafers of plastic like a priest displaying the host. Occasional cries and exclamations broke the silence. Narrowing his eyes to a squint, Zen tried to look at the sun. Its hazy outline eluded him, but it seemed damaged.

'Look through this,' said a voice he recognized as Irena's.

A piece of blank photographic negative was pressed into his hand. He raised it to his eyes and beheld in sudden terror the pallid disc of the sun occluded on one side, as though by a huge wing.

'You were blinded by the light,' said the voice.

At once fascinated and appalled by the spectacle unfolding in the skies, Zen did not turn for some time. When he did, Irena was nowhere to be seen. The landscape still had a ghostly pallor, but the eclipse had passed its peak and the light was gradually recovering its former vitality. The Carabinieri official materialized at Zen's side.

'That's a nasty-looking cut you've got there, *dottore*,' he said. 'Quite fresh, too, by the look of it.'

He pointed down the hill, where the Bugatti could just be seen turning on to the road back to Alba.

'It seems that your suspect in this alleged crime has escaped.'

Zen looked Pascal in the eye.

'You must think I'm mad.'

The *maresciallo* made a puffing noise and performed a full-body shrug, indicating that he wouldn't hold a little thing like madness against a colleague.

'But there's actually a good reason for this farce,' Zen went on. 'I have preliminary evidence leading me to believe that Bruno Scorrone was murdered. A full autopsy will prove that, and this gives us a pretext for ordering one. Can you call one of your men out here to guard the corpse until the ambulance arrives? Meanwhile I'd like to have a chat with you in private.'

Pascal returned his stare for a moment.

'Well, this will set people's tongues wagging!' he said. 'All right, I'll play along. But you'd better be right about this, *dottore*. If it turns out that this really is a farce, I won't be able to show my face in public again.'

While the *maresciallo* strode off to find a phone, Zen did some preliminary damage assessment. By now the light had almost completely recovered, and with it his grasp of the situation. He anxiously reviewed what he could remember doing and saying during his own partial eclipse. Most of it seemed acceptable, given the circumstances, although no doubt disconcertingly erratic to those who had not abused the substance in question. But there was one aspect that he felt less confident about, something he had now forgotten but which he could sense lurking at the fringes of his consciousness like a stage villain concealed behind a curtain.

'*Buon giorno, dottore.*'

Andrea Rodriguez was wearing a black suit whose cut and fabric suggested board meetings and power lunches rather than funerals.

'Manlio insisted that I come and greet you,' she continued in her laboured but correct Italian. 'This is his coming-out party, you see, and he's nervous about his reception. "They'll never forgive me if I don't go," he said, "and if I do, they'll cut me dead."'

She nodded towards a knot of men standing in the centre of the courtyard.

'He was wrong, I'm glad to say. But he thought that being seen fraternizing with you might be pushing his luck, so he sent me instead. Most of these people have rearranged their schedules specially in order to be here, you see, and then you burst in and cancel the whole event on some specious pretext. You're not very popular with the locals just now, I'm afraid.'

Zen conceded the point with a nod.

'Neither am I,' Andrea Rodriguez added. 'It's not easy being a foreigner here, particularly when everyone expected you to be a man.'

The ironies of the situation had been borne in on Zen the day before, after their introduction at the Vincenzo house. In Italian, Andrea is a man's name; in English, he had learned, a woman's. When Aldo Vincenzo had read a letter addressed to his son and signed 'Andrea', he had drawn the seemingly obvious conclusion: the real reason why Manlio refused to entertain his suggestion of forcing a marriage with Lisa Faigano was that he had 'come out' during his stay in California.

Although undeniably Californian, Andrea was not only female but of Italian descent on her mother's side, her father stemming from one of the pre-settlement Spanish families. Manlio had been so insulted by his father's intransigent attitude that he had refused to explain.

'Why should I deign to correct someone who assumed he already understood everything?' he had demanded rhetorically. 'In the end, I assumed, the truth would come out and I would be vindicated. Instead, my father died as he had lived – in ignorance.'

All this should have made Zen and Andrea natural partners, as outsiders and rejects from the community. But he saw things differently. Perhaps it was the last sigh of the hashish, undulating up from the bottom of his cranium like long weed from the seabed, or perhaps just a natural bloody-mindedness, but instead of accepting the olive branch being extended to him, Zen turned on the American with a bureaucratic glint in his eye.

'I think you told me that your mother's family was Sicilian, *signorina*,' he said, emphasizing the final, status-diminishing epithet.

'That's right.'

'From where, originally?'

'A village called Corleone, up in the mountains behind Palermo. My grandfather emigrated in 1905, and . . .'

Zen's expression intensified.

'Corleone, eh? A notorious hotbed of the Mafia. No doubt you still have connections there. A word in the right ear, some cash up-front, plus a promise of more to come when the Vincenzo property is sold . . . After the village *festa*, Manlio lures his drunken father out to the vineyard where your hired assassins are waiting. They do the deed, then mutilate the corpse to look as if the whole thing was the result of some vicious local vendetta.'

'Are you out of your mind?'

Zen looked at her seriously.

'You're the second person to ask me that.'

'Well, maybe you should think about it!' snapped Andrea Rodriguez. 'You've already alienated everyone else here, and now you've made another enemy.'

'I've executed your orders, *dottore*!'

Enrico Pascal was still twenty metres away, but his voice carried clearly to Zen – and to everyone else assembled in the courtyard. The underlying message was made equally clear as Andrea Rodriguez turned her back pointedly on Zen and strode off to join the others.

'The ambulance will here shortly, and meanwhile my orderly has secured the premises,' the Carabinieri official continued in the same parade-ground tones. 'Do you have any further orders?'

'Not at present!' bellowed Zen in return. In an undertone he added, 'Where's the winery?'

'Over there, down the hill,' whispered Pascal, nodding to one side. 'Just follow the track.'

'Meet me there in fifteen minutes.'

Zen turned away. Pascal saluted ostentatiously and marched back towards the house as though he had been dismissed.

Realizing that the funeral ceremony was indeed not going to take place, the assembled mourners were by now heading towards their cars and driving away. Zen walked past them and started at a leisurely pace down the concrete-paved track which connected the Scorrone residence with its commercial appendage, discreetly tucked away out of sight over a ridge of the hillside.

Enrico Pascal appeared exactly fifteen minutes later, driving down the same track along which Zen had walked.

'Make it brief,' he warned, stepping out of the jeep. 'Feelings are running high, I can tell you. You're presently the most unpopular person in the Langhe, and if I'm seen consorting with you . . .'

Zen laughed.

'The most unpopular? I'm glad to hear it. After all the flannel I've been getting from everyone here, it's a relief to be hated and feared again. I need that edge to work properly.'

Enrico Pascal did not dignify this with a reply. Zen sighed.

'All right, I'll make it brief. My first question is what Bruno Scorrone was doing down here yesterday afternoon in the first place. I've taken a look around this installation. I don't know much about vinification, but I can tell high technology when I see it. Once the controls are set, this equipment can run itself. In any case, Scorrone was not exactly in the fine wine business. Why should he cut short his Sunday lunch to come and check on the progress of some bulk wine which he was going to blend and sell for next to nothing anyway?'

'According to his wife, he said that he had to take delivery of a shipment.'

'On a Sunday?'

'We haven't been able to confirm it, but that's not unusual. Bruno preferred to keep his paperwork to a minimum.'

'You mean he was operating illegally?'

The *maresciallo* gestured in an anguished way, to indicate the impossibility of conveying the complexities of the situation to an outsider.

'Let's say that he operated in a grey area, not necessarily crooked but not strictly legal either. Lots of people around here do. On the one hand there are the legitimate demands of the market, on the other the often unreasonable stipulations of the myriad bureaucracies anywhere between here and Brussels. A man has to make a living. Bruno didn't adulterate his wine, at least not usually, but he was sometimes – how shall I put it? – imaginative as to its origins.'

Zen looked around the concrete expanses of the winery. The staff had been given the day off, and in its stagnant desolation the place might have been any one of the ugly, light-industrial complexes of indeterminate purpose which littered the highways of the region. The only sign of its true function came in the form of a number of plastic-covered demijohns stacked on one of the loading platforms. Zen pointed them out to Pascal.

'Do you think that could be the wine that was delivered the afternoon he died?'

The *maresciallo* shrugged.

'Who knows? Bruno did a lot of business on a small scale. You saw the occasional tanker from Puglia or Calabria pulling up here, but it was mainly local products he used. All good stuff, but, as I said, imaginatively labelled.'

Zen led the way over to the cluster of flagons. There was no marking or other indication of origin on them.

'These could have come from anywhere,' he said.

'Oh, I don't know about *anywhere*.'

Pascal walked back to the office at the end of the loading bays, returning a few moments later with a pipette and a glass. Handing both to Zen, he pulled out the rubber bung securing the mouth of one of the *damigiane*, then reclaimed the pipette and lowered it through the layer of olive oil floated on the surface of the wine to keep the air out. He pumped the bulb a few times, and repeated the procedure to expel the wine into the glass. Swirling the wine around, he sniffed deeply.

'Ah!'

He took a large sip, swishing it around his mouth like a gargle, and finally swallowing.

'Yes,' he said.

The procedure was repeated.

'Definitely,' Enrico Pascal pronounced.

Zen stared at him bemusedly.

'Definitely what?'

Pascal emptied the remaining wine on to the ground and replugged the container.

'I'd bet quite a large sum that this particular wine was made by the Faigano brothers.'

'You can tell that just by tasting it?'

A shrug.

'I drink a lot of Gianni and Maurizio's wines and I'd be prepared to swear that this is one of theirs.'

Catching Zen's glance, he added, 'Off the record, of course. Anyway, there's no proof that this is the delivery Bruno came to collect.'

Zen sighed histrionically.

'That seems to be the keynote of this whole case. Lots of hints and indications, but no proof. What am I supposed to do?'

'Ah, well, *dottore*, that's for you to decide.'

Zen got back to his hotel late that afternoon, having hired a local driver to take him to Alba. Above the wavering outline of the darkening hills, the sky was a molten glory, ranging from a creamy peach to a delicate glowing pink like sunlight filtered through a baby's ear. The taxi dropped Zen in Piazza Savona, and he spent some time just wandering around aimlessly, as delighted as a child with the sense of purposeful but mysterious activity all around his brief excursion into the rural hinterland. Nature was neither benign nor malign, his genes told him. However cropped, parcelled and inhabited, it remained other. This was its fascination but also its horror. A few hours was enough.

He crossed to the tree-lined promenade at the centre of the square and spent some time looking over the remaindered volumes offered for sale by the *bancari*. The east end of the central reservation was disfigured by an abstract fountain in early sixties' Civic Modern style, beside which stood a pillar inscribed with the elliptical opening words from the book by Beppe Fenoglio about the heroic and tragic 'Twenty-three days of Alba', when the local partisans precipitately seized control of the city from the retreating Fascists: *Two thousand of them took Alba on 10 October, and two hundred lost it on 2 November 1944.*

As Zen walked slowly round to the entrance of the hotel, his mind was on those eighteen hundred young men whose deaths Fenoglio had celebrated by implication, and the two hundred who had survived. If they were still alive, they would now be in their seventies. How did they view it all, looking back? Had it been worth the suffering, the bloodshed, the deaths? Were they bitter at having fought and risked everything in a desperate conflict for ideals that were almost immediately betrayed or compromised? Or was it simply the most exciting thing which had ever happened to them, an experience never to be forgotten, immune from judgement or regret, like the first time a woman gives herself to you?

His room seemed a refuge, quiet and secure, against these and other doubts. Zen took off his jacket and shoes and collapsed on the bed, closing his eyes for what he thought of as a 'little rest' amply earned by his exertions. When he awoke, it was to the trilling of the telephone. Disoriented and resentful, he snatched up the receiver.

'Yes?'

'Good afternoon, dottore. I trust I'm not disturbing you.'

Zen groaned.

'Who are you?' he yelled into the phone. 'Why can't you leave me alone? What in God's name do you want anyway?'

'To invite you to dinner this evening, if you're free. Seven o'clock, at the Maddalena on Via Gioberti.'

The line went dead. Zen glanced at the clock. It was just after half-past six. At least eight hours had elapsed since he had inhaled hashish courtesy of the prince and his companion, but the room seemed to be moving slightly around him like a carousel which had been turned off but was still revolving just fast enough to make stepping off a hazardous affair. Nevertheless, this was what he was going to have to do. The appointment he had just been offered, whatever its purpose, could not be avoided. If he didn't turn up, it would simply be reassigned to a later date.

His mind went back to the Burolo affair in Sardinia, of which he had spoken to Lucchese, when he had been hounded down and confronted by a gangster he had once sent to prison, who now sought his revenge. This must be something similar, he thought wearily. A policeman inevitably made many enemies. Reaching for the phone again, he called the local *Commissariato*.

'Police!' snapped a voice he recognized.

'Ciao, Dario.'

A brief indignant pause.

'This is the Alba police station! What do you want?'

'Too bad about that penalty,' Zen continued smoothly. 'But Juve are still looking good for the championship.'

'Who the . . .'

'Aurelio Zen, Vice-Questore, Criminalpol, Rome. I have just received a phone call summoning me to a restaurant in Via Gioberti, the Maddalena. I'm to be there at seven, and I have reason to think that the person I am meeting may be armed and dangerous. Quite apart from my own safety, I have no wish to endanger the lives of the other patrons of the establishment in question.'

Dario took a moment to digest this information.

'In view of this,' Zen went on, 'I suggest that a uniformed officer meet me here at the hotel in fifteen minutes and accompany me to the restaurant.'

'I'll see to it in person, *dottore!*'

'I appreciate it.'

'To be honest, there's no one else on duty.'

Ten minutes later, bundled up in an overcoat and with his hat in hand, Aurelio Zen patrolled the grotesquely ample spaces of the lobby, taking care to stay well away from the windows and door where he would be visible from the street.

'Good evening!' said a female voice.

Startled out of his increasingly paranoid meditations, he turned to find himself facing the young woman who had introduced herself to him as Carla Arduini. She, too, was dressed to go out.

'*Buona sera, signorina.*'

For a moment she seemed inclined to linger, and perhaps to say something else, but to Zen's relief she walked on and vanished through the revolving door. The last thing he needed at this point was any further complications, such as her taking him up on the dinner invitation he had thoughtlessly extended the previous evening for reasons he could no longer remember. These speculations were abruptly cancelled by the appearance of a uniformed figure carrying a machine-gun with the air of someone not only prepared but eager to use it.

'*Dottore!*' he said hoarsely, catching sight of Zen.

'Good evening, Dario.'

The young policeman scanned the lobby rapidly, as though armed enemies might be concealed anywhere. Failing to locate them, he consulted his watch.

'Shall we go?'

'Not just yet.'

'But it's time.'

'Never turn up when you're expected,' Zen pronounced solemnly. 'Keep them waiting. Their nerve will start to fray and they'll be more likely to make a mistake.'

Dario nodded as though all this made sense.

'Let's have a drink here and arrive about ten minutes late,' Zen told him.

At the bar, Dario ordered a Coke, Zen a *spumante*.

'Are you from these parts?' he asked the patrolman, pushing the muzzle of the submachine-gun aside.

'Yes, sir.'

'Whereabouts?'

'Barolo.'

'Do you know anything about a woman named Chiara Vincenzo? Widow of the late lamented Aldo.'

'She was my great-aunt.'

Zen stared at him.

'Is everyone here related to each other?'

'Well, not *everyone*. Not incomers.'

Zen gave him a still harder look.

'Present company excepted, of course!' Dario responded hastily.

'I understand your great-aunt Chiara died recently,' said Zen, pressing his advantage.

'That came as no surprise. She had been suffering from cancer for some time.'

'How old was she?'

'Sixty-one.'

He made an apologetic gesture.

'Women normally last to seventy at least, sometimes ninety.

But Aunt Chiara seemed to have lost the will to live a long time ago. There was a story about some tragedy in her youth which she never got over, I can't remember the details.'

'So she died just before her husband?' asked Zen.

'I suppose so, yes. A matter of weeks.'

'*Cherchez la femme*,' Zen intoned with a superior air.

'Pardon?'

'Nothing.'

He glanced at his watch.

'Let's go.'

Outside, the streets were dark and almost deserted. A fine drizzle was falling, backed up by a powerful but lazy wind lolling around like a drunken braggart at the street corners. The few pedestrians about glanced nervously at the tall man and his armed escort, and hastened past.

As they turned into Via Gioberti, Zen began to have serious doubts about the wisdom of his plan. If there were an assassin, resentment with a rifle, this is where he would be waiting, in a doorway or at a window opposite the restaurant. He would take down young Dario first, then the unprotected Zen. But it was too late to back out now.

There were no shots. When they reached the Maddalena, Dario burst inside ahead of Zen, brandishing his machine-gun. The restaurant was packed, but when Zen made his entrance, there was not a sound to be heard. Everyone in the place had come to a halt in the midst of whatever they were doing, the waiters poised in mid-delivery or removal of dishes, the diners stilled, forks half-way to their mouths.

'Aurelio Zen,' he heard himself say. 'I'm meeting someone for dinner. Has he arrived?'

A deferential elderly man in a suit and tie emerged from behind a desk.

'*Sì, certo*,' he said imperturbably, as though the appearance of armed men in uniform were a daily occurrence. 'This way, please.'

Accompanied by the ever-watchful Dario, Zen and the head waiter traversed the crowded room and another beyond it, to come to rest at a table at the very rear of the premises. It was occupied by Carla Arduini. She and Zen stared at each other in silence for a long time. Then the head waiter coughed self-consciously.

'You may go,' Zen told him. 'You too, Dario.'

The patrolman pulled him aside.

'This could be a set-up, chief! They put this young woman out front to get you relaxed and off your guard while the killer awaits his chance . . .'

'I don't think so.'

Dario looked distinctly disappointed that the promised excitements and risks of the evening had come to nothing, leaving him to return to his routine duties at the police station.

'Don't you think I should take a seat at one of those tables over there and just keep an eye on things, just in case?' he asked hopefully.

Zen scanned the room.

'Those tables seem to be reserved.'

Dario smiled and patted his machine-gun.

'Believe me, I'm not going to have any problem getting seated.'

Zen sighed and nodded.

'All right. I'll have some food sent over. But don't wave that thing around too much. You'll scare the customers.'

Dario grinned impishly.

'We'll get great service, though!'

Indeed, waiters appeared with extraordinary promptness, bearing menus and wine lists of such complexity that Zen finally shrugged and said, 'Just bring me something good to eat. A warm starter and a main course. I don't care what it is, as long as it has truffles grated thickly all over it.'

He glanced at Carla Arduini, who nodded.

'The same for me.'

'And take some over to that lad over in the corner with the gun,' Zen added. 'He gets nervous if he isn't fed properly.'

When the flurry of attendance had died away, he looked up at his companion.

'So it was you?'

She nodded. Zen lit a cigarette and studied her.

'And who is your collaborator? The man on the phone.'

'I have no collaborator.'

'But that voice . . .'

'It's an electronic device which alters your voice to any register you desire,' Carla Arduini explained. 'I bought one and hooked it up to my telephone at the hotel. It can make you sound like a man, a woman, a child, even an opera singer. For my purposes, a slightly metallic man's voice seemed best.'

Zen puffed away, studying her face closely all the while.

'And what were those purposes?'

She smiled wanly.

'I planned to make a series of threatening phone calls, each with a vague clue to the mystery, and leave you to twist slowly in the wind, tormented by nameless fears. I'm not sure what I planned to do after that. I certainly didn't intend you any physical harm, despite my threats. I just wanted to scare you.'

She gestured to the table where Dario was sitting.

'It certainly looks as if I succeeded.'

A bottle of wine arrived. Zen poured them both a glass and drank his off at a gulp.

'So why me? Or is it the police in general you have it in for? Did you just pick any officer at random?'

'No, it was personal.'

Their first course arrived with the same promptitude as the menus, a mound of homemade pasta buried under a fall of truffle flakes so thick as to almost overflow the bowl.

'Personal? We met for the first time two days ago, *signorina*.'

'Yes, but I already knew who you were, you see. And as soon as I saw a news report saying that you had been sent up here to investigate the Vincenzo murder, I decided that I had to act.'

She paused.

'No, "decided" is the wrong word. Something decided for me. Even at the time, I remember asking myself what I hoped to gain. But it was irresistible. So I booked a room next to yours in the hotel, and here I am.'

Zen wound a portion of truffle-scented noodles around his fork and began to eat. At least the food made sense.

'Amalia mentioned your name only once,' Carla Arduini went on, her own meal still untouched. 'We'd had a terrible row about nothing, one of those things that happens when you have an adolescent girl and her mother living too closely together. I understand now that I just resented her control. I wanted to create my own nest, my own way. It's a very basic instinct.'

She pushed her dish of pasta away.

'I can't eat this.'

'You don't like it?'

'I just can't eat it. I can't eat anything.'

Zen clicked his fingers. A waiter instantly materialized.

'The *signorina* is feeling unwell. Please cancel her main course and offer this to my colleague over there.'

He pointed to Dario, who had already cleaned his plate. The waiter looked around uncertainly.

'The one with the . . .'

'Exactly.'

The waiter vanished.

'So you and your mother had a row,' Zen continued, pouring himself more wine. 'I still don't see where I come into it.'

Carla Arduini pushed a breadcrumb around the white table-cloth.

'She made me swear not to tell anyone, never to mention it, least of all to you. I think that she had decided never to tell me, but the truth came out the night we had that stupid argument. I said something cheap and cruel, taunting her with not having a man, with not being able to hold the father of her child. I even accused her of feeling jealous of me. Several boys were taking an interest in me at that point, and she seemed to disapprove. I realize now that she was just being cautious. She didn't want the same thing that happened to her to happen to me.'

Waiters arrived with more food. Zen waved them away.

'And that's when she told you?'

A nod.

'That's when she told me about Via Strozzi, number twenty-four, in Milan, where she used to live. That's when she finally revealed the pain and the shame she had been hiding all those years with no one to comfort her, no one to support her, no one to hold her at night . . .'

Zen coughed awkwardly and lit a cigarette.

'And that's when she told me . . .' Carla Arduini began, and then broke off, cradling her head in her arms.

'Well?' demanded Zen with an air of exasperation. 'What did she tell you?'

The young woman's face rose from her arms like the eclipsed sun Zen had beheld that morning: vast, obscure and terrible.

'She told me the name of my father.'

And so, without warning, it all starts again. He had always known this, he realized now, ever since that morning out on the sandbanks of the *Palude Maggiore* in the northern lagoon. The trip, the longest he and his friend Tommaso had ever attempted, took a whole day's hard rowing there and back, so they'd filched some blankets and an old army tent and camped out for the night on an island whose name, if it had one, he'd never been able to discover.

At dawn the next morning, as the dull, exhausted light strained to heave the insensible darkness off the lagoon like an elderly whore trying to get out from under a drunken client, he had wandered down to the shoreline. Tommaso was still asleep, emitting the thin, raucous snores which had kept Zen awake for much of the night. Where the glaucous water met the liquid mud, marsh birds puttered about like mechanical toys, their beady eyes on the look-out for food. An aeroplane passed high overhead, its remote presence merely emphasizing his solitude. The only other sound was an irregular succession of splashes somewhere nearby, like fish leaping or a bird diving.

When he first came on it, the stream seemed nothing much. Its gently flowing water, draining down from the marginally higher surface of the island, had cut a passage through the mudbank left by the receding tide, carving out a sequence of miniature bends, ravines and ox-bow lakes which had made him feel as though he were seeing the whole countryside from the plane which had just passed over. He had never been in a plane, of course.

He settled down to watch his private River Adige, gradually peopling the banks and highlands, surveying towns and villages and connecting them by road and rail, when a vast region of this imaginary terrain – a whole mountainside, with half the plateau beyond – cracked off and, with a terrible, slow inevitability, tumbled into the stream with one of the loud splashes he had heard earlier. The fractured surface thus exposed, as rugged and dense as a split Parmesan cheese, was riddled with scores of tiny red worms twitching frantically this way and that.

In the end he had stayed there so long that Tommaso started calling for him, warning him that they should start for home and the inevitable interrogations and punishments which awaited them. It hadn't taken Zen long to work out that the landslides were the result of erosion by the stream, undercutting the cliffs it had created, but he was never able to predict where or when the next collapse would come. Outcroppings which looked shaky, worn and fragile seemed to survive for ever, while a fat chunk of ground you had just walked across with total confidence would suddenly reveal the tell-tale hairline crack, then slowly peel off and plunge into the current, damming it briefly before being scoured away.

For a time he had tried to influence the outcome, protecting one stretch with clumps of rushes and pieces of driftwood, undermining another with a stick. It was only after he had almost fallen into the stream himself, when the bank he was standing on suddenly gave way beneath him, that he understood that this process had its own rules which he could no more understand or alter than the scarlet worms wriggling helplessly in the exposed innards of the mudbank.

Which was how he felt now, hundreds of kilometres away and still more hundreds of years – or so it seemed – distant from that childish experience. *Something had happened*, that was clear, but he had no idea what it was, still less what it meant or might portend for the future. All he could do, as he rose at eight minutes past ten the next morning to address a meeting of the Alba police detachment in the city's central *Commissariato*, was to try to remain faithful to this insight.

'I have called you together to review recent developments in the Vincenzo case,' he said in a speciously confident tone, 'to explain my current thinking and outline the measures to be taken at this point.'

He looked around the narrow table, meeting and assessing everyone's gaze. Present, besides himself, were Vice-Questore Tullio Legna, Ispettore Nanni Morino, and the only woman to have attained the higher echelons in the Alba command, one Caterina Frascana.

'Since my arrival here,' Zen continued, 'we have been groping in the dark, stumbling into unexpected obstacles and talking to ourselves in mirrors. There's been nothing solid to go on, no leads which didn't turn out to be equivocal, nothing but insubstantial theories and disturbing rumours which could never be put to the test. It's as if we've been collectively dreaming, even hallucinating.'

His audience sat in an awkward silence, as though at a concert of modern music, unsure whether it was over and time to applaud.

'But that's all in the past now!' Zen exclaimed. 'We can't go on living with these doubts and uncertainties. The time has come to act, to put these nebulous suspicions to the test and determine the truth once and for all.'

The three police officials looked at him oddly, as well they might, since his speech was not directed at them but at a young woman they had never met. Zen had spent so much time wondering what to say to Carla Arduini at their rendezvous later that morning that he had quite neglected to prepare his discourse to the colleagues whom he had summoned to this meeting.

'Someone once remarked that while fruit flies seem eager to drown in the wine you are drinking, they never show any interest in the discarded dregs,' he went on with an air of slight desperation. 'Perhaps you've noticed the same thing in your own lives. I know I have.'

The two men nodded sagely, but Caterina Frascana screwed up her face in a frown.

'Fruit flies?' she repeated.

Zen gave her a haughty glare.

'I was speaking metaphorically, *signora*.'

'Oh.'

La Frascana was clearly going to be a problem, thought Zen. The two men would sit there through any amount of bullshit, cowed into submission by Zen's hierarchical eminence, but the woman's eyes were lively and her sharp, alert face seemed predisposed to break into a mocking smile at any moment. With her around, he was going to have to try harder.

'As a result of private initiatives I have undertaken, we now have a promising opening which with your support I intend to exploit to the full. I refer, of course, to the death of Bruno Scorrone. The autopsy and forensic examination I have ordered will, I believe, determine that Scorrone did not die accidentally, as everyone had assumed, but was in fact murdered.

'According to Enrico Pascal, Scorrone went down to the winery that afternoon to pick up a delivery of wine. He didn't say where it was from or who was bringing it. But when I inspected the site, I noticed a number of flagons of wine standing on a loading dock. They are unmarked, but Pascal tasted the wine and is of the opinion that it was made by the Faigano brothers.'

Caterina Frascana finally released the laugh she seemed to have been struggling to repress.

'I'd love to see someone trying to make that one stand up in court!'

Her laughter died away in silence.

'I mean, you can't hope to make a case against anyone on that basis, *dottore*,' she added in an exaggeratedly respectful tone.

Zen gazed at her in apparent astonishment.

'I have no interest in making a case against Bruno Scorrone's killer. My task is to solve the murder of Aldo Vincenzo. I assumed that that was understood.'

Tullio Legna recrossed his legs fussily.

'But what's the relevance of this Scorrone business to Aldo's death?' he asked.

Behind a confident smile, Zen was thinking furiously. What *was* the connection? He knew there had seemed to be one the previous evening, as he sat in his room reeling from Carla Arduini's revelations and trying to anchor himself by getting a grip on work.

'I was reading in the paper the other day that the beating of a butterfly's wings in a South American jungle can cause a hurricane thousands of miles away,' he began.

Caterina Frascana stifled another laugh.

'Good thing we don't have butterflies that size here!'

'The fruit flies are bad enough,' murmured Nanni Morino.

Zen did not deign to glance at them.

'The same thing applies to this situation. There's no point in our sitting around here trying to do everything by the rules. That would be like a group of eighteenth-century philosophers struggling to understand a world which is only explicable in terms of chaos theory.'

This time, the three officials exchanged a meaningful glance.

'I'll bear that in mind, *dottore*,' said Tullio Legna, with an elegant little bow. 'But what exactly is your point?'

Alone at the head of the table, Zen gave a disappointed sigh.

'I assumed that that was obvious to the meanest intelligence. Very well, then, I'll spell it out for you. Three men have died. My interest is only in the first, but the other two appear to be linked to that event in various ways. The knife found at Beppe Gallizio's house may well be the one used to kill Aldo Vincenzo. Bruno Scorrone was in turn an important witness in the Gallizio affair.'

'The forensic tests on the knife are not complete,' Tullio Legna objected. 'As for Scorrone, he merely mentioned having seen a truck near the scene. He didn't make a sworn statement, and the person implicated turns out to have an alibi. With all due respect, *dottore*, I don't quite see what measures we can take on this basis.'

Zen slapped the table with a force which startled even him.

'We can stir things up! If we don't understand the connection between these crimes, neither does anyone else. We can exploit that fact to crack this conspiracy wide open.'

'Conspiracy?' queried Nanni Morino with an incredulous grin.

'Exactly! A conspiracy not of silence but of chatter. Down south, if you try to get people to cooperate with the police, they give you sullen looks and clam up. Here they smile and buy you a drink and you can't shut them up, but the net result is the same.

Everyone knows who killed Aldo Vincenzo, just like they knew that Lamberto Latini was sleeping with the tobacconist's wife, and their response is to take refuge in garrulous evasiveness. They'll tell you anything else you want to know, and a lot of stuff you don't, but not that. Well, we're going to dig it out of them just the same, and Scorrone's death is the lever we're going to use. Any questions?'

This time, no one dared speak.

'Very good! Now to the details. I want Gianni and Maurizio Faigano brought in for questioning. They are to be transported and detained separately, under armed guard at all times.'

'On what charge?' asked Tullio Legna.

'Suspicion of illicit trafficking in wine without due permits and papers.'

'But we have no proof.'

'I'll deal with that. As soon as the brothers have been taken away, I propose to institute a search under a warrant I applied for before coming here. I'll either find something or fake it.'

Tullio Legna frowned, then smiled nervously.

'Is this how they operate down in Rome?'

'It's how *I* operate, wherever I may be, when the situation requires irregular measures. I take full responsibility for the means used and the eventual outcome. All I ask of you is prompt and efficient compliance with my orders. Do I have it?'

'Of course, *dottore!*' his cowed subordinates assured him.

'Good. Let's get going. I want an impressive show, the might of the state in action. Bring in some men from Asti if necessary. Put the fear of God into everyone concerned and give the neighbours something to talk about. I'll return here as soon as the warrant is signed, and I'll need a car and driver at my disposal. Any further initiatives will be decided after I have interrogated the Faigano brothers.'

He surveyed the table.

'Any questions?'

There were none. Zen collected his overcoat from the hook near the door and left. In contrast to the shocked hush he had created in the room upstairs, the street was buzzing with activity and noise. Traffic was backed up by a builder's truck attempting an almost impossible manœuvre to reverse into the entrance to a building under renovation, and a variety of horns sounded at intervals like an orchestra warming up. The air was crisp and sunny, but distinctly colder than it had been, the first hint of winter's rigour making itself felt.

Zen walked briskly up the street to the main piazza, feeling well pleased with his improvised performance. He had been true to his insight. Something had happened. The psychic stalemate he had suffered from for so long had been broken. Life had returned and things were on the move again. What more could anyone ask?

The far end of the piazza was closed off by the sober, restrained façade of the cathedral, a plain mass of brickwork broken only by a rose-window and a few saints in niches. Zen searched the curved portal for Carla Arduini, but there was no sign of her. They had agreed to meet here at ten o'clock, and it was now almost a quarter past. Zen felt a sense of his former paralysis return, like a cloud skimming the sun. He could boss the Alba police detachment about as much as he liked, but if Carla decided not to go through with it after all, there was nothing he could do about that.

He was about to turn away when she appeared from a nearby café, waving and calling out. Still some distance away, she stopped, confronting him.

'Are you sure this is a good idea?'

Zen nodded decisively, his sense of energy and purpose flooding back.

'Absolutely! It's the only way.'

He led her around the corner, into the sheltered, decrepit courtyard of the Palazzo Lucchese. As before, Irena answered the bell. This time she was fully dressed, but seemed flustered.

'The prince is playing,' she announced.

The sweet clamour of some plucked instrument tickled the lugubrious silence of the massive hall.

'How charming!' exclaimed Carla Arduini, gliding effortlessly past Irena. 'I just love music. Is he really a prince, this friend of yours?'

She strode off down the hallway towards an open door at the far end. Irena watched with a look of panic.

'Wait! You can't go in now!'

But Carla could and did, followed after a moment by Zen and the distraught Irena. It was a large corner room, spacious and completely bare except for an instrument like a small piano, with a painted lid and a Latin inscription on the body. But the sound which emerged was more like a band of gypsy guitarists than a piano: precise, sexy and urgent, with stabbing chords and rapid passage work in the high range and a dark, sonorous bass which rebounded off the walls and floor like gunshots.

At the keyboard, Lucchese looked imperious and incisive, all his anachronistic airs and graces scorched away by the intensity of the music. There were lots of wrong notes, or what sounded to Zen as such, but they were lost in the sheer impetus of the playing, intent only on completing its preordained trajectory, impervious to flaws and lapses.

At length the cascade of notes ended. To Zen's horror, Carla Arduini started to clap.

'Wonderful, just wonderful! I wish I could do that.'

Lucchese pushed back his stool and stood up, inspecting the intruders with a glare whose pedigree bespoke generations of arrogance and condescension.

'Do what?' he demanded after a terrible silence.

Zen was about to intervene, to try to save the situation, but too late.

'Play Scarlatti like that, of course!' Carla burbled on. 'And what a magnificent instrument! Is it a Ruckers?'

The prince's glacial hauteur was instantly replaced by an expression of almost childish pleasure.

'Absolutely! Originally, that's to say. It was remodelled by either Blanchet or Taskin a century later, of course.'

'Of course,' nodded Carla.

There was a brief pause.

'And to whom do I have the honour . . .?' Lucchese began.

'My name's Carla Arduini, and this is . . .'

The prince shot Zen a sour look.

'I know who he is.'

'. . . my father,' Carla concluded.

'Your father?'

'We think so,' Zen put in. 'Now we want to find out.'

A beam of sunlight projected into the room between them. On the other side, Lucchese's dim figure moved around the harpsichord and emerged into the glare.

'First, let's talk about this absurd charge that's hanging over my head for having mutilated Scorrone's corpse.'

Zen gestured languidly.

'No problem. I've subsequently ascertained that you were merely carrying out a recognized medical procedure at the request of your deceased cousin. All charges have been dropped.'

Lucchese glanced at him.

'Very well. I fancy the bass needs a tune-up, Irena.'

'So do I!' retorted the latter, stalking out of the room.

Lucchese shook his head sadly.

'These highly strung modern instruments are so hard to keep sweet. So you want a blood test, is that it?'

'If that's what it takes,' Carla replied.

'Oh, and I want these stitches removed,' added Zen. 'If one more person tells me that it's a nasty-looking cut I've got there, and quite fresh, too, by the look of it, I won't be responsible for my actions. Then give me your bill and I promise never to disturb you again.'

Lucchese led them towards the door.

'Ah, but I may still have to disturb you, *dottore*. Remember our agreement? Until that matter is resolved, my charges remain pending.'

'What if I just run off without paying?'

Lucchese turned to him.

'You've been doing that all your life,' he said, his delicate fingers exploring the scar on Zen's brow. 'Look where it's got you.'

Minot was under his truck, completing an oil-change, when Anna started barking. He listened intently to the sound of the approaching vehicle, then gave a satisfied nod. He'd been expecting this visit all day.

'*Basta!*' he yelled at the dog, which subsided into repressed whimpers.

Minot crawled out from under the truck as the Carabinieri jeep drew up alongside. The door opened and Enrico Pascal clambered out with ponderous gravity.

'Minot,' he said.

'*Marescià.*'

The two men stood looking at each other, trying to divine the exact nature of the silence, the shape and heft of their unspoken thoughts.

'Good thing you came by,' Minot began. 'I was going to call you anyway.'

'You were?'

'I've had a word with the friends I was out truffling with that night we were talking about.'

Enrico Pascal appeared to reflect.

'Ah, yes. And?'

'And they say it's all right.'

'Do they?'

'Yes, they do.'

Enrico Pascal swept his eyes up and down Minot's faded check shirt and corduroy trousers.

'Nasty stains you've got there.'

Minot pointed to the truck.

'I've been changing the oil.'

'It looks more like wine to me. You didn't have a demijohn break on you, did you?'

Minot hesitated just a moment.

'As a matter of fact, I did.'

Pascal shook his head.

'Temperamental buggers. Sometimes you can set them down with a wallop and nothing happens, other times they crack apart if you just look at them the wrong way.'

He sniffed deeply.

'Over at Bruno's, was it?'

Minot flashed him a look of genuine shock.

'Bruno's dead!'

The *maresciallo* nodded morosely.

'Shame about the funeral. It's this busybody we have up from Rome, you see, on account of the Vincenzo business. He decided to start throwing his weight around, and there was nothing I could do.'

'So why did you mention Bruno?'

Pascal looked up at the cold blue sky.

'Well, shortly before he died Bruno took delivery of a consignment of wine. We think it came from the Faigano brothers, and I naturally assumed that you handled the carriage for them. You normally do, right?'

'Not this time. I didn't even know about any delivery. You've probably got the wrong supplier. Bruno used to buy wine from all over the place.'

'That's true.'

A silence fell.

'Well, I can always check with Gianni and Maurizio, I suppose,' Pascal remarked, as though to himself. 'I don't know when I'm going to find the time, though. This man from Rome has really stirred things up, I can tell you, what with impounding Bruno's body and ordering an autopsy . . .'

'What?'

Pascal smiled and shook his head.

'Absurd, isn't it? And of course the family are absolutely furious at the idea of their beloved relative being cut up, all on account of some sliver of glass which this Zen claims to have found in his neck.'

There was another long silence. Pascal heaved a long sigh.

'So who were those friends you were out with the night Beppe died?'

Minot did not reply for some time, and when he did it was in a strange, halting voice, as though he was still learning this new skill but had not yet mastered it.

'Gianni and Maurizio.'

Enrico Pascal opened his eyes wide.

'What a coincidence.'

The *maresciallo* stuck his fingernails under his starched collar and scratched his neck.

'Well, I'll be off,' he said.

Minot watched the jeep drive away. At the crossroads outside the village, it turned left, away from the Faigano property. He released the breath he had been holding all this time, leapt into the truck and revved up the motor. Why all these problems now? Was he losing his grip, his instinctive sense of what was and was not possible? At any rate, the key to the whole matter remained the Faigano brothers, he thought, pushing the truck as fast as he dared down the winding road. As long as they backed him up, he was in the clear. The trouble was that he didn't know *what* they would do.

That was the problem with people, you could never be sure how they would react. If only they were like the rats, a collective whose apparent individuality was in fact an illusion, and whose behaviour was totally predictable. But people weren't like that. They could do the craziest things, as Camillo had when the Fascists captured him. Instead of shutting up and taking his chances, he had danced – *danced* – in front of his captors and told them that, yes, he was a partisan and proud of it, and that they were doomed by history.

They'd shot him, of course, but not before he had taunted them one last time, when the Republican recruit detailed to pull the trigger had funked out and started to shake. One of the other prisoners, who had watched the whole scene, later reported what happened next. 'So Camillo looked at the boy, and he smiled. "Go ahead and shoot," he said. "You're only killing a man. Nothing will change."'

People did things like that all the time. Maybe Gianni and Maurizio would, too. What could he do to sway them, other than recite the usual formulas about their mutual interest and so on? Suppose they decided not to listen? Suppose, like Camillo, they just didn't care? Since Chiara's death, Gianni didn't seem to care very much about anything.

It didn't give him much to work with, not nearly enough, in fact. Perhaps he should try an alternative approach. Unpredictability, after all, was a game two could play. The thought of Chiara Vincenzo reminded him of Aldo's death. That was what the cops were really interested in. Beppe and Bruno were just distractions, although inextricably linked to that main event. And if the Faigano brothers refused to help Minot, why should he protect them any longer?

Not only did he know exactly why and how Aldo had been murdered, but he could explain the grotesque and ferocious mutilations inflicted on the corpse as well. Once the truth about that crime had been established, the culprit would automatically become the chief and only suspect in the Gallizio and Scorrone killings. A community such as this didn't run to two murderers, any more than it ran to two lawyers or newsagents. One was both necessary and sufficient, and once he was identified, no one would think of looking any further.

Minot pulled into the courtyard of the brothers' house, strode up to the door and knocked hard several times. He had made his decision, and was in no mood to be kept waiting. There were footsteps inside and the door opened, but the person who appeared was not Gianni or Maurizio but the famous 'busybody from Rome' about whose activities Enrico Pascal had complained so bitterly.

'I was looking for the Faigano brothers,' Minot said hesitantly.

'Come in.'

Caught unawares, Minot obeyed.

'And Gianni and Maurizio?'

'They're not here.'

'Out among the vines, are they? It's a busy time of the year for wine-makers.'

The other held out his hand.

'I think we've met. I'm Aurelio Zen. You were kind enough to give me a lift the other day. Minot, isn't it?'

Minot clasped the proffered hand and gasped audibly. He turned away, trying to evaluate the inspiration which had been clear and powerful enough to force the spasm from him. He needed time to think it through properly, but time was just what he didn't have. Gianni and Maurizio might return at any minute, but until then he was alone with the policeman in charge of the whole investigation – and no one would ever know that he'd been there!

'Come through to the kitchen,' the official told him, leading the way. 'I want to show you something.'

The kitchen was where Gianni kept his butcher's knives, lined up on the chopping block by the sink. One quick thrust would be enough, with a towel around the handle to eliminate fingerprints and staunch the blood. 'Do it!' said the voices in his head. What was that phrase the priest had explained to him once, long ago? *Nihil obstat.*

'Who's this?' the policeman asked, pointing to a framed photograph standing all alone on one shelf of the sideboard. It was a studio shot, obviously quite old, showing a young girl dressed all in white, with a lace headscarf.

Minot hesitated. The question had no relevance to his plans, but he had grown up in a world where figures of power – schoolmasters, priests, commanding officers, policemen – were licensed to ask questions, and where you were expected to reply or face unpleasant consequences.

'Chiara Cravioli,' he said, eyeing the array of gleaming knives.

'Cravioli?'

'Aldo Vincenzo's wife.'

'But why is her photograph here?'

Before Minot could answer, the door opened and a teenage girl with an armful of schoolbooks walked in. She stared at both the men.

'What are you doing here?'

Aurelio Zen inclined his head slightly.

'We met at the market in Alba at the weekend. I'm a police officer.'

'Where's my father?' demanded Lisa Faigano. 'What's happened?'

'I'm afraid that your father and uncle have had to go into Alba to answer some routine questions.'

The girl dropped her books on the table.

'And what about you, Minot?' she demanded, seemingly more annoyed by his presence than that of the policeman.

'I was hoping to see Gianni and Maurizio. No one told me they'd been arrested.'

'They haven't,' put in Zen quickly. 'We're just taking statements from a number of people, including them. There's nothing to worry about.'

Minot coughed.

'Well, I'll try again later.'

He sidled off to the door as if expecting to be stopped at any moment. But there was no challenge, and a moment later his truck roared away.

Left alone together, Lisa Faigano and Aurelio Zen surveyed each other warily.

'Would you like a coffee?' the girl said at last, as though grasping a little desperately at the rituals of hospitality.

'Thank you.'

Zen had no interest in the coffee, but it would give him a pretext to stay longer without producing his search warrant. Lisa Faigano's unexpected appearance had thrown him off-balance. Once Gianni and Maurizio were safely in custody, Zen had descended on the house and dismissed the patrolman on guard and his driver, telling them to return in an hour. He had wanted to be alone with the house, free to prowl and pry at will, to let the silence seep into his soul and reveal its secrets.

The arrival of Minot and then the girl had put an end to all that, and while he could have seen the former off the premises easily enough, he could hardly throw Lisa Faigano out of her own home. Nor did a bureaucratic approach seem likely to be fruitful. The brutally official questions he could so easily have posed sounded, as he rehearsed them in his mind, off-key and inappropriate. If he was to get anything out of her, Lisa had somehow to be managed. But how?

'You're the one they sent up from Rome about what happened to Vincenzo,' the girl remarked as she filled the coffee machine.

'That's right, *signorina*.'

'What's that got to do with my father and uncle?'

Zen hesitated. It was hard to know who he had to deal with. The girl was at a stage where she could look thirteen one moment and thirty the next. Untuned features and awkward gestures suggested the former, but her brown eyes were shrewd and wary and did not give the impression of missing very much.

'Nothing, so far as we know. But there appears to be a link to another crime which occurred recently, to which they may be material witnesses. Naturally we need to question them, if only to eliminate this possibility, and they have therefore been invited to headquarters to make their depositions. I'm glad to say that they were happy to comply.'

This was a lie. According to the officers who had carried out Zen's orders, the Faigano brothers had been anything but happy at being hauled off at gunpoint in armoured vans emblazoned POLIZIA, the whole operation being conducted under the malicious scrutiny of their neighbours. They were particularly unhappy at losing a day's work at a time when the weather finally seemed to be firming up for the vintage. But their happiness was not Zen's concern.

'When will they be back?' Lisa asked, serving Zen his coffee.

He gave a helpless half-shrug.

'That depends.'

'So what am I supposed to do?'

'About what?'

'About dinner, of course! There's hell to pay if it isn't on the table on the stroke of seven, but if they're not back by then ...'

Zen coughed.

'I think you can take it that they won't be home to dinner, *signorina*.'

'Not tonight at all, you mean?'

'Are you worried about being alone?'

She laughed.

'On the contrary! I can finally get through an entire game with no fear of being interrupted.'

Zen stared at her.

'I play chess with this friend, you see,' Lisa told him, sweeping a stray strand of hair off her face with one finger. 'But either Dad or Gianni usually needs to use the phone at some point, and then everything's ruined.'

Zen sipped his coffee and tried to look interested.

'Perhaps you could go over to your friend's house?'

Another laugh.

'Hardly! He lives in Lima.'

Zen looked at her, smiling determinedly.

'Lima,' he repeated.

'In Peru. Gianni got a computer last year to keep track of the accounts, and then when Aunt Chiara died she left me some money and I arranged for an Internet connection. But there's still only one phone, so when they need to call someone, I have to go off-line.'

Zen nodded in a kindly, avuncular manner. The poor girl was clearly living in a fantasy world, imagining that she was playing chess on the telephone with Peruvians! Living all alone in this cold, comfortless house with a pair of grumpy, demanding geriatrics must have pushed her over the edge.

'The last time I had an evening free was when Dad and Gianni went to the *Festa della Vendemmia*,' the girl burbled on, her face alive with genuine enthusiasm for the first time. 'It looked like we would finally get a chance to play a whole game without interruptions. I'd just tricked Tomás into a knight sacrifice which left him in a very weak position, when in walks Gianni and tells me to get off the line! Result, Tomás got twenty-four hours to analyse the situation and look up his reference books, and he came back and beat me.'

She heaved a sigh of frustration.

'I wonder who your uncle could have called at that time of night,' murmured Zen idly.

There was no answer, and for a moment he thought that the girl was trying to think of a suitable lie. Then he realized that she was still fretting about her missed opportunity to defeat Tomás.

'What? Oh, it was Aldo Vincenzo. I overheard him telling Dad about it afterwards.'

Zen finished his coffee and set the cup down.

'What did he say?'

'I don't know, I just heard the name. They clammed up as soon as I came in, as usual. I'm just a child, you see, and need to be protected from the harsh realities of life.'

Zen gave her an understanding smile.

'And then they went to bed, I suppose.'

'Dad did. Gianni went down to the cellar to check on something or other.'

'And you? Didn't you stay up to finish your game with Tomás?'

'No, I went to sleep. Tomás would have been playing a different game by then. He has six or seven on the go at any one time, with people all over the world.'

A vehicle pulled up outside. Zen walked over to the window, then went to the door and called to the uniformed officer getting out of the police car.

'Wait there! I'll be out shortly.'

He came back into the room.

'How do you get down to the cellar?' he asked Lisa.

'There.'

She pointed to a door in the corner.

'But there's another way in, too, I suppose. For deliveries and so on?'

'At the far end of the house,' she confirmed. 'A flight of steps goes down from the yard. Why are you asking all these questions?'

'I'm just trying to get things straight in my mind. Just two more questions, and I'll leave you to get on with your homework.'

'Actually, I'll probably watch TV!'

Zen nodded and winked conspiratorially.

'I'll try to keep it brief. You mentioned just now that you inherited some money from an Aunt Chiara. Is that her picture?'

He pointed to the framed photograph. Lisa nodded.

'It was taken the day she was confirmed. Isn't her dress fabulous? I wonder what became of it.'

'So Chiara Vincenzo was your aunt?'

Lisa laughed.

'No, no, not really. I just called her that. And we never called her Vincenzo. She was always Signora Cravioli here.'

'Did she come here often?'

'Once a month or so. She walked here across the fields and stayed for about an hour. She'd never learned to drive, you see.'

'Why did she come?'

Lisa thought about this, as if for the first time.

'I'm not really sure. She used to sit in the front room with Gianni, and . . . I don't know what they did, really. They didn't seem to talk much. It was odd, I suppose. But she was always very kind to me, bringing me little presents, some fruit or a cake she'd baked. I just took it all for granted.'

Zen was silent for so long that the girl eventually added, 'And your second question?'

'Ah. I'm afraid that's a little more delicate, *signorina*.'

Lisa Faigano gave an embarrassed laugh.

'Go on.'

Zen looked down at his shoes.

'Did Manlio Vincenzo ever propose marriage to you?'

'Manlio? Of course not!'

'He never mentioned the matter?'

Lisa blushed charmingly.

'He mentioned once that his father was keen on the idea. But that was just to warn me, in case I heard about it from someone else. It could have been an awkward situation.'

'So neither of you took the idea seriously?'

'Of course not!'

Zen walked over to the dresser and inspected the photograph again.

'Did you tell your father or Gianni about it?' he asked, without turning round.

Lisa hesitated.

'I wasn't going to, but someone must have gossiped. We met in the village, and there were lots of people coming and going. One of them must have told Dad, because he brought it up over dinner.'

Another pause.

'I used to have a bit of a crush on Manlio at one time you see,' she said all in one breath. 'Just silly adolescent stuff, nothing serious. He never even knew about it, and I'd have died if he'd found out. But I used to keep a diary at the time, and my father read what I'd written about Manlio. He got in a raging fury and made me swear on Mamma's grave never to see him or to speak to him.'

Zen finally turned to face her.

'Did he explain why?'

'No. He just said there was a very good reason which he would tell me when I was older. But I was scared. I'd never seen Dad like that, so intense and angry. Of course I started imagining all sorts of things. I thought perhaps we might be related, Manlio and me. I'd always wanted a sibling, and it didn't seem that far-fetched an idea, not round here. You hear all kinds of odd stories. About that man who was just here, for instance.'

'Minot?'

The girl's cheeks turned even brighter pink.

'They say his father was also his grandfather, if you see what I mean.'

Zen clearly didn't.

'I mean that his mother was abused by her own father and Minot was the result,' Lisa said quickly. 'I don't know if it's true. He's an odd sort, keeps to himself, and people are a bit afraid of him for some reason. They may just have made it all up, but I've heard similar things about other people, back in the old days. There wasn't much else to do, I suppose, and this area was so isolated. Half the folk in the village had never even been to Alba.'

Zen scribbled something in his notebook.

'When did you meet Manlio in Palazzuole?'

'Oh, that was later, after he got back from abroad. He phoned and said he had something important to discuss, and would I meet him at the bar in the village. I didn't see why not. I'd completely forgotten about Manlio by then. Besides, I'd heard he'd met someone in America. Anyway, that's when he told me about Aldo's plans. He was just being kind, trying to protect me in case the whole thing came out somehow.'

'And how did your father react when he heard that you'd disobeyed him?'

Lisa looked away, out of the window.

'It was even worse. He wasn't angry. He just marched me to the telephone, made me phone Manlio and then stood over me while I told him never to call me again and a lot more cruel things I don't want to repeat.'

'What did Manlio say?'

'He said, "Very well," and hung up.'

There were tears in her eyes now.

'Why does it all have to be horrible? I don't understand! I just don't understand.'

Zen was about to go and comfort her, but then thought better of it.

'Well, thank you, *signorina*,' he said, putting his notebook away. 'I'm sorry I've brought back painful memories, but you've been very helpful. I'll naturally let you know when you can expect your father and uncle home again. But supposing all this takes longer than I thought, is there somewhere you could go?'

'There's my aunt in Alba, my real aunt. But Dad's not in any real trouble, is he?'

'Not so far as I know. And, believe me, I'm just as anxious as you are to get this whole thing over with. In fact I can't wait to get out of this place, to tell you the truth.'

The girl made a face.

'You're not the only one.'

'Where are you going?'

'To Milan, to study mathematics.'

'When?'

'Next year. More precisely, in ten months, two weeks and six days. Do you know Milan?'

'I used to work there.'

Lisa looked at him eagerly.

'Is it as ghastly as everyone says?'

Zen smiled.

'It's even worse. Crowded, noisy, dirty and dangerous. I'm sure you'll have a wonderful time there, *signorina*. If I don't see you again, let me wish you the best of luck.'

He opened the door and walked out, leaving the girl standing all alone in the large, empty house.

'We want a lawyer,' said Gianni Faigano.

'That's right,' his brother added. 'We have a right to legal representation.'

It was twenty-past five in the afternoon. The sky was dulling, draining away to the west, chased by the long night coming. Aurelio Zen took off his overcoat and hat and laid them on the desk in the centre of the room.

'A lawyer?' he said. 'Whatever for?'

'To protect our legal rights,' replied Gianni.

'With regard to what?'

'Whatever this is about.'

Zen sat down behind the desk, surveying the two standing men. There was a hard wooden stool facing the desk, but the only other chair was occupied by Nanni Morino, resplendent in a tweed jacket, canary yellow pullover, sky blue shirt and red tie. A legal notepad was propped open on his knee, and in the intervals between taking down the proceedings in shorthand he concentrated on picking his teeth with a blade unfolded from a Swiss Army knife.

'What do *you* think it's about?' Zen asked the Faigano brothers.

'How the hell are we supposed to know?' snapped Gianni. 'The last time I saw you, you claimed to be a reporter for some paper in Naples!'

'It's for you to tell us what it's about,' Maurizio insisted stolidly.

'Or our lawyer,' added Gianni.

Zen surveyed them with an expression of bewilderment.

'It's about *wine*, of course.'

The two brothers conferred briefly and silently.

'Wine?' echoed Gianni.

'That's right,' said Zen. 'Specifically, the undocumented shipment you made to Bruno Scorrone the other day.'

The ensuing silence was broken by the click of Nanni Morino's dental aid returning to join its numerous relatives and then the squeaks of his pen.

'That's all?' Gianni Faigano blurted out.

Zen frowned.

'What else would it be?'

Maurizio's relief was evident in his laugh.

'Well, you know, it's just that we heard that you'd been sent up here from Rome to investigate Aldo Vincenzo's murder. And then you tried to pump Gianni about it over lunch, so when your men came to bring us in we naturally assumed that . . .'

The scene was a second-floor office in the Alba police station. It was small and dingy and had been unused for some time. A thick layer of dust covered every horizontal surface like a natural secretion.

Zen got up from the desk and, with some difficulty, opened the window. It was evidently the first time in years that this had been done, and the musty, enclosed odours lingered in the air, mingled with currents from the cool darkness outside and the sounds of merriment and sociability drifting up from the street below.

'Scorrone?' Gianni Faigano remarked with exaggerated casualness. 'Sure, we sent him some wine from time to time. When we had a back stock we couldn't shift, or needed some cash right away. Bruno could always use some good stuff to bulk out his blend.'

He paused and shot Zen a shrewd glance.

'But I don't understand why someone like you should be taking an interest in this sort of thing, *dottore*. We might have been in technical violation of some law or other, but people round here do it all the time. It's like borrowing a little oil or a couple of eggs from a neighbour. There's no call for you to round us up at gunpoint over something like that.'

'Let's stick to the point, shall we? The sooner we get this

cleared up, the sooner you can go home. Scorrone's widow has testified that he went down to the winery after lunch to take delivery of a shipment of wine. We know that the wine was yours . . .'

'We haven't admitted that,' Gianni put in sharply.

'You don't need to, although you would have improved your position by doing so. Scorrone kept an informal account book in which he recorded all shipments and deliveries, with the name of the producer, quantity and price paid. You're clearly identified as the source of the two thousand litres of red wine due to be received that afternoon.'

He gave the brothers a moment to digest this piece of misinformation.

'So what do you want from us?' asked Maurizio.

'The name of the person who made the delivery.'

Maurizio Faigano glanced away. Zen looked at his brother, who was studying a battered filing cabinet in the corner with mute intensity. A succession of disconnected noises wafted up from the street like fragments of wind-borne seed.

'It was Minot,' said Gianni.

Zen nodded.

'I know.'

As though stunned by the failure of some party turn, Gianni Faigano stared at Zen with genuine rage.

'Then what are we doing here, if you already know? First you tell us this is all you need to know, and now you claim that you knew all along!'

Zen fixed them with an intimidating glare.

'The results of the autopsy held today confirm that Bruno Scorrone died as the result of injuries sustained in an assault with a broken bottle, the body later being dumped in the wine vat where it was found. Your friend Minot is thus our prime suspect at this point. I needed corroboration from you that he had indeed visited the winery at about the time Scorrone was killed.'

He looked back at the window, his back turned to the two brothers, observing their reflections in the glass.

'Now we come to the matter of motive,' he said. 'After searching your house under the terms of a warrant I obtained this morning, I went to see Enrico Pascal, the local Carabinieri official. He told me various things of interest, notably that Bruno Scorrone had made verbal allegations which appeared to implicate this Minot in the death of Beppe Gallizio.'

'What's all this got to do with us?' demanded Maurizio Faigano.

Zen turned round.

'According to the *maresciallo*, Minot is citing you two as his alibi in the Gallizio affair.'

Another quick, mute, fraternal glance.

'Apparently he claims that you were all three out after truffles that night. Is that correct?'

Silence.

'Well?'

'I want a lawyer,' said Gianni.

'So do I,' said Maurizio.

Zen stared at them for a long time. Then he turned to Nanni Morino, who was just concluding another page of hieroglyphs.

'How many cells do we have free?'

Morino consulted the ceiling.

'All of them, at the moment. It's been quite quiet recently.'

'How many is all?'

'Six. They're down in the basement, three on one side and three on the other.'

Zen nodded lugubriously.

'Do you like music, Morino?'

'Music? How do you mean?'

'I mean that half the cells here are going to be occupied overnight,' Zen remarked dreamily, 'and I don't want any possibility of conversation between the detainees.'

It took Morino another moment or two to get it. Then his face lit up.

'I've just got a new Sony boombox! Eighty watts RMS, with a superbass feature that makes the walls bulge.'

'And what sort of music do you have?'

'At the moment I'm into salsa. That's a sort of Latin-American dance music which . . .'

'Is it loud?'

Morino's smile widened.

'It's loud.'

Zen yawned lengthily.

'Excellent. In that case we can treat our house guests to an all-night crash course in the wonders of Latin-American culture.'

He picked up the phone.

'Dario? Who else is on duty? All right, put him on the desk and get up to room 201 right away.'

'Are you proposing to hold us here overnight?' demanded Gianni Faigano.

'That's right.'

'On what charge?'

'Illicit trafficking in wine and probable tax evasion. You have indicated that you will not respond to my questions without the presence of a lawyer. It is too late to obtain the services of an *avvocato* at this hour, so I am obliged to detain you until tomorrow.'

There was a rap at the door and Dario appeared.

'Take these two down to the basement,' Zen instructed him. 'Put them in separate cells as far apart as possible, and stay down there until relieved. I want you to make sure that they don't have a chance to communicate before or after they're locked up. Understood?'

Dario nodded.

'No problem. Come on, you.'

'And our third guest?' queried Nanni Morino as the door closed. 'This Minot, right?'

'Ah, you're the quick one!' murmured Zen with a hint of irony. 'Yes, I'm afraid you're going to have to drive out to Palazzuole tonight and bring this character in.'

Morino got to his feet.

'It's been a pleasure to watch you at work, *dottore*! Round here, of course, we don't have much call for those kind of skills, but it's a privilege to watch a virtuoso in action.'

Zen gestured awkwardly.

'There was nothing to it, really.'

'Nothing to it? On the contrary! The way you manipulated that pair into giving crucial evidence against this friend of theirs, and then pinned them down on an alibi which both they and we know is false . . . It was masterly! And your strategy was a stroke of genius. When everyone was expecting a frontal assault on the Vincenzo case, you attack instead on the flanks with Gallizio and Scorrone. All three murders are linked, of course, so if you nail this Minot for one of them, it's just a matter of time before we get him for the others as well.'

He started towards the door.

'Just a moment!'

Nanni Morino turned back with an expectant look. Zen coughed and, perhaps by association, lit a cigarette.

'Thanks for the compliments.'

'I meant every word,' Morino assured him. 'It was an inspiration and a privilege to . . .'

'But we seem to be at cross purposes. I want this Minot brought in so that we can go to work on him. But I don't think he did it.'

Morino stared at him in amazement.

'You don't?'

'No.'

'Then who did?'

Zen jerked his forefinger towards the floor.

'Our friends downstairs. At least, one of them.'

Nanni Morino looked down, scratching his eyebrow, as if reviewing the facts. Clearly they didn't add up.

'I don't quite . . .' he began.

'Come and sit down,' Zen told him.

Morino did so. Zen dragged his chair round from behind the desk and seated himself opposite the young inspector.

'All right,' he said, 'let's go through the whole thing point by point. If we're going to work this case together, we'd better get our agenda clear.'

The telephone woke him, a salvation as cruel as a harpoon descending fathoms to skewer a drowning man and haul him, gored but alive, back to the surface. Blind blunders with the lamp followed, then the brutality of light masking a tumbler of water which spread a glistening trail across the glass-topped table before rolling over the edge and landing on the ingrowing nail of his big toe. And when he finally got the receiver to his ear . . .

'*What's going on? I heard screams. Are you all right?*'

He did not answer.

'*Hello? Are you there? Is everything all right?*'

'Yes,' he said at last. 'Yes, everything's all right.'

'*I'm sorry if I woke you,*' the robotic voice went on, '*but I heard what sounded like someone yelling and I was worried. I thought you might have set the bed on fire or something.*'

Zen took a succession of quick, short, shallow breaths.

'Is it you, Carla?'

'*Of course it is!*'

'You sound funny.'

'*Do I? Oh, shit! Wait a moment . . .* '

Various clicks and grunts.

'Sorry about that!' Carla Arduini resumed in her own voice. 'I'd forgotten to disconnect the attachment I was using. No wonder the man from room service has been giving me odd looks.'

Zen glanced at the clock, marooned in the puddle of spilt water. It was twenty past five in the morning.

'I'm sorry if I disturbed you,' he said. 'I must have been having a nightmare.'

'What about?'

'I can't remember. Anyway, I hate discussing dreams. It seems

179

to give them a credibility they don't deserve, don't you think? It's like someone who mumbles things you can't quite catch, and then when you ask him to speak up looks hurt and says, "Never mind, it doesn't matter."'

'Or those pieces of modern art entitled "Untitled".'

'Exactly,' said Zen, although he couldn't really understand the connection.

There was a pause.

'Well, good night,' said Carla.

'Good night.'

Zen hung up with a sense of disappointment and loneliness. Sleep was out of the question, at least for the moment. His facetious persiflage about the insignificance of dreams had been pure bravado. While it was true that he couldn't remember the precise content of the nightmare from which he had been awakened, its malign aura informed his every thought like the memory of an ancient atrocity in which he was somehow implicated.

His eye fell on the pile of papers he had brought back from the police station the night before. Confused memories of the case he was involved in surfaced like episodes from his dream, the events dimly recalled but their significance lost. When he outlined the whole thing to Nanni Morino, it had all made perfect sense, but now he had lost the connecting thread.

Then it came to him. The Faigano brothers! That had been the insight he had suddenly but quite characteristically had the day before, the sensed presence of a pattern which abruptly made the hitherto disparate elements of the puzzle picture snap into place. Long ago, after the war, Gianni Faigano had been in love with Chiara Cravioli, but Aldo Vincenzo had raped her and thus forced a marriage to obtain ownership of the family's land. That was motive enough for the killing, and it also explained the subsequent mutilations. The violator's body had been violated, the offending parts cut away and destroyed.

Lisa Faigano's testimony showed that Gianni had made a phone call to the Vincenzo house that night, and had subsequently gone down to the cellar, from which he could easily have left the house without being observed. Manlio Vincenzo had testified that his father received a phone call at about the same time, and had then gone out for a walk claiming that he needed 'to get some air', had discouraged his son from accompanying him and finally provoked Manlio to return alone by an extraordinary and gratuitous display of brutal rudeness.

Let us suppose, Zen had told Morino, that Gianni Faigano lured his loathed rival out to the fields under some specious pretext and stabbed him to death. Manlio Vincenzo is arrested for the killing and everything looks good for Gianni, until he discovers that Zen has been sent up from Rome to conduct a fresh investigation. Sooner or later, he knows, the love affair between him and Chiara Cravioli *in Vincenzo* must come to light. The time to act is now, but he needs a suitable scapegoat.

He selects Minot, whose reputation as an odd and potentially violent recluse with dark secrets in the family cupboard makes him a perfect choice. Minot is also an associate of the Faigano brothers, so his movements are relatively easy to predict. One night when both Minot and Beppe Gallizio are out after truffles, Gianni enters the Gallizio house through the back door, which sticks slightly and is never locked. Using gloves to prevent fingerprints, he takes Beppe's shotgun and leaves the knife with which he killed Aldo Vincenzo on the kitchen table. He then lies in wait for Gallizio . . .

'What about Minot's truck being seen down there?' Nanni Morino had interjected.

'I'm coming to that,' replied Zen with a satisfied smile.

With Gallizio dead, possibly by his own hand, and the Vincenzo murder weapon found in his house, either he or his assailant becomes the primary suspect in the earlier case. But now something unforeseen arises. Bruno Scorrone has noticed a red Fiat truck down in the hollow where Gallizio was shot, possibly belonging to Minot, who is questioned by the Carabinieri. To cover himself, he goes to the Faigano brothers and requests an alibi for the night in question. A less astute pair of conspirators might have refused, but Gianni and Maurizio realize that the same alibi also protects them, and that they can withdraw it at any time. So they agree.

'As for that truck,' Zen continued, 'Minot is not the only person round here with a red Fiat pick-up. It's a common enough model, and it so happens that the Faigano brothers own one too. I saw it at the market here in Alba on Saturday.'

Nanni Morino nodded dumbly.

'Ah,' he said.

'So when Bruno Scorrone contacted the local *maresciallo* and mentioned the vehicle he had seen, Gianni Faigano realized that with one more murder he could complete his grand design. Scorrone had not testified under oath, so once he had been silenced his previous evidence would not be admissible in court. Even better, his death could be made to tighten the noose around Minot's neck. The Faigano brothers – I'm still not sure how much Maurizio was involved – set up a sale of wine to Scorrone and arrange for Minot to deliver it. Then they kill Scorrone and heave his body into the wine vat, leaving a trail of evidence connecting all three murders and pointing straight to Minot, whose sole alibi depends on them!'

He appealed to the younger man in triumph.

'Well, what do you think?'

Nanni Morino shrugged.

'It's ingenious,' he admitted. 'And it all makes sense. But what about Manlio's evidence? He told the judges that his father was still alive in the middle of the night, that he heard him snoring. If that's true, Gianni Faigano couldn't have killed him after the supposed assignation he made by telephone.'

'*If* it's true,' emphasized Zen. 'But when he told the judges that, Manlio was trying to save his own neck. He repeated the same story to me, but he's still a suspect, remember. There is no independent evidence to support his claim. He might easily be lying.'

Morino nodded dubiously.

'I suppose so. But there's another thing.'

'What now?' snapped Zen testily.

'If this was a crime of passion, a premeditated act of revenge for some alleged incident dating back forty years or more, why did Faigano wait so long? Why was he so patient? After all this time, you would think he might have resigned himself to the situation. Why didn't he kill Vincenzo years ago?'

Zen had had no reply to this the night before, and he had none now, but he felt sure that he was on the right track at last. The details would take care of themselves. What he had to do now was to hold on to the insight he had gained, and to get this Minot in the palm of his hand. He was the key to the whole affair, of that Zen was certain.

From behind the adjoining wall came a faint stirring and banging, then a sound of flushing water. Evidently Carla couldn't sleep either. He lay back on the bed and closed his eyes. He wished he could remember Amalia Arduini better, but she had faded to an impoverished set of fixed images, like worn snapshots endlessly reshuffled.

What remained? A vision of her supine and naked, her large breasts lolling around on her chest like half-trained puppies with a mind of their own. He recalled her crying one day at a restaurant when he'd said something – he had long forgotten what – which upset her, and the pleasure with which she greeted him at the door of her apartment in Via Strozzi, as if perpetually amazed that he'd actually shown up. And he also remembered moments when she would drift away from him, when his spell no longer held, and she was sucked back into personal and familial labyrinths from which he was excluded.

He sat up and reached for the phone.

'Carla?'

'Are you still up, too?'

'It seems so.'

'What are we going to do about it?'

A pause.

'I wondered if you might want to drop by,' Zen continued. 'Or I could come there. I mean, you know, just so as . . .'

'So as not to be alone?'

'Yes, that's it exactly. So as not to be alone.'

Another pause.

'I'll be there shortly.'

He hung up and went to put on his dressing-gown. A door closed in the hallway, and then there was a knock at his. Carla Arduini was wearing a stylish orange track-suit and a pair of running shoes. Her hair was combed back and secured by a sweat band. Zen gestured her into the room.

'Well,' he said, 'this *is* odd.'

'Isn't it?'

She walked inside, looking around as though for a place to sit down, but in the end remained standing.

'I was just thinking about your mother,' said Zen, and immediately cursed his thoughtlessness.

Carla gave a hard little snort.

'You never thought about her while she was alive. Why bother now she's dead?'

Zen stared at her in shock.

'Dead?'

She tossed her head.

'But of course! Why do you think I made my move *now*, when I've known about it for years? I could easily have come to Rome and tracked you down. But she forbade me to do so. She was poor and proud. Pride was all she had left, once her looks went. She didn't want to give you the satisfaction of knowing how much you'd hurt her. So I had to wait until she died before doing anything about it.'

Zen was now staring at her with manic intensity.

'Until she died,' he repeated.

A curt nod.

'Which was recently?'

'Back in the spring. A stroke.'

Zen looked away, his eyes narrowing.

'So Irena was right. Of course!'

'The doctor's friend?'

'*Cherchez la femme*,' returned Zen. 'I understand it all now. He had to wait until she died!'

'I don't know what you're talking about, let alone how that bitch Irena comes into it.'

Carla laughed maliciously.

'She couldn't get over the fact that I was able to spot what Lucchese was playing and to name the harpsichord! She obviously doesn't care for competition.'

Zen looked at her, frowning.

'How *did* you know that, anyway?'

'I used to have a boyfriend who listened to classical music a lot. Scarlatti was one of his favourites, and if you've heard one of those clattery, repetitive pieces, you've heard them all.'

'And the instrument?'

'Even easier! It was written right there above the keyboard. *Andreas Ruckers me fecit.* Latin was one of my best subjects at school. But you still haven't told me what that Irena was right about.'

Zen waved the subject away.

'It's not important. Take no notice of me, I'm still half-asleep.'

Carla consulted her watch.

'Why don't we go and get a coffee? There's a place I know which should be open, down by the station. I noticed it the morning you caught the train to Palazzuole.'

'That was you?' exclaimed Zen. 'I remember seeing some woman standing there in the shadows.'

'I heard you rummaging around in here, and when you went out I decided to follow you.'

'And then phoned me later at the Vincenzo house. But how did you know I was there?'

'I didn't. But I heard you tell the guard to let you off at Palazzuole. I thought you might be going to the Vincenzo house, so I phoned up, pretending to be a reporter. To my surprise, the son himself answered, quite rudely, I must say. That confirmed my suspicions, so I kept trying until you showed up. It was a shot in the dark, but it hit the target. God, you must have been scared.'

She smiled wryly.

'How long ago that seems now! Like years, not days. To think that I was set on terrorizing you with anonymous phone calls. But it all seemed to matter so much to me back then.'

Zen gazed at her expressionlessly.

'And now?'

A shrug, brief, almost irritable. Zen looked away.

'I'll get dressed,' he mumbled. 'Then let's go and try this café of yours.'

When they came for him, he was asleep, if you could call it sleep. Once again, there were two of them: one in plain clothes, the other a uniformed recruit cradling a machine-gun.

That first time, the evening before, Minot had just finished eating a bowl of the lentil soup he made every Sunday, and which sat in its cauldron on the stove for the rest of the week. Eating lentils made you rich, his father had told him; every one you swallowed would come back one day as a gold coin. Minot still believed this obscurely, even though he knew that they didn't make gold coins any more.

He'd grated some raw carrot and onion into the warmed-up soup, poured in a fat slick of olive oil and then spooned it up, dunking in the heel of the day-old loaf he kept in a battered canister, where it was safe from his familiars. The lid was decorated with a faded picture of a smiling woman and the name of a once-famous brand of boiled sweets.

When he'd finished eating, Minot sluiced out the bowl under the tap and left it to dry. Then he went next door, sat down and turned on the television, an old black-and-white set given to him by a neighbour who had changed to colour. He could only get two channels, and either the picture or the sound was often indecipherable, but Minot didn't care. He wasn't interested in any of the programmes anyway. He just liked having the set on. It made the room more lively.

He was watching a film when the police arrived. There was heavy interference on the screen, with ghost doubles floating about and the picture skipping upwards repeatedly like the facial tic which used to afflict Angelin when things got tense. But the soundtrack was clear enough, and at first Minot thought that the noise of the jeep drawing up and the imperious knocking was part of the movie. It was only when the rat perched on top of the set swivelled towards the door, nostrils twitching, then leapt down and disappeared, that he had realized his mistake.

He was taken by surprise this second time, but for a different reason. Ever since they had locked him into his cell the previous evening, the air had been throbbing with loud music from a radio which someone had left on somewhere close by. He had tried shouting and banging on the door to get them to turn it off, but all in vain. In the end he had lain down on the bench provided and tried to get some sleep.

The bench made a primitive bed, but Minot was not fussy in this respect, any more than in others. The cot he slept on at home was no more spacious and hardly any softer, but the only time he'd ever had trouble sleeping was when the resident rodents used to scurry over the covers and tickle his face with their feet or whiskers. He'd solved that problem by fixing rounded wooden caps just below the frame, one at the top of each leg, so that the bed seemed to be resting on four giant mushrooms. The rats couldn't climb past the caps, and after that Minot slept in peace.

As he would have done that night, too, if it hadn't been for that damned music! He hadn't made any fuss when the cops told him they were taking him into detention. He'd been more or less expecting something of the sort anyway, ever since the *maresciallo* had taken to dropping in – and to dropping heavy hints. In any case, Minot wasn't the type to give them any satisfaction by getting upset.

But after being assaulted for several hours by that thudding, repetitive, tuneless barrage that he'd heard kids listening to in their cars or at the local café, he was finding it hard to remember the motto by which he lived: keep cool, say nothing, make them show their hand. In the end, he'd drifted off into a state which was neither sleep nor wakefulness, but seemed to combine the disadvantages of both. While in this stressful but disoriented condition, a succession of sounds detached themselves from the hellish cacophony with which he was being tormented, the light in his cell was turned on, and he awoke to find himself confronting the two policemen. The armed and uniformed one guarded the door, the other advanced into the cell.

'Time to go,' he said shortly.

Minot stood up. Time to go, the man had said, but what time was it? Minot never wore a watch, relying on his knowledge of the seasonal and diurnal rhythms, with occasional data from a distant church bell floating past on the breeze. Now he had a panicky feeling of being completely lost. It might be midnight or midday. Both made sense, so neither did.

The policemen gestured him out of the cell and escorted him upstairs. As the pounding of the music receded into the distance, Minot began to feel better. Passing a window on the stairs, he saw that the darkness outside the window, although still seemingly complete, had lost its inner confidence, sensing the inevitable defeat to come. Half-six to seven, he thought automatically, probably nearer seven. By the time the uniformed patrolman knocked at a door on the second floor, he was once again in control of the situation.

His new-found confidence was almost cancelled by the discovery that the officer sitting behind the desk inside was the one from Rome he'd seen the day before at the Faigano house. This was bad news, for it meant that the Vincenzo case was involved. The uniformed man led Minot to a stool opposite the desk and then returned to keep the door, his gun at the ready, while the plain-clothed cop plonked his ample bum down on a stool beside the desk and opened a notepad.

'I suppose you want a lawyer,' announced Zen.

Minot made a vestigial bow, just like everyone used to in such situations years ago.

'A lawyer?' he said, with an air of astonishment. 'Eh, no, *dottore*! A lawyer? He would just waste your time and my money.'

Aurelio Zen looked at him with unfeigned interest.

'Well, that's an original approach, at least.'

He dragged some papers towards him.

189

'All right, what's your real name? Minot is what people call you, but it won't do for our records. Official forms come with blanks which need to be filled in, you understand.'

Minot nodded briskly.

'Piumatti Guglielmo, *dottore*.'

Zen noted this down, then got to his feet.

'Right!' he said. 'You've declined the offer of legal representation, Signor Piumatti. This being so, I shall proceed directly to the interrogation. Present Inspector Nanni Morino and Patrolman Dario . . .'

He glanced at the uniformed man, who responded, 'Tamburino, *dottore*.'

'Date such and such,' continued Zen, 'time whatever, place etc, etc.'

While talking, he had moved around the desk and was now standing directly in front of Minot. Bending forward suddenly, he caught the prisoner by the jaw and pulled his entire head back by a fistful of hair.

'We know you did it, you son of a whore! You'll confess in the end. Why not save yourself any more pain?'

He glanced at Nanni Morino.

'Delete that from the record.'

Zen smiled at Minot.

'Sorry about that. Nothing personal, and thanks for the ride the other day. But I've had just about enough of this sleepy, friendly, crime-free community where everyone has been pissing me around ever since I arrived. I'm in a mood to do a little damage myself, and it's your bad luck that it happened this morning.'

Minot looked him straight back in the eye.

'Go ahead! Beat me up, if that's what you want. But if you think you can get anything out of me that way, you're even more stupid than I thought. I've seen far worse than you!'

Aurelio Zen shook his head slowly, holding Minot's eyes all the while.

'No,' he said decisively. 'You've never seen worse than me, Minot. I'm as bad as it gets.'

A contemptuous laugh.

'I faced up to the Gestapo and the Republican death squads while you were still sucking on your mother's tit! What can you do that they couldn't?'

Zen continued to hold his eyes.

'I can destroy you, Minot. Unless you cooperate, I *will* destroy you.'

Another laugh.

'Go ahead!'

Zen leaned forward, his face a breath away from the other man's.

'Let's talk about your father, Minot.'

The prisoner's eyes flared briefly, then dulled again.

'My father? What has he to do with anything?'

'He had quite a bit to do with your mother, I'm told,' Zen said evenly. 'And not just in the usual way. I hear they had a – how shall I say? – a previous connection.'

Minot froze into a tense stasis.

'Meaning,' Zen continued, 'that they were related not only in bed but by blood. Meaning that your father was also *her* father.'

He straightened up and took a step back.

'Meaning that he fucked his own daughter and that you're the outcome. Meaning that you're not just a bastard but an incest bastard, Minot! A gene pool so swampy that nothing can live there, a cloning experiment gone badly wrong, an abortion on two legs . . .'

Minot sprang up like one of his rats, the raised stool in his hands. But his intended victim was no longer where he had been a moment before and then a huge pain erupted in his body – a pain without precedent, an unthinkable and outrageous intrusion.

'Well done, Nanni,' said Zen.

'No problem, *capo*.'

Minot stared up through a mist of agony at the plain-clothed brute who had kicked him in the groin from behind.

'You son of a bitch! You assaulted me! I'll kill you, you scum!'

'So you admit to murderous tendencies,' commented Zen.

'Note that down, Morino. As for assault, *you* assaulted *me*. That's a crime in and of itself, and I hereby charge you with attacking a police official in the course of his duties and remand you in custody until further notice.'

Minot struggled to his knees, then clambered painfully back on to the stool.

'That was a very silly thing to do,' Zen told him condescendingly. 'Not only are you on a charge, but I'm afraid that my colleagues will be tempted to have some fun at your expense while you're in custody, particularly now that we know how sensitive you are about your family background. It's highly unprofessional, I know, but I have a feeling that some of them won't be able to resist the urge to tease you about it once in a while.'

'You think I chose my stinking family?' demanded Minot, his face taut with anger.

Zen sat down again, tapping the desk with the end of his pen.

'Of course not,' he said in a soft, soothing voice. 'Anyway, I couldn't care less about any of that. But I have a job to do, Minot, a case to solve. And at the moment you're the prime suspect. We have witnesses who tie you into the killings of both Gallizio and Scorrone. The knife used to stab and mutilate Vincenzo was found at Gallizio's house after he was shot. Scorrone told the Carabinieri about seeing your truck close to where Gallizio's body was found, and a few days later he dies, too, and at about the time you made a delivery of wine to his *azienda*. There's a pattern here, in other words, and it points to you.'

He paused, looking Minot in the eyes.

'Unless, of course, you have any alternative suggestions to make.'

'I have an alibi for Gallizio's death,' Minot gasped. 'I was out after truffles with Gianni and Maurizio Faigano. They'll vouch for me on that.'

Zen nodded.

'Yes, but will you vouch for them?'

Minot looked at him acutely, his eyes dilating as though in an attempt to correct some error of vision.

'But they're not . . . I mean, you said . . .'
Zen gave him a devastatingly arch smile.
'Perhaps you shouldn't believe *everything* I say,' he suggested.

Subject: interrogation of Faigano, Gianni Edoardo
Present: as above
Place and date: as above
Time: 08.11

z: Not until ten? But I have an important case which I'm . . . Do
you realize who you're talking to? The suspect in question
has requested the presence of a lawyer, as is his statutory
right, and now you tell me . . . I thought I was in Piedmont,
not Sardinia. Very well. All right. I'll call back then. Dario,
take him back down.

G: Wait a minute. What was that about?

z: You told me last night that you weren't prepared to make further statements without legal representation, Signor Faigano.
I've just contacted our pool of court-appointed lawyers – I
take it you don't have someone on retainer yourself? – and
find to my astonishment that the bastards . . . Substitute
'lawyers' for 'bastards', Morino. That they don't get in to
work until ten o'clock. I apologize for disturbing you. Were
you asleep?'

G: What do you think?

z: It's too early to think. I'm just doing my job, that's all. At least
I'm awake, unlike those lawyers. Maybe a coffee would help.
If anyone's open at this hour. There's a place I went to earlier,
down by the station, but . . .

G: Alberto's, on the corner where we met the other day. He's
open as soon as it's light. He makes no money to speak of till
mid-morning, but that's the way Alberto is. If he isn't working, he's fretting.

z: Got that, Dario? I'll have it strong and short, in fact make it a
double. And you?

G: The same. Why's he taking notes?

Z: That's his job. OK, Dario, off you go. No, leave the gun here. If Signor Faigano's right, you won't have any trouble getting served. Oh, for Christ's sake, Morino, you're not writing all this down, are you? This isn't part of the interrogation, you idiot.

Z: For Christ's sake, Morino, why aren't you writing this down? That's your job, you idiot. Don't tempt me, Morino, I've had a hard night, just like Signor Faigano. Did you like the music we laid on, by the way?

G: It was all right. But we've got better stuff at home. My niece Lisa knows someone in Latin America who sends her tapes of the real thing, not these tame commercial groups.

Z: Your niece has good stuff, all right.

G: Meaning what?

Z: Speaking of her friend in Peru, she told me that she'd had to interrupt a chess game they were having the evening of the *festa* because you needed to make an urgent telephone call to Aldo Vincenzo. Oh, you don't want to talk about that without your . . . I quite understand. No problem.

Z: I've been talking to Minot.

G: Who?

Z: What the hell's his real name? Thank you, Morino. Signor Piumatti, popularly known as Minot, seemed convinced that you and your brother would give him the alibi he so desperately needs in the Gallizio case. Which would be a problem for me.

G: A problem? Why?

Z: Because this Minot is my principal suspect in the Vincenzo case. The problem is that I have no substantive evidence. It's all a matter of circumstantial detail, a chain of connections and inferences. And, like any chain, it's only as strong as its weakest link.

G: Meaning?

Z: The alibi I just mentioned. If Minot was out after truffles with you two the night Bruno Gallizio was killed, you see, then he can't have killed Gallizio and planted the knife smeared with Aldo Vincenzo's blood at the house. In which case there's no proof that he killed Vincenzo either, and I'm back at square one.

G: That phone call.

Z: Yes?

G: I did make it.

Z: To Aldo Vincenzo?

G: Yes.

Z: A few hours before he was killed.

G: I didn't know he was going to be killed.

Z: Of course not. But it was very late at night, and you'd both been at the *festa* earlier. Why didn't you tell him whatever it was then?

G: Do you have children, *dottore*?

Z: Two, as it happens.

G: A boy and a girl?

Z: How did you guess? And you, Signor Faigano?

G: I've never had this great responsibility. But my brother . . . To me, Lisa's like the ghost of some child I never had. I'm sorry, this sounds crazy.

z: Not at all. I understand exactly what you mean. Unborn children are as real as the dead, after all. Or as unreal.

G: So when I heard that Vincenzo wanted that son of his to marry Lisa, I . . . Maurizio was calmer than me – how strange! He said there was nothing in it, that it was not like the old days any more, when a man could just . . . When he had this power to . . .

z: But you were not so sure.

G: He was right, of course. I knew that. But when Vincenzo started shouting at his son that evening across the table, calling him impotent and I don't know what else besides, and then dragged Lisa's name into it . . .

z: What did he say?

G: If you're that interested, you can find out from other people. There were plenty of them there, the whole village. It was about breaking a woman, the way you break a horse. I didn't say anything at the time. It would only have drawn attention to his insults, and he would have repeated them still louder. But as soon as I got home I called him up and told him that if he ever mentioned my niece's name in that way again . . .

z: You'd kill him. Good for you. I'd have done the same.

G: I didn't say that.

z: It doesn't matter. Now about this alibi. Are you prepared to swear in court that you were with Minot on the night Beppe Gallizio died? I need to know, you see, before I decide what to do next. God, this coffee certainly hit the spot. Careful with that gun, Dario. There's one more thing you should know before you answer, Signor Faigano. After I'm finished with you, I'm going to have your brother up here and put exactly the same question to him. If your stories don't match, of course, then that's the end of that. You'll both be entirely discredited as witnesses and will have no influence whatsoever on future developments. Just a thought.

G: There's a problem.

Z: (grunt)

G: I need to talk to Maurizio.

Z: First it's a lawyer you want, now it's your brother. Maybe I should just have Dario take you downstairs and beat the shit out of you. Delete that, Morino. Dario, as you were. Very well, Signor Faigano, what do you need to talk to your beloved brother about?

G: It's only fair. He's in it as much as me.

Z: In what?

G: I can't tell you until I've talked to Maurizio.

Z: Or maybe I'll take care of it myself. Why should Dario have all the fun? Have we got any rubber truncheons, Morino? All right, get the little bastard up here. Jesus Christ, I can remember when interrogations used to be run by the police officer in charge. Now it's like room service. Give me this, bring me that, and where's the drink I ordered?

As above, plus Faigano, Maurizio Ernesto.

Z: Take off those cuffs and sit him down here. All right, Signor Gianni, he's all yours.

G: It's about Minot.

M: (gesture)

G: That alibi for the night Gallizio died. The *dottore* wants to know if we will support it in court. He thinks Minot is responsible for that murder and the other two as well, but he can't arrest him if we say we were out with him after truffles when Bruno was shot.

M: (gesture)

G: (shrug)

M: (shrug)

G: We're prepared to answer your question, *dottore*. But there's a complication we want you to know about. Minot has had a hard life in many ways. He's never really been accepted, you understand what I mean? As a result, he can be extremely vindictive on occasion. This might be one of them.

Z: Don't worry, I can look after myself.

M: But what about us?

G: He won't like us if we withdraw his alibi. He'll probably tell you a pack of lies about us to get even. That's the only reason we hesitated about cooperating.

Z: I'm used to dealing with lies. But why did you agree to perjure yourselves in the first place?

M: We didn't.

G: We never swore an oath that this was true. We never even had any dealings with the police until you showed up. We were just doing a favour for a neighbour, that's all.

Z: Putting yourself at risk with the law, and all out of the kindness of your hearts? That's quite a favour.

G: Well, he sort of made a threat, too.

M: Not really a threat, but . . .

Z: What did he say?

G: He said he'd found some evidence connected to the Vincenzo case which could look bad for me, and that as former partisans we should all stick together.

Z: You fought together?

M: That was long ago.

G: Not for Minot. It was the only time he's ever really been accepted, you see.

Z: Did he tell you what this supposed evidence was?

G: A button.

Z: That's all?

G: From one of my jackets.

Z: What about it?

M: He said he'd found it near the spot where Vincenzo was killed.

Z: And what was he doing there?

G: He didn't say.

Z: Did he show you the button?

G: No. He just mentioned it in passing, as though it wasn't important. It was just a hint, not a threat.

Z: Have you lost a button recently?

G: There's no woman to take care of us any more, except young Lisa, and she's too modern to know anything about sewing. I've got a lot of missing buttons. What does that prove?

Z: Nothing. Even if Minot does have a button to show me, and we could match it to your jacket, it doesn't amount to evidence of anything. Minot does deliveries and other work for you on a regular basis, so I've been told. He could have picked up one of your stray buttons, or even snipped it off. There's nothing to tie it to the Vincenzo murder.

M: That's what I thought. But Gianni said, 'If the police drag us into this, we'll never hear the end of it, and people will say there's no smoke without fire. Better to agree to what Minot wants.' And I saw what he meant. We didn't know we would be dealing with a man like you, you see. Most of the cops round here are ignorant arseholes.

z: Delete that reference, Morino. So do I understand that you unreservedly withdraw the story that you were out with Minot the night Beppe Gallizio died?

g: (nod)

z: Say it, please.

m: Yes, we do.

g: That's right, we do.

z: So what *were* you doing?

m: Watching television.

z: Was your daughter there?

m: She was staying with her aunt. Her school's here in Alba, so she can go straight there on Friday, help us out at the Saturday market, then come home after school on Monday. I'd like to telephone her, by the way, to let her know that everything's all right.

z: That can be arranged. Well, I do believe we're finally getting somewhere. I'm afraid I'm going to have to detain you for a little longer, until I've had a chance to interview Minot again. After that, the situation should sort itself out quite quickly. Take them down, Dario. Oh, and turn off the music. Apparently it's just making us look bad. That'll do, Morino. Save your wrist for our next client.

Aurelio Zen's next client was at that moment sitting on the edge of the wooden bench which had also served him as a bed. All things considered, Minot was in good form. The music which had tormented him all night had abruptly ceased, and the rest he could easily live with. Indeed, it was even to his taste: bare, spartan, unfussy and impersonal.

Even the dimensions suited him. The house he had inherited from his mother was much too large for his needs, and he felt its size and scope not as a liberation, full of potential, but as a lack – of security, of controllable space. He had attempted to compensate for this by using just two rooms, the kitchen and the *sala* next door, but he was always aware of the rest of the house spreading its wings around him like the night sky, cold and dark and uncontainable.

By contrast, the cell they'd put him in was perfect. Already it had taken on the reassuring smell of his body, as close-fitting and homely as another set of clothes. Minot's reluctance to wash himself or his garments was a staple joke in the local community, but when he overheard such comments – which was rarely, for people had learned to be guarded in his presence – he was not offended. His habits in the matter of personal hygiene had nothing to do with slovenliness or indifference. On the contrary, they were deliberate. Without those intimate odours to prompt him, he would have lost track of who he was.

And who was he? 'An incest bastard', the cop from Rome had said. Minot had gone for him then, riding a sudden surge of the energy which came to him at times, investing him as though with a halo of *corpo santo*, the fabled fire of Saint Elmo sometimes seen at the height of great storms at sea. His own storms, though as fierce, were no longer lasting than those of the physical world. Now, seated in his homely cell, he could calmly review what had happened, and make his plans accordingly.

During his brief fit, he had tried to assault the policeman with a stool before two witnesses, both cops themselves. They could put him away for months before the case even came to trial, and then for at least a year or two after that. More to the point, he would have no chance to return to the house and conceal or destroy the evidence stored in his fridge. If that came to light, it was all over.

And if he went to prison, it would. For years the villagers had speculated about Minot's character, beliefs and ancestry, and always failed to pin him down. Somewhere in the house, they would argue, the key to the mystery must lie hidden: a set of documents, a photograph album, a bundle of letters. Some of the bolder ones would find their way in and search the place. They wouldn't find what they were looking for, but they would find what was there.

The cosy security of his cell was therefore an illusion. His first priority was to obtain his release, and to do that he would have to make a deal. The problem was that this Aurelio Zen was as much an unknown and perhaps unknowable quantity to Minot as he himself was to his neighbours. In a way, they made a pair.

Minot smiled, instinctively covering his mouth, although he was alone and unobserved. That was the line to take, he realized. This Zen was not interested in the deaths of Gallizio and Scorrone. He had made it clear that the only thing he was concerned with was the Vincenzo case. That was what he had been sent up from Rome to solve. Once he had done so, he could go home, leaving the local authorities to mop up after him. Minot could deal with them, he felt sure. It was just a question of easing this unpredictable outsider out of the picture.

So when the patrolman named Dario appeared to escort him upstairs, Minot was feeling reasonably confident. This feeling strengthened when he was ushered into the room upstairs. One glance revealed that Aurelio Zen was tired – not just from lack of sleep, like Minot himself, but tired of the case, of his colleagues, of the town, and perhaps of life itself. He has other things on his mind, thought Minot, more important things. All he wants is a quick and tidy solution to this mess he finds himself in, and I can give it to him.

This sense of ease and assurance was soon put to the test, however.

'The Faigano brothers have changed their minds,' Zen announced once Minot was installed on the penitential stool.

'About what?'

'About your alibi for the Gallizio murder.'

Minot managed a puzzled smile.

'About *theirs*, you mean.'

Zen shrugged wearily.

'The alibi works both ways, of course. But they claim that it was you who asked them to provide it, and that you did so with menaces.'

This was a shock. Minot had expected Gianni and Maurizio to stick to the story that the alibi had been cooked up for their mutual convenience, to avoid unnecessary interference from the authorities. Instead, they had done the one thing he had never anticipated, something explicitly forbidden by the code he had invoked in discussing the matter with them. They had told their mutual enemy the truth.

Or rather, they had told him what they believed to be the truth. There was a difference, and a moment later Minot realized that he was free to take advantage of it, now that the brothers had by their own treachery renounced the freemasonry of the former *partigiani*.

'Menaces?' he laughed. 'What could I do against two of them, both bigger than me?'

Aurelio Zen did not answer immediately. He was eyeing Minot in a way the latter found distinctly disquieting. Then he looked away at the window. The darkness outside had given way to a limp, unhealthy light which clung to every surface like some greasy substance strained through a piece of dirty muslin.

'They said you tried to blackmail them with some story about a button,' Aurelio Zen replied, with an ostentatious yawn.

'How do you mean?'

'A button that you supposedly found, supposedly at the scene of the crime, and which supposedly belonged to a jacket supposedly owned by Gianni Faigano.'

'That's ridiculous.'

'I know,' said Zen. 'I told them so. It's all hearsay, and from someone who – if you'll excuse me saying so – doesn't exactly command huge respect in the community.'

This was the crux. Minot consulted his inner voices. 'Do it!' they said. As always, he obeyed.

'Supposing it wasn't a button?'

Aurelio Zen emitted another massive yawn.

'I don't really give a damn what it was you told them, Minot. I'm more interested in why you tried to extort an alibi for yourself in the Gallizio affair.'

'But I didn't. It was Gianni and Maurizio who asked me to give them one.'

'That's not what they say. And, as you just pointed out, there are two of them. Besides, how could they have come up with this story about the button unless you tried to pressure them?'

'That's obvious. They suspected that I had some evidence against them, but they didn't know what it was. So to cover themselves, they invented this story about the button. I'm afraid you've been misled, *dottore*. This has nothing to do with the case you're investigating. It's a personal matter between me and the Faigano brothers.'

'You mean I don't come into it?' murmured Zen.

Minot looked at him with an almost solicitous air.

'Of course you do, *dottore*! Without you, I can't do a thing.'

He gave Zen a crafty glance.

'But without me, neither can you.'

Catching the incredulous gaze of the official taking notes, Zen quickly stood up, as though to assert his authority.

'Allow me to remind you that you are in detention pending being charged with assault on a police officer, Minot.'

'I didn't lay a finger on you, *dottore*. You were much too quick for me.'

'It's the intent that counts.'

'But what if my intent has changed? Supposing that I intend to cooperate fully with your investigation into the murder of Aldo Vincenzo, and that I'm the one person who can provide proof that will stand up in court. Would that be enough to get the charges against me revoked?'

Aurelio Zen stared at him.

'You were right. You don't need a lawyer.'

Minot fought to contain his exultant emotion.

'So you agree?'

'Agree to what?'

Minot regarded him fixedly.

'I give you conclusive evidence of the killer's identity. In return, you drop all charges and release me unconditionally.'

Zen snorted.

'It'll take more than a stray button to get anyone convicted, Minot. And to get you released.'

'There *is* more.'

'What?'

Minot smiled conspiratorially.

'Ah, well, that would be telling, wouldn't it? And I can't very well do that until I know that you're going to keep your end of the bargain.'

The plain-clothed cop shifted awkwardly in his chair.

'Listen, *capo*,' he said, 'I don't think you should be . . .'

'That'll do, Morino.'

Zen turned to Minot.

'All right, so what do you propose? You can't expect an unconditional discharge until I can evaluate what you're offering in return, and you're apparently not prepared to reveal that until I've handed over the papers, signed and sealed. In short, you don't trust me and I don't trust you.'

Minot nodded slyly.

'So we need to find a third party. That's what we do in the

truffle business when we're dealing with some outsider, use a go-between we can both trust.'

'You mean a lawyer?'

Minot laughed.

'Someone we could trust, I said!'

'Do you know someone?'

'Plenty of people, *dottore*, but you don't know them. So let's look at it the other way round. Can you think of someone round here that you trust? The chances are that I'll know them, too, and perhaps we can do business.'

Zen considered a minute.

'I suppose there's Lucchese . . .'

Minot glanced at him in surprise.

'You know him? Perfect.'

'This is highly irregular, *capo*!' protested Morino.

'Shut up,' Zen told him, lifting the phone. 'And strike all references to a deal from the record. Hello? Ah, good morning, *principe*. This is Aurelio Zen.'

Minot did not bother to listen to the ensuing one-sided conversation, preoccupied as he was with reviewing his own position. As always, he had acted instinctively. That was his great strength. Plans that were not made could not be exposed later. It was just a question of checking that his spontaneous words and actions were consistent with the apparent facts of the case. He did, and they were.

'. . . take receipt of the item and of the papers which I will give you,' Zen was saying into the phone. 'I will then examine the former and, if satisfied, authorize you to release the latter to the said third party. Agreed? Very good.'

He hung up and looked at Minot.

'Lucchese agrees. Where is the evidence in question?'

'At my house. I'll go and pick it up, then bring the evidence back to the Palazzo Lucchese in person.'

'Don't trust him, *capo*!' Morino burst out. 'I'll take a couple of men and go over the place with a fine-tooth comb. Whatever's there, we'll find it!'

Knowing what was at stake, it took Minot all his nerve to smile disdainfully.

'I could have it on me right now and you'd never find it,' he replied in a matter-of-fact tone.

Zen shot him a keen look.

'It's small enough to conceal, then?'

Minot smiled.

'You could hide it under one finger. Or on it, for that matter.'

'A ring?' snapped Zen. 'Without continuity of evidence, that's no more use than your famous button!'

Minot stood up and stretched lazily.

'What have you got to lose, *dottore*? If you don't like the product, you don't have to go through with the deal. But you will, I promise you that. Just get the papers for my release written up. We've wasted enough time as it is.'

As ten o'clock sounded, at various intervals and pitches from bell towers all over town, Aurelio Zen mounted the steps of the Palazzo Lucchese and pushed the recessed brass bell beside the door on the first floor. He rang five times, ever more lengthily, then sat down on one of the shallow stone steps leading up to the next floor and lit a cigarette.

The bells ceased and silence fell. Somewhere inside the building, Zen could now make out a brittle tinkling sound he associated with adjacent wineglasses in the sink of his apartment back in Rome when the neighbouring refrigerator rattled into action. At length another sound intervened: a dull, regular clumping, as if someone were pounding with a hammer. It was coming, he realized, from the steps below. A few moments later an elderly woman emerged, formidably breathless, on the landing. She turned on Zen a face so creased and contoured that it could have been classified as an historic site, produced a large key from her dauntingly capacious handbag and set about unlocking the front door.

'Good morning,' said Zen.

Much to his surprise, the crone responded with a complacent smile. Dear God, he thought, she used to be a beauty.

'I'm here to see Prince Lucchese,' he continued, standing up. 'My name's Aurelio Zen. He's expecting me.'

The woman sighed and made a compendious gesture suggesting that the prince was a busy man, even slightly eccentric in his way, and not to be held to prior appointments or arrangements; that she herself had been battling with this situation for longer than she cared to remember; and that if Zen had just arrived, he should join the queue.

'Wait here,' she told him. 'I'll see what I can do.'

The door closed behind her. Zen resumed his seat and smoked quietly for some time. Eventually the door opened again and a withered hand waved impatiently.

'The prince will see you now.'

Inside, the sense of spacious gloom and dilapidated gentility was unchanged, like a museum exhibit preserved under a bell jar. The old woman indicated a door to the left at the end of the hall.

'In there.'

It was yet a different room from his previous visits, as though the prince had decided to give Zen a gradual guided tour of the palace. This one was a sort of antechamber, as long and narrow as a corridor, but with a hexagonal bay at the far end. The walls were bare, the ceiling high. A small teak table, an embroidered sofa and a darkened cane chair were the only furnishings. Lucchese was sitting in the latter, resplendently casual in the now-familiar silk dressing-gown.

'Ah, there you are!' exclaimed Lucchese in a tone of irritation. 'I almost changed my mind about this business after speaking to you. My upbringing does not permit me to display spontaneous emotion, but when you rang earlier, I was working on the allemande from Bach's D major partita. Do you know Wanda Landowska's famous *mot* on the subject? She'd had an argument with another musician over stylistic issues. "Very well," was her parting shot, "you play Bach your way and I'll play him his way!" This morning, for the first time, I felt I was playing Bach his way, and then the phone rings . . .'

A gesture.

'What did you make of Arianna?'

'The cleaning lady?'

'My mother, actually.'

Zen gulped.

'I didn't realize . . .'

'My real reason for agreeing to see you,' the prince continued evenly, 'has nothing to do with this hand-over you called about. For various reasons, not least a demand I received this morning from the electricity company, leads me to think that the moment has come for me to present my bill. Before doing so, however, we need to conclude two pieces of outstanding business. The first concerns your recent tendency to somnambulism. What time is this Minot person arriving with the "item" you wish to appraise?'

Zen snapped his fingers apart and together again.

'An hour? Maybe less.'

'In that case, we're going to have to deal with this more peremptorily than I would ideally wish,' Lucchese replied, flexing his own fingers with a loud detonation of joints, which apparently caused him no discomfort. 'My preliminary analysis has led me to the conclusion that you have recently suffered the loss – or, what is almost more disturbing, the unexpected re-appearance – of a child, sibling or parent. Is this in fact the case?'

Zen nodded.

'Which?' demanded Lucchese.

'All three.'

The prince stared at him in disbelief.

'I recently discovered that my mother's husband was not in fact my father,' Zen explained. 'Also that I have a half-sister living in Naples.'

'That's two,' Lucchese prompted him in a deliberately unempathetic tone.

Zen gazed down at the puddle of unclean light forming on the floorboards as the sun grazed up against the cloud cover outside.

'A former girlfriend of mine also informed me that she was pregnant, and that I was the father. She subsequently announced that she had had an abortion. In which case, I have lost a child as well.'

Lucchese's mask of professional indifference withered and crisped like a letter thrown on a fire. He rose and embraced Zen warmly, patting his back.

'In a case like this, *caro dottore*, it's not a question of trying to work out why you were sleepwalking, but of asking ourselves why you didn't throw yourself off the nearest high building! You must have the constitution of a rock.'

211

Unseen, Zen smiled wearily.

'Several times, I thought I might be going mad.'

'A sure sign that you weren't.'

Lucchese released him and reached into his pocket for some papers which he shuffled about nervously.

'I needed to get that straight, you see, because of the second piece of business I mentioned. I refer, of course, to the results on those DNA tests you wanted done. They arrived this morning.'

Zen stared at him as though in terror.

'So soon? But I thought . . .'

'My brother runs the lab in Turin which processes these things. I arranged for your samples to be moved to the top of the list.'

'And what . . .? That's to say, are we . . .?'

Lucchese did not reply. Zen sighed.

'It's bad, then.'

'That depends. It's certainly definitive. I talked to my brother in person this morning, and he made that absolutely clear. So I wanted to make sure that you are aware of the potential consequences, psychological and otherwise, and to assure myself that you are strong enough to cope with it.'

Zen stared at him bleakly.

'I can cope with anything. It's my speciality.'

The prince resumed his seat, looking over the papers in his hands.

'Nevertheless, let's just run over the background story. You say this woman Carla approached you at your hotel, claiming to be your daughter. Do you have any reason to believe her?'

'I had an affair with her mother once, long ago. In Milan,' he added, as though this explained everything.

'You realize that if she were proven to be your daughter, you would have to take on various legal and financial responsibilities that might well be onerous?'

Zen shrugged.

'I just want to know the truth.'

Lucchese gave him a smile spiced with a grain of contempt.

'So, in theory, anyone could just walk up to you in a public place, having done a little research on your former mistresses, and claim to be your love child?'

Zen turned away to the window. Down in the Via Maestra, a host of strangers passed to and fro in eager intent or sociable procrastination.

'I'm no more credulous than the next man,' he said. 'But I suppose that having just lost Carlo . . .'

'Who?'

'That's what I decided to call the child Tania was carrying. I decided that it was a boy, and I named him Carlo. So when a young woman named Carla appeared, claiming to be my daughter . . .'

He swung around to confront Lucchese.

'But my feelings are not important, *principe*. If Carla Arduini is my daughter, I'll do the right thing by her, whatever it may cost me.'

Lucchese rose to his feet and made a slightly ironic bow.

'Your words do you credit, *dottore*. But, as it happens, you can relax. The tests carried out by my brother reveal beyond a shadow of a doubt that this Arduini woman is not related to you in any way whatsoever.'

Zen gazed at him in silence.

'Are you sure?'

'Positive.'

He held out the papers to Zen.

'It's all here, not that it will make any sense to you – or to me, for that matter. But my brother has assured me that it's absolutely conclusive. Despite her impressive musical expertise, this Arduini woman is clearly a common gold-digger, out for what she can get. Luckily you have the might of science on your side, *dottore*. Tell her to try her luck elsewhere, or sue her for slander if you want. The courts will back you all the way.'

Zen took the papers and glanced at them abstractedly.

'Thank you,' he mumbled.

Lucchese frowned.

'Aren't you pleased?'

'I suppose so. It's just a shock, that's all. I'd assumed . . .'

'In the past, lots of men have been caught that way! But thanks to the miracles of modern technology, we can now get at the truth. Which in this case turns out to be a lie.'

The doorbell sounded. Lucchese rose and left the room. Zen subsided on to the sofa and sat looking over the results of the DNA tests. At length the prince reappeared.

'Minot has returned,' he announced. 'This is the item which he referred to. You have five minutes to examine it, following which you may question him if you wish. The item itself will remain in my keeping for the meantime. May I have the papers which you are offering in exchange, by the way?'

Zen produced a long brown envelope from his coat pocket and handed it over. Lucchese perused the contents briefly, then passed Zen a crumpled piece of cheap paper which felt empty. He opened it gingerly, disclosing a sliver of what might have been plastic, translucent except for a brownish smear on one side.

'What is it?' he asked.

'A fingernail, by the look of it,' the prince remarked, inspecting the object. 'From a male adult, in his fifties at least, used to manual work, and not overly fastidious about personal cleanliness. Oh, and he uses scissors rather than clippers to trim his nails, but you'd spotted that, of course!'

Zen handed the object back to Lucchese.

'Kindly send Minot in here,' he said.

Borrowing the tactics once used by Mussolini at his desk in the ex-Venetian embassy in Rome, Zen forced Minot to traverse the long distance from the door, hat in hand, before deigning to acknowledge his existence with an imperious glare.

'*E allora?*' he barked, once Minot had come to rest before him. 'A fingernail. So what?'

Minot smiled.

'So whose, you mean.'

Zen stared up at him from the cane chair which Lucchese had occupied earlier.

'Look, Minot, I know you're an unsophisticated fellow, but evidence is only admissible in law if there's an unbroken sequence of links – each duly witnessed and notarized – leading back to the scene of the crime. Some broken fingernail, whatever its provenance, is of no more use to me than that button we were talking about earlier.'

Having brushed the seat of his trousers in a perfunctory way, Minot perched on the edge of the embroidered sofa and leant forward. Despite that symbolic gesture towards the prince's furnishings, he did not seem overawed by his surroundings, still less by Zen's presence.

'Let me make an admission, *dottore*,' he whispered in a voice which was barely audible even to Zen.

'Get on with it!'

Minot looked from one side of the space to the other, as if checking that they were alone. Satisfied, he leant still closer to Zen.

'Aldo's body wasn't discovered by that police dog, as everyone thinks.'

Zen stared at him.

'It was discovered by me,' Minot went on. 'I was trespassing on the Vincenzo's property the morning after the *festa*, after some truffles I thought might be hiding in a bank at one end of the vineyard. Instead, I found Aldo.'

He made a large gesture.

'Imagine how it feels, coming on something like that with no warning, and with the mist so thick you can barely see where you're going! At that moment I became a child again.'

'How do you mean?'

Minot looked at him.

'Children notice what's close to them, what's near enough to touch and hug and hold. That's what I did then. I looked at the earth at my feet, so as not to have to look at that obscene apparition! There was something glinting there, as the light caught it. I picked it up and put it in my pocket as a kind of talisman against the horror.'

He leant back and raised his voice to a normal level.

'A couple of days later I was over at the Faigano house, helping them with some work, and I noticed that Gianni was missing a fingernail from the index of his right hand. I thought no more about it at the time, but later I remembered the thing I'd found beside Aldo's body, and realized that it was a fingernail. A fingernail with blood on it.'

Zen shrugged.

'If you tear a nail, it bleeds.'

'But the blood on this nail is on the outside, too, *dottore*. What if it's not Gianni's?'

The two men confronted each other in silence.

'I can't proceed on the basis of your word, Minot.'

'Of course not. But you have ways of finding out the truth about these things. You did it with the knife they found at Beppe's house. You can do it with the evidence I'm offering. I'm just telling you in advance that what you'll find is that the nail is Gianni's and the blood Aldo's.'

Zen looked at him with a curious, glazed expression.

'So they did it?' he asked.

Minot laughed apologetically, as though not wanting to offend the outsider who had only now realized the self-evident truth.

'Of course! Everyone knows that.'

Aurelio Zen had already entered the revolving door of the Alba Palace Hotel when he noticed Carla Arduini slipping into a compartment on the other side, going out. He glanced at her, and she at him, and he gestured furiously, pushing the door around so hard that he found himself back outside again before he could stop. Carla had also made the complete circuit, no doubt assuming that he would have exited, so the situation ended as it had begun – her inside, him out, and the door still between them. Zen held up his hand, indicating that she should stay where she was, and then plunged back into the roundabout.

'Carla!' he exclaimed awkwardly, when they were finally face to face.

'I was just on my way to mass. I haven't been for ages, but the cathedral is supposed to be very beautiful, and . . .'

'Meet me afterwards, in the bar immediately to the left as you leave the church,' Zen instructed her, as though giving operational instructions to a subordinate. 'I have something to tell you.'

Carla inspected his expression for a moment, with what results remained unclear.

'Very well. In about an hour, then.'

She strode off into the lively, impersonal bustle of the streets, and Zen went up to his room. He had felt the need for a break before resuming his interrogation of the Faigano brothers, but it had never occurred to him that he would meet Carla Arduini. The news he was going to have to break to her lodged in his chest like the silver spike with which Lucchese had punctured his late cousin's heart.

Zen showered, shaved and changed into clean clothes, then

hastened back outside. The debilitated sunlight had finally broken through the clouds, and although the air was crisp and cool the scene might have suggested summer but for the deep shadows which trenched the street, revealing the fraud. Zen wandered through the purposeful crowds, deferring to their sense of urgency and competence. They all looked as though they knew exactly where they were going and what they were going to do when they got there. By contrast, Zen felt as insubstantial as a somnambulist.

When he reached the bar, there were still fifteen minutes or so left before Carla emerged from the cathedral. Fifteen minutes for him to decide how to express himself, how to phrase the announcement that would put an end to all her hopes. 'I'm afraid I have some bad news . . .' No, that sounded like a policeman addressing the nearest and dearest of the deceased. 'The results of the blood tests we had done yesterday prove conclusively that . . .' Too bureaucratic. 'I would have been proud to have you as a daughter, but unfortunately . . .' Patronizing bastard!

His *cappuccino* cooled and subsided into an unappetizing beige puddle on the counter before him, untouched. Seemingly offended, the barman asked if there was something wrong with it. Zen just shook his head. The next thing he knew, the bells of the cathedral had begun their pagan clamour and the faithful were emerging, blinking, into the sunlight of the piazza. A head taller than the rest of the predominantly menopausal worshippers, Carla was easy to spot.

'How was it?' he asked mindlessly, as she took a place beside him at the bar.

'It was the mass,' she replied. 'What did you expect?'

She ordered an orange soda from the barman and turned to Zen with an unsympathetic eye.

'Well?' she enquired pointedly.

'What? Oh, well, it's nothing really. It's just . . .'

He broke off.

'You see, I'm investigating the Vincenzo case, as you know, and . . . Well, it's beginning to look as though an arrest is imminent. Probably two, in fact. They're local and have a teenage daughter who lives with them. The press has gone quiet about the case recently, for lack of new developments, but when this gets out, they're going to be back in force. I don't want the girl to be hounded, but there's nothing I can do officially. So I was just wondering whether by any chance you might know someone in Turin who has a spare room where she could hide out.'

'For how long?'

'Just a few days, a week at most. Until the media lose interest again. It won't take long.'

Carla Arduini finished her drink and set the glass down with a decisive clack.

'She can stay with me. I'm going back today anyway.'

Zen grasped her arm.

'You're leaving?'

She shrugged dismissively.

'Why not? There doesn't seem much point in staying here, does there? I did what I came to do, or rather failed to do it. It was a silly idea anyway. It's time to put it behind me and get on with my life.'

Now she was avoiding his eyes, looking studiously out of the window at the passers-by in the piazza. Zen took a deep breath.

'About that blood test . . .'

Carla laughed briefly.

'Oh, that! Send me the results when you get them. It'll take months, probably. Anyway, it's of no importance.'

Zen removed his hand from her arm.

'Of no importance? But I thought . . .'

'What did you think?'

'I thought . . .' He paused lamely. 'I thought it was.'

'I used to think so, too, but I've changed my mind. Now it just seems absurd. I mean, here am I, spending a fortune staying for a week at a hotel in a dreary provincial town, and all for what? Because my mother told me a story about having slept with some policeman the year before I was born!'

She sniffed scornfully.

'I wasn't going to tell you this, but when I started looking into this business, I kept running into the names of men my mother had slept with in the years before I was born – and after, for that matter. Not that I blame her for that! God knows, she had little enough else in the way of pleasure. But the chances of you being my real father, Dottor Zen, are frankly next to nothing. She couldn't even get the story straight herself towards the end. Half the time it was you, and half the time it was Paolo or Piero or Pietro. But I had no way of tracing them, so when you showed up here . . .'

She took a two-thousand lire note out of her purse and dropped it on the bar.

'Send this Lisa to the hotel. I'll be glad to take care of her for you. Consider it a way of apologizing for the distress I've caused you. And don't worry, I won't bother you again.'

With a vague, mislaid smile, she turned and walked out.

'Carla! Wait!'

He caught up with her in the piazza.

'Listen, I . . .'

'Look, *dottore*, I don't want to seem rude, but will you please leave me alone? Every time I see you, I'm reminded of what a fool I've made of myself. In a few hours I'll be gone, and I promise that you'll never hear from me again. All right?'

'No! No, it's not all right!'

She looked at him with astonishment.

'And just what is that supposed to mean?' she demanded angrily.

They were speaking so animatedly that a small crowd had formed around them, but Zen had eyes for no one but Carla Arduini.

'You didn't make a fool of yourself,' he said.

She smiled scornfully.

'Very kind, I'm sure. I happen to disagree.'

'Those tests you mentioned? They're already complete.'

'That's impossible.'

'Lucchese's brother runs the clinic where they're done. He put

220

our samples to the top of the pile and faxed the results through this morning. I've seen them, Carla. I'll show them to you if you want, not that they'll make any sense to you, or to me for that matter. But the prince explained them all to me, and the result is perfectly clear.'

They stared at each other with silent intensity.

'Well?' Carla burst out at last.

'I'm afraid it may be bad news. But there's nothing I can do about it.'

'Tell me!'

Zen sighed and looked away.

'The tests prove beyond a shadow of a doubt that you are indeed my daughter.'

Carla Arduini took a step back.

'You're joking.'

'Do you think I would joke about something as important as this?'

He shook his head sadly.

'You're stuck with me, Carla. I may not be much of a father, but you'll have to make the best of it, because I'm the only one you'll ever have.'

There was a seemingly endless silence. Then Carla Arduini rushed at Zen and flung her arms around his neck.

'Daddy!'

'It wasn't in vain!' he murmured in her ear. 'Everything your mother went through, everything you've been through. None of it was in vain.'

She broke the embrace and stepped back, biting her lip.

'I'd given up hope.'

'So had I.'

A ripple of polite applause recalled them to the realities of the situation. The assembled onlookers beamed their good wishes and congratulations, then tactfully dispersed.

'Now then!' said Zen decisively. 'I've still got work to do, but I think this calls for a glass of *spumante*, don't you?'

'It won't work,' said Tullio Legna, chopping his right hand through the air as though to finish off this sickly idea once and for all.

Zen shrugged.

'It might. And if it doesn't, we still have the evidence to fall back on. But that will take longer. I think we should go in for the kill.'

'You really believe the evidence will stand up?'

'Why not? Minot may be an odd type in many ways, but he's not stupid. He knows we can prove or disprove his assertions, and he knows we will. He has nothing to gain by lying, and everything to lose.'

The Alba police chief raised his eyebrows and emitted an expressive sigh.

'He's not the only one, *dottore!*'

Zen frowned.

'What do you mean?'

'Nanni Morino gave me an account of the methods you've been using so far,' Legna continued in a bureaucratic tone. 'I must say that I find them highly irregular, to say the least. I'm not trying to tell you how to do your job, Dottor Zen. Maybe your approach is standard procedure at Criminalpol. I don't know anything about that. All I know is that you've been interviewing individuals without a lawyer present, telling each a different story, and then doing a deal with one of them in exchange for a piece of supposed evidence whose value and authenticity we have had no chance to evaluate. And now you tell me that you're going to invent a pack of lies and use them to get a confession out of someone who wasn't even a suspect until now!'

'He wasn't, was he? Which is somewhat surprising, given the

fact that he had both a strong motive and a perfect opportunity.'

'I wasn't aware of that!' Tullio Legna insisted with undisguised anger.

'Maybe that's why I'm handling this case and not you, Dottor Legna,' remarked Zen sweetly.

He turned to Dario.

'Go and find Morino, then bring the Faigano brothers up here.'

The patrolman glanced at Tullio Legna, who stalked out of the room. Dario followed. Left alone, Zen wandered over to the window, collecting his thoughts for the coming performance. He had no doubts about the course he was taking. The encounter with Carla, and its unexpected but wholly logical conclusion, seemed to have clarified his mind like a breeze carrying off mist. He had been sleepwalking for too long. Now he was awake once more, responsible for his actions, and confident about the result.

Nevertheless, despite the bravado with which he had answered Tullio Legna, he was well aware that it could all go very wrong. He felt like a sculptor confronting a block of expensive marble, sheer to all appearances but with a slight internal flaw. If he selected an instrument of the correct size and shape, and applied it with precisely the proper force at exactly the right place, the whole mass would open up and reveal its inner essence to him, and he could finish his work with ease. But if he miscalculated, he would be left with a botched lump of masonry which no amount of subsequent labour could ever repair.

He turned round expectantly as the door opened, but it was only Nanni Morino, shuffling in with his notepad and a sheepish expression.

'Ah, it's you!' Zen remarked coldly. 'I gather you've been ratting on me to the chief.'

'I was just keeping him informed about developments in the case,' Morino replied with righteous embarrassment. 'He has a right to know what's going on in the section under his command.'

'That's all right. In your position, I'd probably have done the same. There's no reason why you should risk your own career just to follow me.'

'On the contrary, *dottore*,' Morino protested, as Dario ushered in the Faigano brothers, 'I'd follow you anywhere!'

In a barely audible undertone, he added, 'If only out of morbid curiosity.'

'Ah, there you are!' Aurelio Zen exclaimed, going round the desk to greet the new arrivals, his right hand held out. With expressions of mild bemusement, both brothers automatically responded. Maurizio's hand was given a perfunctory shake, but Zen grasped Gianni's and brought it up to his face for closer examination.

'One of your nails is missing,' he observed.

Gianni snatched his hand away.

'So?'

'How did it happen?'

'Working the land isn't a desk job,' Gianni returned with a touch of contempt.

'Do you remember the occasion?'

Gianni looked at his brother, frowning.

'It was when we were bottling last year's wine,' Maurizio prompted. 'Don't you remember?'

'Oh, that's right! I'd forgotten.'

'It's common enough round here,' Maurizio explained. 'And that's not counting the ones from the war. The Fascists used to specialize in that, when they ran out of more inventive ideas. They used to do it properly, with pliers. And slowly. Half the men round here are still missing a few. Once the roots get ripped out, the nail never grows back.'

He glanced keenly at Zen, as though suddenly recalling the situation.

'But why are you asking about this?'

For a moment, Aurelio Zen looked puzzled. Then he waved at Nanni Morino, who was assiduously noting all this down.

'Just "morbid curiosity", to quote my colleague. I'll only need to keep you a moment, and then Dario will take you downstairs and do the necessary for your release.'

The brothers glanced at each other.

'Release?' queried Gianni.

'Yes, it's all over. Once I got the confession, of course . . .'

'Minot has confessed?'

Zen nodded briskly.

'And that's why I need your help. It was off the record, you see. No lawyer present, no witnesses, no notes taken. The cunning bastard waited until everyone else had left, and then confessed to the whole thing!'

Zen burst into laughter.

'I've never seen anything quite like it!' he exclaimed in a tone of aggrieved admiration. 'This Minot is certainly quite a character. He even told me why he'd done it, but as a challenge. "Now try and prove it!" he said. "You won't be able to. There isn't a scrap of evidence. You'll never be able to take me to court, much less get a conviction."'

Gianni Faigano nodded sourly.

'That sounds like Minot all right. But where do we come in?'

'Because I accept his challenge, and to win I need some background information.'

'About what?' asked Maurizio.

Zen gave a declamatory sigh.

'When I searched your house yesterday, following your arrest, I noticed an old photograph on display. It was a portrait of Chiara Cravioli, later Signora Vincenzo.'

The silence which followed had a new quality, like a fresh sheet of sandpaper replacing one worn smooth.

'What's that got to do with it?' snapped Gianni.

'Well, you see, Minot claims that she's the reason he murdered Aldo.'

'That's absurd! He didn't even know Chiara!'

Zen gestured for calm.

'One thing at a time, Signor Faigano, if you please. I'm sorry, it's my fault. I'm telling the story back to front. It's been a long night for all of us, and I'm getting confused. Let's begin at the beginning.'

He sat down, looking over some notes scribbled hastily on the back of various envelopes and departmental circulars.

'Yes, here we are. According to Minot, he and this Chiara Cravioli were lovers long ago . . .'

Gianni Faigano took a step forward.

'That's bullshit!'

'Oh!' called Dario from the door.

His weapon was cocked and levelled. Maurizio gripped his brother's arm and drew him back to his place.

'As I was saying,' Zen continued in the same bored tone, 'Minot claims that he and Chiara used to be lovers. In itself, this is of no particular interest. But he also claims that the relationship did not cease once *la Cravioli* married Aldo Vincenzo. In fact, he went on to say, Manlio Vincenzo is not Aldo's son at all, but the fruit of Minot's loins.'

Gianni Faigano stepped forward again, unable to control himself.

'That's a damned lie! A filthy blasphemy!'

Zen gestured helplessly, as though to apologize for an unintentional gaffe.

'I'm only telling you what Minot said. And the reason I'm mentioning it is in the hope that you might be able to corroborate his story. It would give me a motive, you see, which is the one thing I don't have at present. Once I've got that, I'll call a lawyer and formally charge Minot with murder.'

He got to his feet, shaking his head.

'But first I need a credible reason for him to have killed Aldo. If the victim first stole his girlfriend and then claimed Minot's only son as his own, it all makes sense. Even the timing fits in. According to Minot, he'd wanted to get even with Aldo for years, but Chiara had forbidden it. She was apparently a conventional person, in that sense at least, and even though Vincenzo allegedly raped her to force the marriage . . .'

Maurizio grasped his brother's shoulders and held him still.

'. . . Chiara took the view that she was married to him for better or worse, and made Minot swear on the ashes of their youthful love that he would not harm Aldo. So it wasn't until she died that he was able to carry out his long-premeditated revenge.'

Zen clapped his hands together.

'It's a pretty tale, and of course the press will eat it up. "Ex-partisan kills to avenge teenage sweetheart! A love affair that triumphed over death!" But what I need is independent confirmation of this alleged love affair between Minot and Chiara Cravioli. And that's where I was hoping that you might be able to help.'

He gave the Faigano brothers an inane smile. Maurizio glanced hesitantly at his brother.

'I've never heard anything about that,' he said.

'And you, Signor Gianni?' asked Zen.

Gianni Faigano did not reply. He no longer seemed agitated. He stood perfectly still, gazing down at the tiled floor with an air of almost beatific calm, his features relaxed, his bearing simple and natural.

'Presumably one of you knew this Cravioli woman?' Zen went on. 'To keep her photograph in the living room like that, I mean. I didn't notice any other pictures.'

'I knew her,' said Gianni Faigano at length.

'And was she in love with Minot?'

'Of course not! The whole idea's a joke. A sick joke.'

Zen shrugged.

'Minot isn't anyone's idea of Adonis, to be sure, but women can be funny that way. It isn't so much the looks that get to them, I always say, it's the force of personality. And Minot certainly has plenty of that, even now. Forty years ago, I can see him bowling over some impressionable young girl and . . .'

'It's an obscene pack of lies,' Gianni Faigano stated in a quiet, hard tone. 'A total travesty of justice.'

Zen frowned.

'I don't see how justice comes into it. Minot's not even under arrest yet. But since you two apparently can't help me, I'll have to try elsewhere. Somebody must know something. Why would Minot make up a story like that?'

'Because he's a dirty, scheming, treacherous piece of shit!' retorted Maurizio Faigano.

'Possibly, but I still don't see what he hopes to get out of lying about it. Anyway, the local newspaper has been trying to get an interview from me ever since I arrived. This might be the moment to arrange for a non-attributable leak. I'll make sure Minot's story about him and Signora Cravioli gets maximum exposure and hope that something comes of it.'

'You mustn't do that,' Gianni Faigano said with an air of finality.

Zen looked at him oddly.

'I mustn't?' he repeated with a sardonic smile. 'And why not, might I ask?'

For a moment it seemed as if Gianni was not going to answer this question. Then he pushed his shoulders back and looked straight at Zen with an air of renewed resolution.

'Because it would make a mockery of everything.'

'I don't know what that's supposed to mean,' Zen said impatiently. 'In any case, I have no choice. There's a murder to solve, and this is the only way to do it.'

'It's not the only way,' replied Gianni Faigano.

Zen stared at him in silence.

'What would you need to get a proper confession?' Gianni asked. 'Not a teasing perjury like the one Minot tried to make you fall for. I mean something that would stand up in court, and which no one could challenge?'

'Well, we'd need a lawyer to represent the deponent and certify that no improper methods had been used in obtaining the statement . . .'

He waved his hands helplessly.

'But it's no use! Minot will never repeat what he said under those conditions.'

'I'm not talking about Minot,' Gianni Faigano remarked, as though Zen should have grasped this obvious fact.

'Then who?'

Maurizio grabbed hold of his brother once more, but with a desperation which suggested that he knew the effort to be futile. Gianni Faigano brushed him off and turned to Aurelio Zen with a perfectly serene expression.

'I killed Aldo Vincenzo. Get a lawyer up here and I'll tell you the whole story.'

Like some children, the following day was born with a mild, sunny disposition which time merely focused and intensified. The air was still and bright, with just a hint of winter to add some welcome edge, the sky a flawless, bleached blue whose diffident haziness made it seem infinitely distant and desirable.

On such a day, Zen felt, it would be a kind of sacrilege to stay cooped up in Alba, particularly after the spectacular break-through which had crowned his labours and brought his mission to a triumphant conclusion. He therefore arranged for a car to pick him up at his hotel and prepared to perform in person a task he could equally well have accomplished by telephone, or dele-gated, or even neglected.

Before doing so, he called Carla Arduini. Following Zen's dec-laration in the piazza outside the cathedral, her planned return to Turin had been delayed for twenty-four hours, at his expense. At this rate, he explained, outlining the successful conclusion of his investigation, they might even be able to leave together – with or without Lisa Faigano, who had angrily rejected Zen's offer of asylum from the press once she learned that her uncle and father had been arrested for conspiracy to murder Aldo Vincenzo. In the meantime, at any rate, he had an errand to run in the country near Palazzuole. Would Carla care to join him?

Twenty minutes later they were sitting side by side in the back seat of an unmarked police car provided through the offices of Tullio Legna. The only aspect of the situation which troubled Zen's pleasure was that the Alba police chief himself was at the wheel. On the surface, Legna was his usual urbane self, but Zen quickly detected an undercurrent of pique, not to say hostility, in his continual expressions of amazement at the way in which Zen had 'succeeded where all others had failed, and in so short a time, knowing nothing of the people and background involved'.

Despite his conviction that Legna had insisted on acting as chauffeur in order to spy on Zen's last hours in his domain, and possibly even wring some last-minute credit from a casual indiscretion, Zen appeared to take it all in good spirits. He had merely been lucky, he claimed, and sooner or later the truth would have emerged anyway. But when they reached the gates to the Vincenzo property, he told Legna to pull up and let them out.

'My daughter and I will walk the rest of the way.'

'But don't you want me to stay and run you back to town?' Tullio Legna protested.

Zen shook his head with a polite smile.

'It's a private call which may take some time, and I'm sure a busy man like you has plenty to do. Particularly in the present situation.'

'What do you mean?'

'There's still the Gallizio and Scorrone cases unaccounted for,' Zen reminded him. 'Gianni Faigano explicitly denied any part in those events, and there's no clear evidence linking him to either. Now that the Vincenzo affair has been cleared up, I imagine there's going to be a lot of pressure on you to make an arrest in the two unsolved killings.'

He held out his hand to Legna.

'In a perverse way, I'm sorry it's worked out so smoothly,' he recited with an unctuous smile. 'It would have been good to have been able to stay longer and see some of the wonderful things which the Langhe has to offer. But I'm eager to get back to my family and friends, and at least I had a chance to sample the famous white truffles and some good wine. It's been a pleasure working with you. If there's anything I can do for you once I'm back in Rome, don't hesitate to contact me. *Arriverderci!*'

Taking Carla by the arm, he started off briskly down the track leading to the Vincenzo property, leaving Tullio Legna no choice but to drive off.

'You still haven't explained why we're here,' Carla pointed out mildly.

'Officially, because I need to tie up a few loose ends. But really that's just a pretext. The fact is that I wanted to spend my last day here out in the country with you.'

He hoped this was the right answer. Carla seemed to agree, or at least to feel that she ought to appear to do so, squeezing his arm affectionately. The rapport between them inevitably felt a little strained, since each felt the need to reassure the other, and slightly resented this.

Reciprocity went this far, but Zen's view of the situation was inevitably different from Carla's. They both might be wondering how, or even whether, the relationship would work out, but he alone knew that it was not a destiny but a choice, and one that he had made; a lie he had sponsored in the interests of maintaining what had seemed a greater and more important truth.

So in addition to whatever doubts Carla Arduini might have about this dramatic turn of events, Zen had to deal with a succession of nagging internal queries about whether he had done the right thing. It had seemed a good idea at the time, but then so had all the failed initiatives which littered his personal history, and which he now saw quite clearly for the disasters they were. Why should this be any different?

That logic, though, would induce paralysis. Life was not a spectator sport, he told himself. You couldn't opt out, and you couldn't ever be sure of doing the right thing. All you could hope for, perhaps, was to do the wrong thing better, or at least more interestingly. Acquiring a twenty-something daughter about whom he knew next to nothing certainly promised to be interesting – and if it goes seriously off the rails, a weasel voice reminded him, you can always tell her the truth.

They walked in silence down the track, through the mild air and the strata of sunlight, the Vincenzo house gradually emerging from behind its screens of soil and vegetation. There was a low rumble of machinery at work somewhere, as well as the distant and disconsolate barking of the dog, but the house itself appeared deserted. Zen freed himself from Carla's arm and strode across the courtyard to the main door, which lay wide open. He knocked, without effect.

'Hello?' he called inside.

The silence bulged lightly, like a silk drapery with a faint draught behind it. Zen rapped again, more loudly.

'Anyone home?'

He was on the point of turning away when an elderly woman suddenly appeared in a window on the second floor.

'*Sì*'

'Signora Rosa?' asked Zen.

'Well?'

'We came to see Dottor Manlio.'

The woman sized them up shrewdly for a moment, then pointed to a row of buildings at the far end of the courtyard.

'They're making the wine,' she replied, and disappeared inside.

Zen thanked the empty window and then walked with Carla across the courtyard towards the line of adjoining sheds, each a different size and design, which had apparently been added to the main structure at different periods as needed. The first few additions were similar to the main house and the other outbuildings surrounding it, but by the end of the row the idiom had changed to the efficient brutalities of modern construction.

Open steel doors in the concrete-block wall of this section revealed signs of activity within. The mechanical rumble grew louder as they approached, then was swallowed by the louder racket of a tractor pulling a cart laden with garishly coloured plastic baskets containing bunches of dull, bruise-blue grapes. A group of young people emerged from the building and started carrying the baskets inside, helped by the driver of the tractor. Zen and Carla followed.

The scene inside resembled some light-industrial plant rather than the picturesque squalor which Zen had always associated with wine-making. The floor was a bleak, runnelled expanse of poured concrete, the roof an exposed matrix of metal girders and corrugated sheeting, the lighting provided by glaring fluorescent strips hanging from the beams.

In the middle of the floor stood a raised trough made of stainless stecl, lined on either side by women of all ages. Within this ran a wide rubber belt, like a supermarket checkout, upon which the grapes that had just arrived were unloaded. These precessed slowly past the waiting lines of women, whose nimble fingers darted in among the clusters, sorting out the spoiled or unripe grapes. The fruit which passed this test tumbled into yet another gleaming machine at the end of the belt, connected to a wide metal tube which ran at a slight angle straight into the end wall.

There were so many people coming and going in the shed that it was some time before Zen recognized Manlio Vincenzo, standing at one end of the conveyor belt, scrutinizing the work of the women to either side and occasionally leaning out to inspect a cluster of grapes more closely. It was still longer before he looked up and noticed the presence of the two intruders.

'Well?' he said sharply. 'What do you want?'

Zen gestured vaguely, as though at a loss.

'Just a word with you, Signor Vincenzo. But I can see that you're busy. I'll phone later, perhaps.'

Manlio Vincenzo ducked under the inclined metal tube and came towards them, frowning.

'Oh, it's you, Dottor Zen!' he exclaimed, his expression changing to one of guarded welcome. 'I hope you haven't come to arrest me.'

They shook hands.

'On the contrary,' said Zen. 'In fact I have some good news.'

Manlio smiled warily.

'That's always welcome. I made the decision to start harvesting yesterday. I don't trust this weather. Too stable, too settled. All we need now is a hailstorm and the whole harvest could be wiped out.'

He glanced at his watch.

'We're almost finished for the morning, as it happens. Can you stay to lunch, *dottore*? And of course . . .'

233

He looked at Zen's companion.

'My daughter, Carla Arduini,' Zen told him.

'Delighted to meet you, *signorina*, although it's a far from ideal moment. Who was it said that no one should watch sausages or laws being made? He should have added wine.'

He waved at the moving belt.

'This is only the first stage, of course, but I'm doing a much more rigorous triage than we used to in the past. Since this will be the first and last vintage that I will oversee, I wanted to do an exemplary job.'

He glanced at Zen.

'Tell your Roman friend to invest with confidence. This is going to be a quite exceptional wine. At a quite exceptional price, naturally.'

'I don't think the price is a problem.'

'Unless you set it too low! The market's so hot these days that you can sell practically anything as long as it's expensive enough. But if you don't charge stellar prices, the serious collectors will sneer at you. "Why, anyone could afford that," they think.'

He gestured towards a door in the wall.

'Let's go and find Andrea.'

Manlio Vincenzo led the way into the next part of the connected sheds, closing the door carefully behind him. In the sorting room which Zen and Carla had first entered, there was little evidence apart from the bunches of grapes themselves that wine was being produced there, rather than knitwear or ceramics. In the room in which they now found themselves, this fact was primary and dominant, confirmed by a pervasive stench at once as heady as petroleum and as dank and dark as hanging meat or rotten leaves.

The space was almost entirely occupied by a number of huge fermentation vats made of deeply stained oak banded with metal. The pipe which had disappeared into the wall next door emerged here at the same inclined angle, running up to a level above the vats, into one of which it discharged a gush of rich red juice. Manlio waved to a woman standing on a ladder attached to the side of the vat being filled. He climbed up to join her and peer down into the internal cavity. They had a brief discussion, then came down to join their impromptu guests.

Once Carla and Andrea had been introduced, Manlio led them outside into the blissfully fresh air.

'You'll have to forgive Rosa,' he warned Zen. 'She's a little eccentric at times, but a wonderful housekeeper. I shall miss her.'

'Is she leaving?' asked Carla.

'No, we are,' Andrea replied.

'I hope we're not inconveniencing you,' said Zen.

Manlio laughed.

'At vintage time Rosa cooks for everyone, including all the student pickers and the sorting ladies. It's a sort of informal *festa*, and there's always too much food. Rosa grew up on a big farm, but now she lives alone in an apartment in the village with no one to care for except herself, and she doesn't care about herself. So at this time of year, it's as if the world has suddenly started to make sense again. Lots of people around, masses of food being served, a scene of chaos and purpose. I'll swear she looks about ten years younger!'

As promised, the meal was copious, simple and good: home-made pasta ribbons with a wild mushroom sauce, followed by roast chicken and a selection of fruit. Several of Manlio's neighbours who were helping him out with the vintage joined them at table, so the subject which had brought Zen there was not raised until the meal was over and the neighbours had returned to work, along with Andrea, who quickly sized up the situation and suggested that Carla join her.

When Zen and Manlio Vincenzo were alone, the younger man poured them both another glass of the wine they had been drinking, regarding Zen in the manner which he recognized by now as an invitation to make a fool of himself by commenting on the beverage in question.

'Interesting,' he remarked urbanely, choosing an adjective which seemed promisingly vague.

The look which Manlio Vincenzo gave him suggested that this was not quite enough.

'A very long finish,' Zen added. 'Which brings me to my reason for troubling you today, Signor Vincenzo. As I mentioned earlier, I have some good news. We have made an arrest in the matter of your father's murder. It is supported by a full and voluntary confession, not to mention various pieces of material evidence. There is thus no doubt that the judges responsible will confirm your unconditional discharge within a few days. In short, your legal worries are over.'

Manlio Vincenzo nodded coolly.

'So who did it?'

Zen lit a Nazionale with the air of someone who didn't care if the bouquet of the wine was adversely affected.

'My report to the judiciary will conclude that the crime was a conspiracy between Gianni and Maurizio Faigano, although the former has tried to take all the blame on himself.'

Manlio started forward so suddenly that he upset his water glass.

'The Faigano brothers? But that's absurd!'

He picked up his toppled glass mechanically, frowning.

'There was that stupid business of my father trying to talk me into marrying the daughter, but I explained the whole thing to her privately, and of course it came to nothing. Why on earth should the Faiganos have wanted to kill my father?'

Zen slurped some more wine into his glass, blinking from the cigarette smoke which had got in his eyes.

'According to the confession deposed by Gianni Faigano before me and a court-appointed lawyer in my office yesterday, the motive for the crime dates back more than four decades. Signor Faigano claims that he and your late mother, Chiara Cravioli as she then was, were sweethearts at that time. They planned to marry, but since Gianni was unemployed, Chiara's father would not approve the marriage. It was at this point that your father entered the picture.

'What happened next is based on Faigano's account of what your mother told him when she explained why she was breaking off their unofficial engagement. There is no proof that it is true, and at this late stage there probably never will be, but your father allegedly went to Signor Cravioli and asked permission to court his daughter. This was readily given, since Aldo Vincenzo was a man of property and an excellent match.

'As for Chiara, she agreed to the engagement, partly out of fear of her father and partly to provide her with a screen behind which she and Gianni could continue, however infrequently, to see each other. Whenever Aldo tried to fix the date of the marriage, she pleaded for more time, hoping that he would eventually lose interest. But he didn't, because his interest wasn't in her but in the Cravioli property, which would come to Chiara when her parents died.

'And then one day – this is all according to Gianni Faigano, I repeat – Aldo took her out for a drive in the country, and in a wood down by a river he raped her. Repeatedly. And then he looked at her and said, "From now on, I won't bother you any more. Let nature take its course. If you're with child, I'll marry you and legitimize my heir. If you're not, I'll put it about that I've had you, and you'll be ruined unless you accept me. The choice is all yours, *signorina*."'

Manlio Vincenzo was staring down at the spreading stain of damp on the tablecloth with the silent intensity of a gambler watching a spinning roulette wheel. The door opened and Rosa appeared, a creature from another world, blithe and unconcerned.

'*Vattene!*' barked Manlio rudely.

The old woman looked at him as though he had struck her, then shuffled out again, slamming the door behind her. Manlio glanced up at Zen.

'Go on.'

Zen crushed out his cigarette.

'Well, it turned out that Chiara *was* pregnant. She went to Gianni, explained what had happened and what she had to do as a result, which was to marry Aldo. Her child was more important than her feelings, and her duty was to ensure its future by marrying the father. Gianni broke down and wept at this point of his confession. He said that that day was the blackest in his entire life, for he couldn't fault her logic, despite the fact that it put an end to any chance of happiness for either of them.

'Chiara duly married your father, only to suffer a miscarriage in her eighth month. Gianni claimed that your father struck her while they were having an argument, but that may be malicious gossip. At all events, almost ten years passed before you were born. And all that time, and ever since, Gianni Faigano carried this terrible secret about with him. At their last meeting before the marriage, Chiara had explicitly forbidden him to denounce or harm the man who had raped her and whom she was now forced to marry. That was why he could do nothing until she died.'

There was a long silence. Then Manlio looked up at Zen.

'But is it true?'

Zen stared at him coldly.

'I don't criticize your wine, Signor Vincenzo. Please accord me the same professional courtesy. The truth of the matter is, of course, for the courts to decide, but let me tell you that if you'd been present in the room when Gianni Faigano made his statement, sobbing and distraught, you wouldn't doubt its truth.'

He lit another cigarette.

'Besides, who's going to confess without the slightest pressure to a murder he didn't commit?'

'I suppose you're right. It's just that I've never thought of Gianni as a killer. He might *want* to be – who hasn't? – but he never struck me as someone who could actually bring it off.'

'When you've had as much experience as I have, Signor Vincenzo, you realize that murderers don't have forked tails and horns on their heads.'

'I'm sure you're right, *dottore*. In any case, this is certainly good news as far as I'm concerned. Not only that, but you've helped me make a decision that I've been dithering over for days. Or rather, you've helped me realize that I'd actually already made it.'

'What decision?'

Manlio smiled.

'Andrea and I have been toying with the idea of selling up here and moving to Chile. It's an exciting place for wine these days, and she knows a lot of people there. We have an option on some land in the Maipo Valley, which is their equivalent of Napa. My idea is to retain a few non-DOC fields here in Piedmont and replant them with Cabernet, Merlot and Syrah, from which I would make an unofficial "signature" wine I could sell for a fortune to collectors less single-minded than your Roman *intenditore.*'

He raised his right forefinger.

'And because Chile's in the other hemisphere, their vintage is in January and February. Andrea and I could make our wine down there, then fly back here to look after this end of things. Two harvests a year, and perpetual summer! What more could anyone want?'

'It sounds delightful.'

'Yes, but at some level I was still undecided. After what you've just told me, I have no further doubts. The land my father acquired in the way you've just described will be tainted for as long as it remains in the Vincenzo family. I knew nothing about this terrible story, but my intuition was correct. I'll make this one last vintage of Vincenzo Barbaresco, and then put the property on the market. Thanks to you, *dottore*, my mind's made up!'

He looked at Zen and gestured to the door.

'Shall we go and see how the women are doing?'

Minot was the way he liked it: alone. His recent forays into the world had been entirely successful. That was why he was able to be alone. That was success, to so arrange things that they left you alone.

It was almost dawn by the time he got home. A bitter, recalcitrant glimmer had begun to infect the darkness, revealing the extent of the devastation caused by the gales which had swept the region for the past week. Bare tree limbs poked the sky like reinforcing wire bereft of its concrete cladding. Stripped of their fruit, the vines looked like a beaten army, their serried rank and order a hollow mockery.

Still worse were those fields whose owners had gambled on the good weather holding out another precious few days, and whose harvest now languished in a heavy, sodden, putrescent mess beyond retrieval. Like the invaders they were, the wind and rain had come from the north, sweeping down without warning and laying waste to whatever remained of the summer; an impersonal obliteration, impartial and absolute.

But what was bad for wine was good for truffles, as traditional wisdom had it, and this local saying was borne out by Minot's bag that night. He had spent over eight hours skulking through groves of oak and linden with Anna, encouraging the hound with the constant muffled chant, '*Péila cà jé! Péila cà jé!*' He then excavated the heavy clay the dog pointed out with his mattock, revealing the nest of tubers, and finally teased out the buff-coloured nuggets and stashed them safely away in his pocket. Anna had meanwhile been bought off with a dog biscuit, a token of her master's appreciation.

He must have gathered over a dozen truffles, several the size of new potatoes, and more than half of the superior female variety. Depending on where he placed them, he could be looking at almost a million lire for his night's work. For Anna's work, rather, but she was no more demanding than the rats. The biscuits, at a few hundred lire a box, were enough to keep her sweet. What she craved was to feel appreciated. It was not the gift but the thought behind it which counted. She and Minot understood each other perfectly.

Their relationship went back a long way, well before her legal owner's death. It had started when Minot discovered some hand-written receipts one day at Beppe's house while the latter was absent, proving that Gallizio had earned substantial sums of money from the sale of truffles supposedly from the prized Alba region, but in fact imported from such far-off and unfashionable localities as Lombardy, the Veneto, Emilia-Romagna and even Umbria.

It amazed Minot that Beppe was capable of such entrepreneurial initiative, and still more that he would be fool enough to keep the evidence stashed away in an unlocked drawer, like a bunch of love letters! There it was, nevertheless, and once he had outlined to Beppe the likely consequences of such documents falling into the hands of the *fisc* – tax evasion plus commercial fraud was a lethal combination – it had proved relatively easy to negotiate a compromise permitting Minot to borrow Anna for his nocturnal expeditions on those occasions when Beppe was otherwise employed.

Unfortunately, and through no fault of his own, this arrangement was to lead to Beppe's untimely demise. It had all started when one of the Faigano brothers had mentioned hearing Anna barking from the neighbouring Vincenzo land on the morning of Aldo's death. That chance remark had tied them all together like one of those cords they used to have on the railway, running back from the locomotive to the guard's van, for use in case of emergency. Once it was pulled, the whole train ground to a halt, while the tell-tale sag in one compartment pointed to the guilty party.

So Beppe had to go. The prospect of having Anna at his unrestricted disposal had helped to stiffen Minot's resolve, but it had still been a wrench. He had never killed anyone like that before, coldly and calculatedly, with malice aforethought, and it rattled him. The actual deed had been simple enough. Having 'borrowed' Anna the day before, he had painted her paws with a dilute solution of aniseed, imperceptible to the human nose but gross olfactory overload to another dog, in this case a half-wild pup which Minot had saved from drowning with the rest of the litter and kept to guard the house. A crash course involving the undiluted aniseed and some chunks of ham and cheese did the trick, and the snuffling pup led Minot all the way from Gallizio's house to the wood he had elected to work that night. After that it was just a matter of heading home, tossing the corpse of his strangled guide into a thicket on the way, and then returning at his leisure in the truck to confront Beppe with his own shotgun. He had seemed as startled as the puppy by the outcome – as helpless and as hurt.

Leaving the bloodstained knife at Beppe's house had been a last-minute inspiration, and Minot had to admit to himself that it had not really been taken as he had hoped. Anna's barking, Beppe's death and the murder weapon had seemed to form one of those triangles with which he had been tormented at school, an absolute and irrefutable demonstration of the facts of the case leaving no margin for further doubt. *Quod erat demonstrandum*, the police would conclude, and that would be that.

But he hadn't counted on the arrival of this outsider, and the impact which his ignorance and innocence would make on subsequent events. Aurelio Zen didn't even know that Anna had been heard in the Vincenzo vineyards that morning, still less that Beppe had been in trouble over his truffle dealings. He couldn't see the beauty of the solution which Minot had created for him, was utterly unappreciative of its clarity and elegance. Instead of grabbing the simple outcome on offer, he had blundered about like a myope who has lost his glasses, ignoring all Minot's thoughtful clues and overturning his carefully crafted design.

Nevertheless, everything had turned out for the best, he

thought, as he reached his house and tethered Anna to the eye-bolt in the wall before taking out his key; unlike poor Beppe, he was scrupulous about locking up. A scabrous rustle announced that the rats were still about. Minot took off his coat and opened the jar in which he kept his 'white diamonds' safely tucked up in a cloth napkin.

An astonishing avalanche of scent instantly invested the room, spreading out in successive waves, each more powerful than the last, until every other odour was buried beneath count-less strata of that infinitely suggestive but fugitive *profumo di tartufo*. Even the speedy conspiracy of rats fell still and silent, as though acknowledging this massive new presence in their midst. Minot set the jar down on the counter. Later he would sort and weigh his catch, then drive into Alba and see what sort of deal he could strike. But first a bite to eat. It had been a long night.

As soon as he opened the fridge, he realized that it had broken down yet again. The light did not come on, and everything inside was at the temperature of the room, chilly but not cold. This did not surprise him. He had picked the thing out of the ravine on the outskirts of Palazzuole, where the villagers had dumped their garbage since time immemorial, and it had only ever worked intermittently. He used it mainly as a secure cupboard, the one place that even the most enterprising rodent could not enter.

Then he caught sight of the glass jar on the top shelf and smelt something even stronger than the truffles: the stench of bad blood. Hare, he had told Enrico Pascal! That had been a close call, although keeping the container and its contents had certainly paid off in the end. Enough was enough, though. Even Minot had his limits, as his suddenly queasy stomach reminded him. He was still hungry, but the thought of food was now an abomination.

He removed the jar full of curdled blood and bits of flesh and set it on the counter next to the one in which he had brought back this night's catch. They were identical, down to the shreds of yel-low label still adhering to the glass and the white lids bearing the name of a well-known brand of jam. Despite his slight nausea, Minot couldn't repress a satisfied smile. Yes, everything had

243

turned out for the best, and in ways he couldn't have imagined, still less planned for!

When he had brought back this trophy, for instance, he'd had no clue how vital it would prove. At the time it had seemed a mere whim, a fancy which had taken him. Even that other time, when he'd picked up the nail which Gianni broke off during the bottling, had been little more than a sudden inspiration, a vague hedge against some undefined threat. But when he'd put the two of them together – like the commonplace and inert chemicals they'd used to make bombs during the war – the results were literally explosive.

And just as effective, he thought, walking through to the living room. How easily he had manipulated events, vanishing from the picture he himself had painted like one of those anonymous daubers of old church frescoes, leaving the credulous and ignorant to gawk at the colourful scenes he had created, but no clue as to the identity of the artist.

Except there was, and it was faked. That was why Gianni Faigano's confession still rankled. It was one thing to leave one's work deliberately anonymous, quite another to have another break in, scrawl his signature on the drying pigment and claim it as his own. That was worse than cheating. It was . . . What was that word they'd used in the paper at the time of the wine scandal Bruno Scorrone had been implicated in? Something like 'plague'. No one had understood until the village pharmacist had explained over cards the next day that it meant passing someone else's work off as your own.

That's what had happened now, and it hurt as bad as any plague sore. It was he, *Minot chit*, who had done the work and taken the risks, and here was Gianni Faigano insolently muscling in to claim the credit! Of course the end result was the same, in a sense, but it didn't feel the same. Minot had expected the Faigano brothers to deny everything indignantly, as befitted the innocent men they were. Then the results of the tests would come back, the scientific analysis of Gianni's fingernail which Minot had dipped into that jar filled with Aldo's gore. They would never be able to talk their way out of *that*!

But to his dismay, they hadn't even tried to. Instead, Gianni Faigano had freely confessed to killing Aldo Vincenzo in revenge for the outrage he had visited upon Chiara Cravioli so long ago. What a heap of shit! Gianni had never had the balls to take on Aldo, and he damn well knew it. He also knew what everyone else in the village knew, or at least suspected – that although the teenage Chiara might have fancied herself in love with Gianni in a misty, moon-struck adolescent way, she had been genuinely swept off her feet by Aldo, who was twice the man Gianni would ever be.

The truth of it was that what she had felt for Gianni was not love but pity, or at best a cloying sort of companionship. 'Gianni is the best girlfriend Chiara ever had,' Aldo had sarcastically remarked apropos of his wife's clandestine visits to the Faigano house. But now Gianni had indeed taken his revenge, not on Aldo but on the whole community. With one deft stroke he had rewritten history, casting himself as the romantic hero who bided his time patiently for years, obedient to his beloved's wishes, and then exacted a terrible price the moment she was in the grave. What a figure to cut! True, he would be condemned and sentenced to life, but everyone would secretly murmur, 'What a man!' in admiring tones. Women would write to him in prison, and the media would tut-tut over the murder while gleefully celebrating the fact that the great days of chivalry were not dead after all.

Even if Minot were to come forward and confess – not that there was any prospect of that! – he would not be believed. People wanted a story, and unlike Gianni he could not offer that. They wouldn't want to hear the truth, that on his annual pilgrimage 'to lay flowers on Angelin's tomb' and clean out the unsuspected truffle bed he had found, Minot had been surprised by Aldo Vincenzo, who could not sleep and had come out to check on the progress of this problematic harvest.

They certainly wouldn't believe, and for that matter Minot could never explain, why this chance encounter had led to death. Planning and executing Beppe's killing had been a new experience for Minot, the exception to his proven rule: to follow his instincts. He had done so with Angelin, and, before that, with *Minot gross* up on the roof. He had done the same with Bruno Scorrone that afternoon at the winery, and with Aldo. Something in Vincenzo's swaggering, contemptuous manner had been the trigger. Without even thinking, Minot had responded with a single blow from the *zappetto* he carried to excavate for truffles. It had caught Vincenzo high up on the forehead, a nasty blow which had laid him on his hands and knees, dazed and bloody.

Even then, he might have gone no further. But the consequences of stopping now seemed worse than those of continuing, so he'd taken out his knife. When Aldo saw that, he had spat out a word which proved to be his last, a dialect term so grossly insulting, and unfair, that subsequent events took on the momentum of a dislodged boulder rolling downhill. When it finally came to rest, Minot's brain kicked in again. As a rule he preferred to make his killings look accidental, but that was not possible here. So he decided to go to the other extreme.

Remembering the angry scene between Aldo and his son at the *festa* the night before, he had dragged the gutted, blood-drenched corpse over to the vines and lashed the wrists to the wire supports. Then he bent down and added one last touch, something so macabre that no one would ever believe that this was anything other than a coldly premeditated act of personal revenge.

His first thought had been to stuff the severed genitals into Aldo's mouth, the way they used to with informers during the war. But something restrained him, some sixth sense that possession of these glaringly absent items might enable him to tip the balance at some time in the future, should he ever come under suspicion. So he'd taken out the jar he'd brought to collect truffles in and scooped the slop in there instead.

And once again his instincts had not betrayed him. He'd got away with it, more completely than he could ever have imagined. His feelings of anger about Gianni's false confession were completely irrational. What did it matter, after all? If Faigano was so keen to act the great lover that he was prepared to accept a wrongful conviction for murder, let him rot in prison.

All around, the rats were out, speedy, furtive presences swarming in the shadows at the corners of the room, some bolder individual occasionally darting diagonally from one patch of imagined refuge to another. There was no refuge, of course. With a couple of blasts of his shotgun Minot could have turned the room into a bloodbath. He could do that any time he wanted, which was why he had no interest in doing so. Minot was above the rats, in the scheme of things. Nothing they did could threaten him, and his generosity or patronage was entirely at his own discretion. He could exterminate them any time he wanted, so he let them live.

Which reminded him that it was time for their feed, if not for his. Then off to Alba, maybe stopping at Lamberto Latini's restaurant to see what sort of price he could get there. He got to his feet, creating a brief scuffle among the more impressionable members of the pack, and went back into the kitchen to fetch some bread.

When he returned, the rats had taken over the entire floor, scurrying this way and that, looking up at him as expectantly as dogs. Minot broke the bread into irregular crusts and tossed them out like fireworks. The rats went crazy. Fights broke out, blood was drawn, and a chorus of shrill squeals scored the silence like nails on a blackboard. Minot laughed and cut more bread, flinging each piece into a different corner of the room so that the rats surged forward like a wave that lapped and broke over the morsel which instantly disappeared down the throat of some animal quicker or more aggressive than the rest. Given enough time and patience, you could tame anything, thought Minot with a flicker of contempt. Anything except him, that was. He could not be tamed, and those who had dared to try had paid the price.

It was time to go. Minot put on his coat and reached for the jar filled with truffles. Then he noticed the other, identical jar. Thank God he hadn't gone out leaving that sitting there on the counter in plain view! With a reputation for shady wine transactions such as he had, even transporting and disposing of it in the wild was a risk. Suppose he got stopped by some officious police patrolman who insisted on searching the truck? Maybe it would be best just to bury it in his vegetable garden. He could do that unobtrusively enough, then rinse out the bottle and reuse it. Waste not, want not. It was a question of how far gone the contents were. If they'd started to decompose seriously, he'd have all the village dogs round there, scratching and sniffing. The neighbours might get curious.

Minot unscrewed the lid cautiously. The smell was definitely on the high side, but not unbearably so. On the surface floated a small grey pouch of flesh which he realized with a shock was Aldo Vincenzo's penis. He smiled wryly, thinking of the power that organ had once wielded, of the pain and damage it had wrought. It had transferred the Cravioli estate to the Vincenzo family and made a hollow, self-pitying mockery of Gianni Faigano's life. Look at it now!

It was at this moment that Minot felt a delicate shiver at his wrist, and looked down to see a rat sniffing at the open jar. Immediately some atavistic trigger was thrown. The rats were welcome to his bread, even some stale cheese or ham on occasion. When it came to human flesh things changed. Without the slightest reflection, Minot lashed out at the beast with his left hand, knocking it on to its back. It lay there, its pale furry stomach exposed and feet wiggling, as if astonished at this unwonted aggression. With a snort of disgust, Minot smashed his fist down on top of it.

But the rat was no longer there. With an astonishing spiral leap, it twisted up and around and sank its incisors into Minot's hand. He yelled and lashed out with his other hand, knocking over the glass jar, which shattered on the floor. The rat had already vanished, along with all its fellows.

Minot inspected the wound. It looked insignificant, just a couple of punctures below the thumb. The real problem was the incriminating mess on the floor. With a heavy sigh, he set about cleaning it up, scooping the solid items on to an old newspaper and mopping the blood into a pail. He did his best, but in the event it wasn't good enough to escape detection by the forensic team which arrived a week later. Aldo's blood had not only coated the tiles but seeped into the cracks and crevices in the grout between them, from which it was laboriously removed, analysed and identified. Soon afterwards, police dogs discovered the shallow pit where Minot had hurriedly buried the whole mess. The case against Gianni Faigano collapsed and, protesting his guilt to the last, he was released.

But that was all in the future. Having completed his clean-up, Minot drove off to dispose of his truffles, which he did at a price which astonished him. As for the bite, he thought nothing more of it. There was a small red swelling and an irritating itching sensation, but that gradually subsided.

It wasn't until the following day that other symptoms manifested themselves, a sort of feverish lassitude which felt like some virus or other; a mild case of flu, perhaps. Then that evening, while he was heating up some soup, Minot suddenly collapsed. To his astonishment, he was unable to get up again. In fact, he could hardly move at all, except for an occasional convulsive jerking of his limbs. He tried calling for help, but all that emerged was a feeble croak.

Minot was a notorious recluse, and several more days passed before his disappearance was remarked on. In the end it was Lamberto Latini who found him, having called by arrangement to collect an order of truffles placed during Minot's earlier visit. By then nearly a week had gone by, and the corpse was almost unrecognizable. Denied their usual food, the rats had had to make do with what there was.

Acknowledgement

The days are past when Poe could get away with having a character demonstrate his wine connoisseurship (in *The Cask of Amontillado*, a few echoes of which may be discerned in the second chapter) by claiming that a rival 'cannot distinguish Sherry from Amontillado'. To protect myself from similar or worse gaffes I appealed to the incomparable Jancis Robinson, who very kindly read the manuscript and made numerous suggestions, many of which have been incorporated in the final text. Needless to say, responsibility for the opinions voiced by my characters, as well as for any subsequent errors, is mine alone.